But as she watched his gaze grow warm, then drift lower, settling on her mouth, her knees went weak.

Stop being an idiot. Move away from the hunk.

But she didn't. She didn't move an inch—and then it was too late because her hands lifted suddenly and encircled his neck, and at the same instant she leaned toward him, Wes tugged her onto his lap. His strong arms banded around her waist.

"That's better. Much better, isn't it, honey?" With a surprisingly gentle smile, he brushed his mouth against hers.

Fire shot through her. Instant red-hot fire.

You're doomed, she thought.

And kissed him back.

They didn't seem to know how to stop kissing. Annabelle found her senses whirling like a merry-go-round as his warm lips tasted hers slowly, gently, before eventually traveling down her throat to nibble at her collarbone. When she moaned with pleasure, he returned his attention to her mouth, kissing her deeply, and then deeper still, like a starving man who couldn't get enough.

Neither could she.

He wasn't just tasting her, he was savoring her. And she was savoring him right back. . .

"[Montana] was a stunning and perfect backdrop for this story of loss, love, and learning to let go in order to find love again . . . A beautiful tapestry of home and heart."

—*That's What I'm Talking About*

Withdrawn
Sunflower Lane

JILL GREGORY

B

BERKLEY SENSATION, NEW YORK

THE BERKLEY PUBLISHING GROUP
Published by the Penguin Group
Penguin Group (USA) LLC
375 Hudson Street, New York, New York 10014

USA • Canada • UK • Ireland • Australia • New Zealand • India • South Africa • China

penguin.com

A Penguin Random House Company

SUNFLOWER LANE

A Berkley Sensation Book / published by arrangement with the author

Berkley Sensation Books are published by The Berkley Publishing Group.
BERKLEY SENSATION® is a registered trademark of Penguin Group (USA) LLC.
The "B" design is a trademark of Penguin Group (USA) LLC.

For information, address: The Berkley Publishing Group,
a division of Penguin Group (USA) LLC,
375 Hudson Street, New York, New York 10014.

ISBN: 978-0-425-25983-2

PUBLISHING HISTORY
Berkley Sensation mass-market edition / November 2014

PRINTED IN THE UNITED STATES OF AMERICA

10 9 8 7 6 5 4 3 2 1

Cover art by Hugh Syme.
Cover design by Rita Frangie.
Interior text design by Laura K. Corless.

For Larry, Rachel, and Jason—with all my love.

*And for Ellen Levine, my extraordinary agent and friend,
with deep gratitude for your guidance and friendship.*

Chapter One

❧

LONESOME WAY, MONTANA

Wes McPhee's dusty black truck roared off the highway and zoomed past the gas station on the corner of town without slowing even a fraction. Wes was in a hurry. He accelerated down Main Street without looking left or right, not bothering to admire the shimmering gold and lavender sunset gilding the Crazy Mountains in the distance.

In fact, he didn't even notice.

He paid no attention to the neat storefronts of the little town where he'd spent the first miserable eighteen years of his life. Didn't spare a glance at the profusion of early-summer flowers planted in brightly colored pots lining the streets, or think about the hushed, peaceful quiet tiptoeing through the town as dusk encroached on the peaks of the cottonwoods.

Wes thought about only one thing. Seeing his grandmother; his mother; his sister, Sophie; and her family all in one quick, painless visit—and then getting the hell out of here.

Away from this town, hopefully within two or three days. Four max.

He'd returned to Lonesome Way only a handful of times in the past fifteen or so years, and he didn't miss the place one bit. The pleasant, cheerful streets, the tiny quaintness of it, were still as familiar to him as the knuckles of his right hand, but there were memories here he'd left behind, and he had no desire to get reacquainted with them.

Hitting the gas pedal harder, he just beat the one streetlight that turned yellow on him. Picking up speed, he bulleted through the intersection, but one block down—ironically in front of his sister Sophie's bakery—an elderly woman began crossing Main, her steps slow, unhurried, and deliberate. She cut him a look as if to say nothing was going to stop her from crossing and she would take her sweet time about it.

Swearing under his breath, he had no choice but to slam on the brakes.

He recognized her, of course.

Martha Davies.

Grimly, Wes lifted a hand in a brief, polite salute, though his mouth never softened to a smile.

Martha, one of his grandmother's oldest friends, owned the Cuttin' Loose hair salon, he remembered. Had owned it as far back as he could recall. Gran would be mighty pissed if he ran down her friend, so he waited impatiently as the eighty-something woman in the patterned purple blouse, belted dark trousers, and heavy gold jewelry gleaming at her ears and wrists took her sweet time strolling across the road.

At this rate it would be dawn before he got to the Good Luck Ranch.

Finally the old woman reached the curb. She apparently figured out who he was by that time because, turning slightly, she lifted one spider-veined hand in a regal wave, and shouted at him.

"Is that you, Wes McPhee? If you're here to see your gran, she's staying with your mother on Daisy Lane!"

The few other people still out on the streets all turned and stared at him.

Remind me not to come back for a dozen more years, he told himself ruefully. But he nodded at Martha. "Thank you, ma'am."

It was the exact wrong thing to say. Planting her hands on her hips, she first frowned, then marched back toward him, determination gleaming in her eyes.

"Now, you wait right there, young man."

The light was green but he couldn't go, because Martha Davies was bearing down on him, apparently hell-bent on bending his ear.

"'Ma'am'? Since when do you call me 'ma'am,' Wes McPhee? It's Aunt Martha to you. I've been best friends with your gran for well over sixty years and I knew you when you were a tiny little thing sporting diapers." She waggled a finger at him. "If you're sticking around Lonesome Way for a while, I don't want to hear any more of that ma'am stuff."

With that, a smile broke across her face and he caught a glint of mischief in her faded eyes as she beamed at him through the truck's open window.

"Yes, ma'am—er, Aunt Martha." Wes couldn't stop the answering grin that began at the corners of his mouth and spread up to his eyes. Some things never changed.

Especially in Lonesome Way.

To Martha and his grandmother—and Gran's circle of elderly friends—he'd always be a kid. Didn't matter that he was six foot four, easing toward his late thirties, and that for roughly the past ten years he'd headed up a crack team of the toughest agents in the DEA. That he'd tracked down and rounded up the baddest of the bad guys, investigating, infiltrating, and arresting worldwide drug dealers and heads of cartels—and the terrorists who joined forces with them.

The past three years alone he'd worked undercover in Afghanistan, Pakistan, and Colombia for months at a time, going up against two of the most powerful drug syndicates trying to stream cocaine into the United States. He'd nailed a legendary meth kingpin in the wilds of Colorado several months ago, shortly before leaving the DEA.

During his years as an agent with the Drug Enforcement Administration, he'd gone head-to-head with thugs in the most dangerous cities of the world, bringing down some of the most ruthless terrorists and criminals of the twenty-first century, and yet, not five minutes back in his hometown, he was being schooled by a lady in her eighties for not addressing her in the manner she preferred.

Not ma'am. Aunt Martha.

"So," Aunt Martha said, as if he weren't stopped in the middle of an intersection, and she had all the time in the world. "Tell me something. Are you?"

"Am I what, ma'am—er, Aunt Martha?"

She smiled. "Sticking around Lonesome Way. You've scarcely been back all these years and never for more than forty-eight hours at a time, if I recall correctly. And I'm sure I do."

"Not staying long. Only came to visit my grandmother."

"Because of her accident." Martha nodded knowingly. "Well, I'd think you'd spend more than a *little* bit of time, seeing as you've come all this way. I'm sure you'll want to get to know your niece and nephew a mite better as well, since you're here. Does Sophie know you're back?"

"You're the first to know, Aunt Martha," Wes said drily. He heard another car coming up behind him.

"I'm holding up traffic, Aunt Martha. Better be on my way. And you might want to get home yourself. It's nearly dark."

"Wes, honey, don't be silly. This is Lonesome Way. It's perfectly safe after dark," she informed him affectionately. She headed again toward the sidewalk. "I live just around the corner, you know, so it's not as if I have very far to go."

But as he took his boot off the brake, she suddenly turned back and yelled, "Tell your gran I'll come by tomorrow morning to discuss the parade route!"

Wes shot through the intersection, then hung a right on Squirrel Road. He wondered what she meant about a parade route. Suddenly it hit him—the Fourth of July. Less than six weeks off.

The Fourth was huge in Lonesome Way. When he was a kid, the town had held bake sales, quilt auctions, and a parade every year on the Fourth.

So. The tradition continues.

But it was only June. Early June. Wes knew he'd be long gone before the Fourth of July rolled around. His mother had emailed him about his grandmother tumbling off the curb outside of Benson's Drugstore. How she'd lost her balance, and ended up lying in the street with a concussion and a broken wrist.

Wes figured it must be gnawing at her to be laid up and waited on.

Ava Louise Todd was nothing if not independent, active, sharp as a bayonet. She was at once the sweetest and most imperial little woman he'd ever met. She had grace, guts, and instincts—along with a twinkle in her eye that Wes had always loved.

He missed her. Of course, he missed his mother and sister, too. But he'd carved out a very different life for himself in a world far from Lonesome Way. He couldn't set foot in this town without all kinds of memories flooding back, and they sure as hell weren't the warm and cozy kind.

Mainly because Hoot McPhee was a bastard. A dead one now.

But Wes always associated stepping into his family home on Daisy Lane with an explosive confrontation with his father.

That mean, demanding, ultra-critical son of a bitch had

made his family's life a living hell. Nothing anyone in his family did had ever been good enough for Hoot. Especially nothing that Wes did.

He couldn't be sorry that Hoot was dead. He'd be hard put to it now to resist the urge to slam a fist into his father's face if they ever met up again. For his mother's sake, he'd managed to refrain from doing that—except for once—but it hadn't been easy.

Which was why Wes had taken off right after graduating high school. He'd had too much anger to stick around—he and Hoot likely would have come to blows on a daily basis if he'd stayed.

So he'd made his own way through college and law school, and he'd never looked back. Never asked for a dime. And wouldn't have taken one.

When his father died, Wes had been holed up in the jungles of Colombia, but even if he'd been within a hundred miles of Montana at the time, he wouldn't have gone to Hoot's funeral.

Hell, he wouldn't have crossed the street for Hoot McPhee.

The man had bullied his children and cheated on his wife. He'd made everyone in his family miserable. The irony was, he'd been well respected in the community—until it came out that he'd had affairs with too many women to count, including Lorelei Hardin, the mayor's wife. Only then had his mother finally had enough. She'd kicked Hoot out of the house—*her* house, since the Good Luck Ranch had been in her family for generations—and Hoot had spent the remainder of his days alone in a cabin on Bear Claw Road.

The sky had darkened to deep twilight blue by the time he turned onto Daisy Lane. In the distance, the Crazies loomed against the sky like ominous craggy giants. Night creatures rustled on either side of him in the brush. A bald eagle took flight from a thicket of trees. Then the Good Luck

Ranch house appeared at the end of the dusty road, warm light glowing from its wide windows.

He felt a strange clutch in his stomach.

Home. Or what had once passed for it.

Wes didn't feel as if he'd ever really had a home. He didn't expect he ever would. But now that he'd left the DEA and was starting over after all these years, he wanted to have someplace . . . someplace he could hang his hat, park his truck, and live alone and at peace.

He had a lot of bad memories to leave behind. Memories worse than those of life with Hoot McPhee in Lonesome Way.

He'd seen death, cruelty, greed, evil.

He'd lost friends. Good ones.

Now he needed a change. A small space of peace. He knew he wouldn't find it in the home of his childhood, but this was just his first stop. Someplace on the road ahead, he'd find what he was looking for. The DEA was behind him.

Thanks to a fellow agent's brother-in-law who'd helped him make some key investments over the years, he had a pretty big nest egg saved up. And a new line of work in mind. Along with a hankering for a piece of land, a cabin of his own. Nothing fancy, just a small place close to nowhere with a barn, a corral, and a couple of horses.

Solitude and quiet. A place where he could look at the stars, roam the wilderness and mountains, forget everything he'd done.

And everything he'd seen.

And everything he'd lost.

⌒

Fifteen minutes later, Wes tucked his grandmother's frail, spider-veined hand into his own large palm.

Gran's still-piercing green eyes eagerly searched his face.

"It's so good to see you, dear. How long can you stay? Please tell me you're finally home for good."

"Can't. I'd be lying, Gran." Seeing her forlorn expression, he pressed a kiss to her softly wrinkled forehead. "Hey, c'mon. I'll be here for a few days—at least."

"A few days? Is that all?"

He reacted without thinking.

"Maybe a week." *Wimp,* he thought an instant later. But it was too late to take it back now. "Someone has to make sure you're behaving yourself, right? No more falling and landing in the hospital—you got that, Gran?"

"Trust me, young man. That is not an experience I'd care to repeat." She gave a tiny indignant snort. "Your mother keeps hovering over me as if she expects me to kick the bucket any moment, and that new husband of hers means well, but I'm not used to people constantly popping in and asking me if I need something. Up until this happened . . ." She glanced balefully at the cast that ran from her wrist nearly to her elbow. It was decorated with childish crayon scrawls made by Aiden, her great-grandson. "I was fit as a fiddle, just fine in my own apartment. And I will be again."

"I'm sure that'll be soon, Mom. But only if you follow doctor's orders."

Wes's mother, Diana, spoke soothingly from the doorway. She looked calm now, but she'd let out a scream of shock and excitement when she'd first seen Wes standing at the ranch house door. Her face was still flushed with happiness at having her son home at last.

"I always follow doctor's orders." It was almost a snap. Ava had never liked having to lie about—she'd always been active and independent. And, Wes noted, she didn't appear interested in listening to her daughter telling her what was good for her.

Instead she focused on Wes as if Diana weren't even there.

"Tell me about you, child. What are your plans now that you've left the DEA?"

"Nothing real specific yet. Exploring something with an old buddy—ex–FBI—but I'm not ready to talk about it right now. Just feeling my way."

He leaned back in the chair he'd drawn up beside the bed in what had long ago been his mother's crafts room. It was true; he did have an idea for his future but it was probably going to happen in Wyoming, not Montana, and nothing was set in stone yet. So he wasn't ready to share with anyone.

"You'll stay for supper, won't you, Wes?" His mother shot him a hopeful glance and smiled when he nodded.

"Sure, Mom. Do you think I can walk away from whatever you're cooking? It smells incredible."

"It's just a potato-broccoli casserole."

"The one I love?"

"Of course." A smile curved her lips. She was still a very pretty woman. "Doug's grilling steaks and the salad is already chilling in the fridge. I just invited Sophie and Rafe and the kids for dinner, too. I hope that's okay."

She looked so unsure, Wes felt a stab of guilt. Did his mother think he disliked his family or something? Crap. Rolling to his feet in one smooth movement, he pulled her gently into his brawny arms and gave her a reassuring squeeze.

"I can't wait to see them. Actually, I picked up a couple of gifts for Ivy and Aiden along the way. So bring 'em on."

A wistful look crossed his mother's face. Wes knew she fervently wanted him to stay. For a year, ten years, forever.

Well, he couldn't give her that but he supposed he could give her a week. Maybe two. *And,* he thought resignedly, *in the future I'll have to keep more in touch. Visit more. Call . . .*

He gave her another little squeeze; then his grandmother started in.

"You'll stay here tonight, won't you? In your old room?"

"Don't push it, Gran." But amusement flickered in his eyes. He'd slept in all kinds of places in the past ten years since he'd entered law enforcement, most of them hellholes while he was undercover—some just a few yards of hard ground or mud, without a blanket, much less a pillow—but they'd all be preferable to staying in his old room from high school, under the same roof with his mother and grandmother in the ranch house that his father used to rule with an iron fist.

He needed space, solitude, and silence.

He needed air to breathe.

He wasn't used to being around people. At least not regular, law-abiding people, and certainly not his family.

"I'll probably catch a few winks in the barn."

"The barn?" His mother looked startled. "But it still gets quite cold at night. And there's not even a cot in there anymore!"

This time he couldn't contain a grin. "I promise, Mom, it'll be like the Ritz compared to some places I've been."

"Really? I don't like to think about that," she said quietly.

Damn. Wes stood to his full six-foot-four height, and wrapped his arms around her. She was thin, beautiful, with soft fair hair peppered with gray and dignity in her bearing and an innate gentleness in her artistic soul.

And she worried about him.

He could kill three men in the space of four seconds, but his mother still worried about him as if each day she were sending him off to the first day of kindergarten.

Thank God none of his buddies from the D Unit were here, he decided with a twinge of amusement.

"Then don't think about it, okay?" Giving her a gentle squeeze, he shook his head. "I'm done with the DEA and all that. Unless I miss it too much and decide to go back."

"Wes!"

He grinned.

"How about my apartment?" Gran piped up. "No one's staying there. It's right in town. First floor. I'm paying rent on it so you might as well use it—Martha lives in the same building, you know."

Whoa. Practically roommates with Aunt Martha. There's an incentive.

Wes held up a hand. "I'll figure it out, Gran," he said easily. "Thanks anyway."

Adroitly he switched the subject, asking to see the latest photos of Sophie and Rafe's young son, Aiden, and of Ivy, Rafe Tanner's teenaged daughter from his first marriage. By the time he finished scrolling through them, Sophie and Rafe had arrived with the kids in tow and his mother's new husband called out that the steaks were done.

Fortunately, by then, his mother and grandmother had managed to stop hovering over him like he was some frail little kid they needed to worry about, and not a decorated government agent for whom knife fights, gun battles, hand-to-hand combat, and dead-of-night drug raids were an almost daily routine.

Two months ago, after an extensive undercover stint in Tijuana, he and his unit scored the most important coup of Wes's career—busting Diego Rodriguez and his crew, all of whom were among the biggest suppliers of cocaine in South America.

D Unit had chalked up more than a dozen arrests of key players in that takedown, and Diego's son Manuel, twenty-two years old, deeply immersed in the family business, and with boatloads of blood on his hands, had been killed in a vicious firefight.

So had Wes's partner, Luis, who'd cocommanded the operation. It was supposed to have been his last.

And it was.

But not in the way Luis had thought. He'd been planning

to retire and live with his wife, Carmela, in San Diego for
the rest of his days. Instead he'd lost his life.

And saved Wes's.

Diego Rodriguez had been wounded—badly—but somehow he'd gotten away. Probably the old drug lord had been
dragged off and driven away by his number-one lieutenant,
Cal Rivers, an American thug who'd started out as one of
Diego's bodyguards and advanced in the organization to
primary hit man and confidante. Wes didn't know whether
Diego had ultimately survived his wounds, but it was possible he and Cal Rivers were both still out there—either
deep underground or floating in the wind.

If so . . . sooner or later, one or both would surface again.

Wes had a four-inch scar across his chest from that last
little encounter with Rivers. Not a big deal when he considered all the rest of his nicks and wounds.

But now, after nearly ten years of doing battle mentally
and physically, a new life loomed before him.

And he had some decisions to make.

"Wes, not to sound like Henry Higgins, but I think I've
got it." His stepfather, Doug Hartigan, snapped his fingers
a short time later as Diana circled the dining room table,
serving dessert—scoops of strawberry ice cream to go along
with the frosted lemon cake she'd baked that afternoon.

It had been too chilly once the sun went down to eat
outside on the new deck Hartigan had built. The nights
hadn't begun to warm up yet, so they'd eaten in the dining
room, bright with light and the colorful, twisted floating
candles his mother made, her latest artistic endeavor. They
glowed in a row all along the center of the table.

"I have just the solution for you," Wes's stepfather told
him. Doug Hartigan had taught high school geometry back
in the day, and had a quick, methodical mind. "If you don't
want to stay here or in town, how about the old Harper cabin

on Sunflower Lane? It's close by and I'm sure Annabelle Harper won't mind."

"Annabelle? She's back in Lonesome Way?"

Wes hadn't seen Annabelle Harper since high school. Yet he could still picture the tall leggy blonde with the huge golden brown eyes, the saucily uptilted nose, and a figure that made all the boys drool. Back in high school, she'd had a reputation for being fast, an easy lay.

And for being a bitch.

Several of the guys on his wrestling team had bragged about being with her at some point or another—even if just for one night. Including Clay Johnson, Wes's closest buddy back in those days.

It was Clay who'd told Wes and the others all about how easy it was to get Annabelle Harper naked. How she'd do anything to make a guy happy. After hearing Clay describe how hot she was, and how easy, all the guys lined up to date her.

But once someone broke up with that girl . . . whew. According to Clay, she got hostile in a big way.

Wes had seen that for himself when Annabelle slapped Clay in the school hallway one day, apparently out of the blue. And when Clay had shoved her in response, she'd punched him in the stomach. Wes had been opening his own locker a few feet away, but had needed to hustle over and intercede after Clay grabbed her by both arms and rammed her up hard against his locker.

Of course, Clay never should have put his hands on her, but that girl was trouble any way you looked at it.

"I thought Annabelle left town right after high school."

"She did. Just like you," Sophie told him. "But she came back to stay a year ago. And I'm glad she did. So's the rest of the town."

"Annabelle really stepped up." Lifting Aiden onto his lap, Rafe began rubbing the little guy's back as he spoke.

"She left her whole life and her dance career in Philadelphia to come home and take care of her sister's kids."

"Why? What do you mean? Something happen to Trish and Ron?"

Sophie looked chagrined. "Oh, God, Wes. You didn't hear?"

"There was a plane crash last January. It was terrible—they both died." Rafe's daughter, Ivy, spoke softly, her eyes solemn. "And they had twin little girls at home. Megan and Michelle are only seven. And then there's Ethan, of course—he's ten. So now Annabelle has to take care of all of them. I babysit them sometimes. They're nice kids, and not any trouble at all."

Wes glanced at Sophie in shock. "How did this happen?"

"Ron was regional manager of J. T. Stevenson Lumber," she said quietly. "He needed to go to Portland for a company meeting, and Trish went with him so she could visit her old college roommate who lived there. They were only going to be gone one night, so they arranged for the kids to stay overnight at friends' houses that evening and during the day. But their commuter plane developed engine trouble. It went down over Saddleback Ridge. There weren't any survivors."

Wes sat back and let out a breath.

He'd bumped into Trish and Ron in Merck's Hardware store the last time he'd been home. They'd both looked great—and happy. He hadn't seen Ethan, but they'd had their twins in tow. The girls had barely been of school age, he remembered. Tiny little puffballs of femininity. Little more than toddlers.

Ron had mentioned a friendly poker game coming up at Dave Harvey's home that evening—Dave had been the halfback on the football team in high school and Wes had barely seen anyone from back then in a whole lotta years.

"Stop by if you have time," Ron had suggested. "There'll be tubs of chilled beer. And pizza."

He'd been friendly. Like most everyone in Lonesome Way. But Wes hadn't gone to Dave Harvey's to play poker. He'd still been grieving back then. It was only two months since Cara had died, and he hadn't been in the mood for games or laughs or jokes.

Cara Matthews had been perhaps the toughest DEA agent he'd ever come across—not to mention his partner on more than a dozen cases. She'd actually been more than his partner. She'd been more to him than any other woman he'd ever met.

Cara had been in her mid-thirties, lean, tough, beautiful in an edgy way. They worked well together. Hell, they did everything well together. And she'd saved his butt more times than he could count. He should have been there to save her. If he hadn't been tied up in Sierra Leone when she was assigned to a case in Bolivia . . .

His sister's voice broke into memories filled with regret.

"Why don't I give Annabelle a call and run it by her? She's been wanting to rent out that cabin for extra income. But it needs some repairs first and she hasn't been able to afford them. I know the roof needs to be patched. And some kids threw rocks and broke a couple of windows last summer, but the cabin has heat and a stove and a bed—"

"Now, *that* is an excellent idea." Gran spoke in her take-charge tone. "Wes, the Harper cabin will be like a five-star country inn compared to what you're used to—and it's close by. I bet Annabelle would let you stay there for free, especially if you're willing to do a little fixing up while you're in town. She can't afford to hire anyone. Sophie, why don't you call her and let her know that Wes is in town and needs a place—"

"Gran, I'm a big boy," Wes interrupted before she had him signing a lease. He'd noticed his mother growing quiet during all the talk about Annabelle, and then he remembered why.

Time to change the subject.

"I'll swing by Sunflower Lane and speak to Annabelle myself," he said easily. "Meantime, fill me in on the Fourth of July parade stuff. I'm sure you're still in the thick of all the planning for every community event, as usual."

"Of course I am, dear. But Sophie and Annabelle Harper happen to be working together on the entertainment committee this year. So if anyone can persuade Annabelle to let you stay in the cabin, it's your sister."

Ava Louise Todd was not a woman easily distracted, especially when she set her mind to something. "I'd feel better if you'd let Sophie call her right now and make all the arrange—"

"Gran," Sophie broke in. "Wes has managed to return in one piece from all the hellish places he's worked these past years, so I'm betting he can negotiate a place to stay with Annabelle Harper all on his own. Why don't you let Doug help you into the living room while Mom and I clean up?"

Their mother was already stacking an armload of plates onto the empty casserole platter.

"I'm fine, Sophie. You all go and visit." Diana spoke brightly, but Sophie and Wes exchanged glances, and Wes saw his stepfather frown.

Damn. Obviously, talking about Annabelle Harper still made his mother uncomfortable and Wes couldn't blame her for that. His father's cheating with Annabelle's aunt Lorelei, the mayor's ex-wife, had been the final straw in Diana and Hoot's marriage.

Hoot had been a terrible husband and a worse father, but Diana had pretty much looked the other way until Hoot's affair with the mayor's wife and several other women exploded through the town. Only then had Diana kicked him out. His father had been dead for years now, and his mother was happily remarried, but that didn't mean any mention of Lorelei or anyone related to her didn't still sting.

Maybe he should forget the Harper cabin, after all.

But the moment his mother vanished into the kitchen, and Doug escorted Gran to a comfortable wing chair in the living room, his sister zoomed back into the dining room and placed a hand on his arm.

"Don't mind Mom and Gran," she said in a low tone. "The two of them are just fussing over you because they're so glad to see you. They'll settle down in a week or so."

"Great. I'll be gone by then."

"No . . . really? Wes, I was sort of hoping—"

Her voice trailed off.

He frowned. "Hoping what?"

"That you might stay a little longer. You have no idea how down Gran's been since her fall. But she's positively cheerful now that you're here. Look at her—she's smiling like a young girl. She'll have to wear that cast for a while, and it's going to get hot and itchy and will drive her crazy. She still gets a little dizzy sometimes from the concussion and won't be able to cook or quilt or even dress herself without help for some time. But if you're here, she might not mind all that so much. You always could twist her around your finger and you know it. You were her favorite."

He started to deny this, but she cut him off. "You know it's true. Nobody can cheer her up like you can. But maybe," she said slowly, "you have something better to do? Somewhere to be?"

"Not exactly. But, Soph, that doesn't mean—"

"Come on, Wes, promise me you'll stay through the Fourth of July. Gran would get such a kick out of having you here—showing you off to all of her friends, everyone in town. You used to love that parade and the bake sale and all the food stands when you were a kid."

"Yeah, I loved collecting spiders and eating banana popsicles twice a day back then, too, but I can live without them now."

She grinned. "It'll be fun. You'll see. And by then, Gran's cast will come off and the worst will be over. Think about it."

"I just did. Two weeks, Soph, that's my limit. Or else I'll go stir-crazy."

She shook her head at him, frowning. "You always were more stubborn even than Dad."

"But not half as mean."

"No. Not mean at all." Her frown faded. She squeezed his arm and stood on tiptoe to kiss his cheek. "You're nothing like Hoot. You never were. You're tougher than him, stronger. You're fifty times the man he ever was. You were never a bully, always a defender."

"How do you know I haven't changed?"

Looking down into her eyes, he saw warmth and love deep within them. He felt the same about her. The years and miles couldn't ever change that.

"I know," she said simply. "So think about staying until after the Fourth. By then I'm sure we'll all be sick of you and more than ready to let you go."

"Nice. Very nice, sis."

Sophie laughed at him, and disappeared into the kitchen.

By the time Wes drove back down Daisy Lane that night, he had just about decided to camp out under the stars. Except clouds were already moving in. There'd be rain before morning. And as he turned onto Squirrel Road, he heard thunder rumble in the distance and saw a flash of lightning spark across the cloud-tinged peaks of the Crazies.

The Harper cabin might have a leaky roof and a few broken windows but it would be shelter in the storm. His mother and grandmother would have a fit tomorrow if they found out he'd slept in his truck.

There was no damn way he could take being fussed over and worried about more than two weeks. He'd rather face a gang of human traffickers. He'd be long gone by the Fourth of July parade, but for tonight, he'd bed down in the Harper cabin.

Unless Annabelle Harper said no.

But from what he'd heard of her back in high school, that wasn't likely to happen. According to his old friend Clay, Annabelle was the girl who didn't say no.

Chapter Two

As a storm blue darkness stole over the mountains, Annabelle sat on the front steps of the house she'd grown up in and sipped her coffee.

The front door stood open behind her, and only sweet, calm quiet came from inside.

She'd hear clearly through the screen door if Megan or Michelle called out for her.

Her ten-year-old nephew, Ethan, was no doubt still poring over his book. The title made her smile. *Lost Loot: The Untold Riches Hidden in the American West.*

Ethan was such a *boy*. Fascinated by a book crammed full of information on supposedly buried or hidden treasure, just waiting for him and his friend Jimmy to discover it in their own backyards.

Right.

The author, Peter Lamont, had passed through town on a book tour that took him through Montana, Wyoming,

Colorado, and Utah. He'd spoken to a packed crowd at the Lonesome Way Community Center two weeks ago. Lamont had done extensive research and had determined that a good deal of gold, cash, and jewels stolen from stagecoach hold-ups and bank robberies in the late 1800s were still buried where the outlaws who stole them had hidden them. The outlaws, he'd theorized, had always intended to come back when it was safe to retrieve the treasure, but most times, they'd been killed or arrested before they could do that.

Ethan and his best friend, Jimmy Collier, had listened with rapt attention—no doubt partly because both of their great-great-grandpas had belonged to the notorious Henry Barnum gang. They'd been two out of five outlaws who'd all killed one another off in Montana within months after their successful gold heist.

And with their deaths had gone the secret of what became of that massive chest of gold bars they'd snatched from a Kansas bank in 1878.

Annabelle's great-grandfather Big Jed had been found dead—gut-shot on a rocky ledge on Storm Mountain—less than twenty miles from his cabin on Sunflower Lane. Rumor had it he'd been headed either toward or away from the hiding place of the gang's buried gold when he was murdered.

But no trace of the gold was ever found.

Ethan and Jimmy were completely fascinated by the lore of this treasure.

Or perhaps obsessed is more like it, Annabelle thought, taking another sip of her coffee as a breeze flitted through the trees that flanked the house, and sent her long blond curls flying.

The treasure was all the two boys talked about. After hearing Peter Lamont speak, the boys had pooled their allowance money to buy his book, and pored over it together for hours at a time. They'd made a friendship pact to search for the loot together and split it fifty-fifty when it was found.

This was Ethan's week to keep the book, and he'd been plopped on his bed practically memorizing every map and clue and anecdote each night before going to sleep.

No doubt dreaming all night long about finding lost gold, she thought ruefully. But anything that took his mind off losing his parents was a good thing. When she'd first moved home after Trish and Ron died, Ethan and the girls had asked her every day when their parents were coming back.

Much better to think about treasure than loss, she thought, her own heart aching. She missed her sister so much. Tears momentarily stung her eyes. She knew Trish's kids were suffering even more.

Annabelle had immersed the girls in art and dance classes at the community center this summer, and she'd signed them up to start Brownies in the fall. Ethan, thank heavens, had basketball camp every day along with his dreams of finding lost treasure.

She wanted each of them to hold on to their dreams as long as they could. She didn't have many dreams these days. Only bills. She wasn't making much teaching ballet and tap at the Lonesome Way Community Center, and her own little nest egg from her so-called dance career in LA was dwindling quickly. She wouldn't touch any of Trish or Ron's insurance money—that had been safely invested for Michelle, Megan, and Ethan's college educations.

If she could just get a little bit ahead . . .

She closed her eyes, dreaming of the possibilities. First she'd hire someone to fix up the dilapidated old cabin that had been built by Big Jed, and then she could rent it out. The rental money would help her get by each month and keep all three kids, growing like weeds, in new clothes. The twins really wanted a pony, too, but there was no way that was happening for a while. Not unless . . .

She'd been turning over an idea in her head, thinking about starting a small-scale candy business. Everyone loved her homemade chocolates. Her mother had taught her how to make them when she was in high school and in charge of the Valentine's Day dance. Caramel truffles were her specialty. And if she could just find time to get a small-scale business going, she was sure she could earn some handy extra money making candy from home. She could make treats for birthday parties, anniversary parties, goodie bags, weddings—and maybe even sell a line of chocolates to Sophie Tanner at A Bun in the Oven bakery.

Perhaps there could even be a mail-order business down the road, she thought, her heart lifting with hope at the idea.

The only two things Annabelle liked better than dancing were reading and chocolate. And sex, of course. Not that she'd had any of that in a while . . . not since she'd left Zack.

Leaving Zack.

Hands down the smartest thing she'd done in a long time. She still winced whenever she thought about how blissfully clueless she'd been going into her marriage to Zack Craig. And how much she'd put up with before she got out.

Just about the only good thing about her marriage was the part where she'd left. Somehow she'd been dazzled by his brown-haired, blue-eyed, boy-next-door good looks. By his crinkly, attractive, nice-guy grin. By the successful ad executive career, and his careless sophistication and readiness to buy drinks instantly for a crowd of her friends.

They'd married in the month of June less than six months after they met—and she'd moved out in November. Zack hadn't called her now—alternately begging and badgering her to take him back—in almost three months.

A record. And a relief.

With any luck, that meant he'd finally given up. If the jerk had even a tiny bit of sense, he would.

But then, she reflected, tilting her head up toward the sky as thunder boomed and a jagged streak of lightning sliced the darkness, a man who pushed his wife around and knocked her into a wall if she even spoke to another man in an elevator, who cheated on her with an underage jailbait intern who just happened to be the niece of his firm's marketing vice president, didn't have much sense, did he?

And neither did the idiot who'd married him, she reflected ruefully. And then her cell phone rang.

Speak of the devil. Why wasn't I thinking about Johnny Depp?

Her throat tightened. Reflexively she braced herself as she set her coffee cup down on the step and tugged her phone from the pocket of her white hoodie.

For months after their separation and divorce, Zack had called her almost every other day, in turns harassing her to take him back, and soulfully pleading his case. Doing his best to persuade her to give him another chance.

Like that was ever going to happen.

But one glance at her lit-up caller ID let her relax. It wasn't Zack, thank goodness. It was her best friend, Charlotte Delaney, the petite brunette director of the community center who had never met a mojito she didn't like.

"Annabelle!" Charlotte squealed. "Sit down! I hope you're sitting down! I'm engaged!"

Several incoherent screams of joy followed these words. "Wait, Annabelle, talk to Tim! I have to jump and run around a little. I'm so freaking excited!"

"Charlotte! This is awesome—" Annabelle tried to get in, but Tim Deane's calm voice interrupted her.

"Hey, Annabelle. It's me. If my future wife doesn't break a leg from jumping around like a lunatic, it'll be great. She's going nuts. She grabbed the ring right outta my hand and put it on her own finger the minute I pulled it out of my pocket."

"That's Charlotte for you." Annabelle smiled on the darkened porch. "Congratulations, Tim. To both of you."

Charlotte and Tim had been dating on and off for nearly

a dozen years. First in high school, then a breakup after a year at different colleges; then they got back together for six months, then a huge blowout that had Charlotte crying for two straight weeks. Then Charlotte got engaged to someone else, but after three months she called it off, and for the past two years Charlotte and Tim had been back together, making good and sure before they took the next step.

"You two finally figured it all out," she began, filled with happiness for them, but suddenly it was Charlotte, not Tim, on the phone again.

"I need to freaking show you this ring!" Charlotte was talking faster than ever. "Can we come over? Tim, can we go see Annabelle? I . . . Oh, yeah, okay. You're right. Good idea. Annabelle, we're going to go have sex now. It's okay, Tim. What's wrong with you? It's not my mom; it's only Annabelle. She knows we have sex. Well, yes, my mom knows, too, but I wouldn't bring it up to her and . . . okay. Annabelle, gotta go, but you're the first to know after my mom and Aunt Susie, and I'll tell Tess tomorrow. Tim's going to call his brother now . . . Oh, you're not? Okay, sex first, and calling his brother tomorrow."

"Have fun, you two. Shower planning starts ASAP," Annabelle managed to get in before Charlotte was laughing again and sounding breathless.

"I don't know if I want a bridal shower. I have to check first and see if it's bad luck."

Then she was gone.

Annabelle rose to her feet, a smile curving her lips as she turned to go inside. She wanted more hot coffee and her mind was already whirling with ideas for shower invitations, decorations, and bags of gaily wrapped chocolate candy favors. But as her fingers touched the latch of the screen door, she heard a sound that made her turn back toward the road.

Headlights glowed along the gravel road.

A car was rolling down her out-of-the-way lane.

At this hour?

It couldn't be Charlotte and Tim—that was for sure. And it wasn't a car at all, she realized, peering through the darkness sliced only by the faint gleam of the moon. It was a truck. And it was coming fast.

She squashed the urge to retreat inside and lock the door, to speak through it until she found out who was here this late at night.

She wasn't dating anyone. And she wasn't expecting anyone at this hour.

But this is Lonesome Way, she reminded herself. *Not Los Angeles or New York or Philadelphia. This is a very small, very safe town.*

But still . . . she wasn't exactly *in* the town; she was outside of it. Miles from another house, in a rural, fairly deserted area, and it could be anyone.

Plus, there was that hiker who'd disappeared a few weeks ago in the mountains. Sheriff Hodge had called off the search only yesterday without finding a trace of the man. No one knew what had become of him.

She drew a breath as the black truck pulled up twenty feet from her front steps, doing her best to ignore the tightening in her throat. But she did reach into the pocket of her hoodie, her fingers closing around the tiny can of Mace tucked in the folds.

A tall man swung out of the truck. Her stomach tightened as he strode toward her but suddenly she sensed something familiar about him.

Impossible to place it . . . but there was something in his walk . . . in those long, purposeful strides. He wasn't just tall; he was big. Muscular. He moved with authority and purpose in the night and she sensed a forcefulness that went well beyond his powerful build.

He had the authoritative walk of a quarterback, she

thought. Or a Navy SEAL. His shoulders were broad, his chest sculpted beneath a white tee and an open leather jacket. His longish hair looked almost as dark as the night sky.

As he closed the distance between them, she drew the Mace out of her pocket and clenched it tightly.

"Stop right there. Who are you?"

She wasn't afraid, not really, not with the Mace in her grip, but she felt tension whipping through her. He advanced one more step, putting him within the gauzy glow of the porch light—and suddenly she recognized him.

She dropped the Mace back into her pocket.

He looked different. Harder, rougher, and fifty times tougher than she remembered. But still . . .

She knew him. Trying to keep her face expressionless, she swallowed hard as memories rushed back.

Bad memories. High school memories.

The man approaching her porch was Wes McPhee. Sophie's big brother. The baddest of the bad boys in Lonesome Way.

And Clay Johnson's friend.

Chapter Three

~

"What are you doing here?" she blurted.

"Hello to you, too, Annabelle."

Wes McPhee's expression didn't change but Annabelle thought she detected a tiny glint of amusement in his deep green eyes. They seemed to shine like a tiger's eyes in the night. Probably a trick of the moon, but still . . .

"I . . . I'm sorry. Aren't you supposed to be . . . in Afghanistan or Tijuana or someplace like that?"

"Keeping track of me?"

Now he did smile. Mockingly, she thought. Back in high school, he'd been like all the other boys, believing Clay's lies about her. She remembered all too well the way they'd looked at her—all of them. Matt, Tobe, Scooter.

Jeering. Scornful.

Wes had always been something of a loner, an independent spirit even back then, but everyone wanted to be his friend. He was handsome, cool, smart—and somehow mysterious. Accepted easily in every clique, all the girls tried to catch his eye. The boys had respected him—and yet, he'd kept his distance from everyone.

Well, he *had* been nice to her that one day in biology class. They'd been assigned to teams to dissect a frog, and she'd been paired with Wes. She hadn't had the stomach for dissecting anything, and was certain she was going to be sick. She must have looked positively green, as green as the frog, because Wes shot her one of those sharp, penetrating glances of his, and then went ahead without a word and completed the entire dissection himself as their teacher graded papers and never looked up.

Annabelle remembered she hadn't even thanked him. She'd been too busy taking deep gulps of air and trying not to run out the door and barf. She'd never liked science. Or math. She liked daydreaming. And reading. And dancing.

Growing up she usually spent most of her time at the Lonesome Way library or the dance studio in Livingston where her mother had taken her and Trish for lessons.

When she wasn't reading a book, she was dreaming about being a dancer. On Broadway. Or in a professional dance troupe. Or in a music video.

She certainly hadn't liked biology. And she hadn't liked frogs, dead or alive.

Wes hadn't needed her help doing that dissection. She was never sure whether he was being kind or just indifferent that day when he went ahead without her. She'd suspected kindness, but it was hard to tell with Wes.

Anyway, all that had happened the year Wes started dating Marissa Fields, and before Annabelle had made the huge mistake of going out with Clay. Before the rumors started and spread, fanning out like an out-of-control July wildfire, before all the kids at Lonesome Way High had started believing she was fast and easy.

A slut.

"Everyone in town knows you work for the DEA." She wiped her hands on her old faded jeans. It took an effort not to stare at him.

Wes was too gorgeous for words. Too big. Too sexy. All that thick brown hair a woman would love to plunge her fingers through. That lean jaw, stubbled with a dark growth of beard, a straight nose, and those piercing green eyes beneath dark brows. Not to mention the hot body that could have starred in a centerfold, except the man the body belonged to looked like posing for a magazine was the last thing he'd ever do.

But anything else? Bull riding, skydiving, battling terrorists in hand-to-hand combat? Oh yeah, he looked like a man who'd step up quickly to volunteer for all of that in a single day.

Fierce, she thought on a breath. Wes McPhee looked fierce. Like a warrior. Big, tough, strong. Dangerous.

And sexy as hell.

Don't even think about it, she told herself, as betraying little sparks of heat flicked everywhere inside her.

Don't go there. You and men spell disaster, remember?

And this man . . . no way. No how. From the looks of him, he was definitely a lot more than she could handle on her good days, and now that she had all these responsibilities, needing first and foremost to be there for Megan and Michelle and Ethan . . .

Men are bad luck. Bad karma. And bad for you. Get rid of him. Now.

"You work in all the hot spots all over the world, right? Sophie's mentioned it. So . . . I just thought . . . you were . . . over there somewhere." She was babbling, but she couldn't seem to stop. "I didn't expect to see you here. If you were anywhere, I'd think you'd be . . ." She broke off suddenly and drew in a breath. "Your grandmother. You're back because of her accident."

He nodded, his eyes unreadable. "My sister mentioned you have a cabin you're looking to rent out. I'm interested."

It was the last thing she expected to hear. She stared at him blankly. "You want to stay in my cabin? But . . . why?"

"It's vacant. And I need a place to sleep."

His tone was patient, as if he were speaking to the town idiot. Which he probably thought he was.

"I don't understand. Can't you stay at Daisy Lane? Or with Sophie and Rafe at Sage Ranch? Your entire family's here. I'm sure they offered to put you up."

"Yeah. They did."

"Then that's what you should do," she told him firmly, and as his gaze pierced her, she suddenly remembered she was wearing her oldest jeans, a hoodie, and a faded gray T-shirt that had a tiny hole at the shoulder. And not a lick of makeup.

"How much do you want a week for the cabin?"

"Wes, this won't work. There's no way. The cabin's in really bad shape."

Brows lifting, he shot her a smile. "Guess you're mistaking me for someone who's particular."

"Most of the windows are broken. They're boarded up. It needs paint—badly. And the roof needs patching; the flooring is kind of a mess—"

"I'll take it."

Annabelle stared. "Why?"

"Need a place. And as I said, I'm not particular. I'll only be here a couple of weeks. Unless my family badgers me into staying for the July Fourth parade."

She did not want Wes McPhee living right down the road—a stone's throw from this house. She *did* want to rent out the cabin and bring in some extra money, but not now, not in the shape it was in, and not to him.

Clay's friend. He'd been there in the hallway that day and stepped in. . . .

Seeing him now made her relive the whole disgusting
sequence of events.

Of course, she'd encountered all of those other guys—
Clay's whole gaggle of friends—in town regularly ever since
she moved back. But aside from Clay Johnson, the others
had grown up nicely and seemed like they didn't even
remember all the old rumors. Scooter had even apologized
to her for lying about what had happened during *their* date.

They'd all lied, probably to save face with Clay, but the
past was the past, and she really didn't care what anyone
thought anymore. The only person she still disliked was
Clay Johnson himself. Because he was a creep and a liar
and some things never change.

But seeing Wes brought it all back—the deserted hall of
the high school that day, Clay's jeering voice as he shoved
her up against her locker . . . and Wes stepping in. . . .

But the past wasn't the only reason she didn't want Wes
living in the cabin. Sure, the memories of that awful time
in her life were one thing, but then there was the fact that
she'd sworn off men and she was gun-shy about relationships, to say the least. And Wes McPhee was just too . . .
too everything.

Too big. Too deliciously masculine. Too tempting. Too
hard-core tough-guy sexy—even that slice of a scar along
his jawline was sexy.

Down, girl.

She couldn't read anything in his face except firm, polite
determination to rent her cabin. But it wouldn't exactly be
smart to have him living practically a stone's throw away.
Every time she saw him, she'd probably think about Clay—
and that wasn't good.

Besides, her aunt Lorelei had had an affair with Wes's
father way back when. His mother surely wouldn't be
pleased if her only son got involved in any way, even as a
tenant, with Lorelei Hardin's niece.

Diana McPhee had always been passably polite to her in town, of course, but out of respect, Annabelle tried to steer clear of her.

The last thing she wanted was to upset the applecart now. She had a ton of responsibilities these days, raising three kids, keeping them in food and clothes, and she didn't need any distractions of the big bad male kind.

Especially from a big bad male who'd almost instantly awakened the tingly waves of heat inside her she'd thought were dead and gone.

"It wouldn't be right to charge rent for the cabin in its current condition," she told him. "Later, when it's fixed up, might be a different story, but you'll be gone by then—"

"How about you don't charge me rent?"

Her brows shot up. The man had some nerve. And he just didn't give up, did he?

He grinned. "I didn't mean that the way it sounded. The thing is, I like my own space. I've retired from the DEA and want to decompress before moving on to the next stage of my life. I'll only be around a couple of weeks. So how about you let me stay in your cabin, and in exchange I'll do some repairs for you. As many as I can get done while I'm here. Then I'm heading to Wyoming to meet up with a buddy of mine, and you can rent it out to the next drifter who comes along. We'll call it even."

"You . . . want to fix up the cabin?"

"Sure. I'm sticking around for my grandmother's sake, but I don't have anything else to do here. I'm used to being busy."

Yeah, I know. Busy catching drug dealers and shooting terrorists. Being a hero. Everyone knew of the danger and courage it took to be a DEA agent.

She was sure he'd have scars all over his body from bullets or knives or whatever. For a moment, staring at his powerful frame, lean and packed with muscle, she wondered how many scars there were, and where exactly . . .

Don't. Don't picture him naked. Don't even go there.

"Bad idea?" he asked, and she realized she hadn't answered him yet.

"I . . . I'm not sure." Since when had she become so indecisive? She didn't want him renting out the cabin, and living so close by. On the other hand, she probably wouldn't see him all that much—and if he'd do the repairs, she could actually rent it out when he left.

The extra money would sure come in handy.

She had three children sleeping upstairs who'd all be going through growth spurts soon enough—she needed to get over herself and be practical.

"You've got a deal." She drew in a breath. "Wait here— my nephew and nieces are asleep and I don't want to wake them. I'll just pop inside and get you the key. I can't take you down and show you the place tonight, because I can't leave the kids alone. But it's only a quarter mile behind the house. There's a dirt track; you just have to follow it. It's pretty rough, and hard to see at night—"

"Not going to be a problem. I'll find it," he said with some amusement.

"Just remember, it's not in great shape." Turning, she hurried up the steps of the porch, opened the screen door, and held it as she looked at him over her shoulder.

"There's heat—at least, I *think* it's working. And there's a small countertop refrigerator. The shower works; I'm pretty sure of that. And you'll find a set of clean linens and towels in the old bureau in the bedroom—"

"No fears. I'll make due. In the morning, after I take a good look around, I'll head over to Merck's for supplies. You can give me a list of what you need done, in case I miss anything."

"You've thought this through." She found herself relaxing, even smiling suddenly, realizing that maybe, just maybe, this could be a godsend. In a couple of weeks, when Wes left, she might actually be able to rent out the cabin. The timing would be perfect. If she found a paying tenant, she'd have an extra windfall by the time school started in the fall, when she'd need to buy the kids their school supplies, books, and clothes.

"Hold on a minute—I'll get the key."

Wes stared after her as she disappeared inside the old ranch house. Wow. A knockout blond beauty in snug jeans, with the golden brown eyes of an angel, and curves that would bring a preacher to his knees.

Whoa. Down, boy.

Annabelle Harper had been hot as a teenager, with her mass of blond curls, those magnificent honey-colored eyes, and that tall, leggy figure, but now . . .

Now, even in an old T-shirt, hoodie, and jeans, she was absolutely, drop-dead stunning. All that curling blond hair tumbling around a delicate, wide-eyed face. A lush mouth it would be mighty sweet to taste. *Oh, man.*

It had taken all of his self-control not to stare at her breasts and imagine how much fun it would be to skim his hands and his mouth all down that slender, sensuous body. . . .

Look, but don't touch, pal, he warned himself as she whipped back out the door a moment later, a lone key clutched in her hand. *No sleeping with the landlord.*

Not that he had much chance of that, not with three little kids running around.

Not to mention the biggie—who her aunt was. There was no way he'd touch Annabelle Harper. Even if she wanted him to—which seemed highly unlikely.

Fact was, she'd seemed in a big hurry for him to leave.

Not that he didn't think he could change her mind about that—if he was inclined. Which he wasn't.

He'd been through enough fireworks abroad, fighting warlords and drug kingpins. He didn't need to stir up trouble in his hometown.

"I'll come by sometime tomorrow and you can let me know what else needs work and what you need," she said a little breathlessly. "I have more towels and linens I can spare—"

"Whatever's there will be plenty. See you tomorrow, Annabelle."

The last glimpse he had of her as he pocketed the key and turned away were her arms wrapped around herself from the cold, her empty coffee mug still resting on the porch steps, her eyes watching him warily in the darkness. The stillness of the night was broken only by the hiss of crickets and the shadow of a lone hawk hunting and swooping through the treetops.

By the time Wes started his truck and drove beyond the old ranch house and onto the narrow dirt road that wound behind it, Annabelle Harper had disappeared. The front door of the house was shut and the porch light off.

Only the warm gleam from the first-floor windows still lit the old place.

Tired from the long days on the road, Wes knew he'd fall dead asleep as soon as he hit the bed in the cabin—whether it had sheets on it, a blanket, pillow, or nothing at all.

The only thing he wanted right then was to somehow stop picturing Annabelle Harper slipping naked into that bed with him.

Because that just wasn't going to happen.

He was passing through. And she had a normal life. She was no doubt looking for a regular Joe, with roots and morals, and a sense of family, of community.

He wasn't that guy, not by a long shot, and he never would be. He'd done things he could barely stand to think about. He'd seen things women like Annabelle couldn't begin to imagine.

Cara could. She'd seen things, done things, too.

But Cara was gone.

No one else could possibly ever get him the same way. And though he hadn't been in love with Cara, Wes knew no other woman could possibly mean as much to him as she had.

He was passing through town briefly, then heading out. Getting involved even on a superficial level with Annabelle Harper was out of the question. He'd crossed a lot of lines in his career, but she had enough going on in her life—and that was one line he wouldn't cross.

So, with the total concentration and commitment that had carried him through nearly forty overseas missions, he gunned the engine and rattled over the bumpy dirt road to the Harper cabin, mentally deleting Annabelle Harper from his brain.

Chapter Four

❧

"We can't be late," Annabelle muttered to herself as she ran toward the base of the stairs.

"Megan! Ethan! Please come down here right now!"

"I can't find my tap shoes." Her eight-year-old niece sounded frantic.

"Did you look in your dance bag?"

"Yes, I . . . Just a minute—oh! Got 'em!"

Annabelle sighed in relief and rushed back to the kitchen, where her other niece, Michelle, was eating Cheerios from the box, chugging chocolate milk, and reading *Harry Potter and the Sorcerer's Stone* all at the same time, oblivious to everything going on around her.

It was only the second day of summer vacation, and Annabelle was scheduled to teach her first ballet class of the season at the Lonesome Way Community Center at nine A.M. sharp. But if Megan and Ethan didn't get a move on, all those little ballerinas between the ages of seven and nine would be tapping their feet waiting.

"Michelle, do you have your ballet shoes?" she asked, quickly smearing a bagel with cream cheese for Megan, who would probably have to eat it in the car if she didn't get to the breakfast table in the next four minutes. With relief she heard Ethan racing down the stairs.

"Mm-hmm. They're in my dance bag, Aunt Annabelle." Michelle, the organized, focused twin, lifted her orchid blue eyes from her book for a brief moment. "I'm glad I'll have two hours to read later when you teach adults," she murmured, then lapsed into silence once again, her attention morphing back to Hogwarts with lightning speed.

Annabelle downed a final gulp of coffee and finished the last bite of her own bagel just as Ethan skidded toward his chair. Her hair was scooped up in a loose ponytail, and she wore a purple leotard under her jeans, and a scoop-necked pink tank. After Michelle's ballet class, she'd teach Megan and Michelle's seven- to nine-year-olds tap class; then she had an hour each of adult yoga and teen jazz, all before lunch. This afternoon she had only one more class—a ballet class for ages four through six.

Then she'd spend an hour or two in the office helping Charlotte update all the files while they brainstormed ideas for the entertainment at the Fourth of July festivities.

She still needed to choreograph a tap routine for the kids to perform in the square after the parade, and design costumes that the kids' mothers could either sew or pull together.

Megan and Michelle were spending the afternoon at their friend Katie's home after their classes today, and after basketball, Ethan was signed up for a class on how to design your own video game, before getting picked up by his friend Jimmy's mom, who was taking the boys for lunch at Pepperoni's Pizza and then over to the park.

A long day, she thought. And arriving late for the first day of class wouldn't be a good way for anyone to start. She forced herself to draw a calming breath as her nephew plopped down at the table.

"I'm ready to roll right now, Aunt Annabelle." Dumping milk from the carton into his cereal, Ethan began shoveling spoonfuls into his mouth. He glanced over at the counter where a strawberry pie perched beside a pair of ceramic apple salt and pepper shakers.

"Can I have pie with my breakfast?"

Her brows lifted. "Nice try. You can have fruit and a bagel—or a blueberry muffin." She pushed a bowl brimming with raspberries and grapes in the center of the table closer to him. "Maybe tonight for dessert you can have pie. And maybe on Sunday for breakfast. I sometimes make exceptions on Sunday for pie."

Grinning, he grabbed a handful of grapes. "Can I have pie when I get home from Jimmy's later? I really like your strawberry pie. It tastes just like Mom's."

"That's because your grandma taught us both how to make it."

"I know. Mom used to tell us that all the time, too."

For a moment a little silence fell in the kitchen. Michelle glanced up from her book, and her lip quivered. Annabelle touched her hand, and smiled at Ethan.

"Your mom made much better cherry cupcakes than I ever did. But my fudge was always better than hers. And we were equally good at baking strawberry pie."

"Mom always talked to us about you," Ethan said in a low tone. "How you were living your dream. She said you almost made it onto *So You Think You Can Dance!*"

"Not exactly," Annabelle said as lightly as she could, relieved when they both started to eat again. "I was close, but not that close."

"Weren't you, like, in the top thirty?"

"Yes, but you needed to make the top twenty to get on the show."

"But you're good!" Michelle set down her book with a thunk. "You're the best dancer ever! Everyone's jealous that we get to have dance lessons at home whenever we want."

"And you were in a movie." Megan sounded breathless as she dashed into the kitchen. Annabelle hadn't heard her come down the stairs, but her tomboy niece slid into her seat like a baseball player sliding home, her straight, dark blond hair poking out from beneath a ball cap. "A movie with Jack Black!"

"I was just an extra." She shrugged, but Megan took a bite of her bagel and spoke with her mouth full.

"But you danced. In a real movie! You did a pirouette, and then that guy dancer threw you in the air!"

For a total of fifteen seconds on-screen, Annabelle thought in amusement. "Listen, if we don't make it to class on time, some angry mothers of your friends are going to throw me, all right. They'll throw me to the wolves. So no more talking—just eating. We'll talk in the car!"

She barely got the words out before there was a knock on the back door.

Charlotte. A smile burst across her face. *She's probably too excited to wait until later to show me her ring. Or maybe it's Tess.*

Tess Stone, her other best friend, was a petite, practical redhead who worked as an accountant and lived on Absaroka Drive, right at the edge of town. She and her husband, John, were expecting a baby in July. *By now Charlotte must have told Tess she's engaged,* Annabelle thought. *Tess must want to talk wedding shower plans. . . .*

"Keep eating," she told the kids, hurrying to the door. "We need to leave in under two minutes."

But when she yanked open the door, it was neither Charlotte nor Tess who stood there.

Wes McPhee loomed over her. He looked hunkier than ever in the crystalline morning light in faded jeans, a white tee, and sunglasses. Along his jaw was the sexiest stubble she'd ever seen in her life.

"Morning."

That killer smile might send countless women to their knees, but Annabelle locked hers in place.

"Uh . . . g-good . . . morning. I . . . didn't expect you so early."

As he pushed his sunglasses up onto his head, she was nearly blinded by the intense green of his eyes. Now that there was daylight, she could see flecks of gray and gold in them. It was impossible not to stare.

"Bad time?"

"Um, yes. We're leaving for town in . . . about thirty seconds, I'm afraid—"

"Dance class," Megan piped up. "We're gonna be late."

Megan was the social, talkative one of the twins, but Annabelle saw that Michelle had actually set down her Harry Potter book and was gazing at Wes as well.

Ethan popped a couple more grapes in his mouth, chewing while he watched Wes with interest.

"My class starts before yours." Michelle flipped her book closed and smiled shyly at Wes. "I take tap and ballet. Ballet is very hard. But I like it."

"Cool." Wes nodded gravely. "My niece, Ivy, took ballet once, I think."

"Oh, shoot. Be right back, Aunt Annabelle!" Shoving back his chair, Ethan bolted toward the stairs. "I forgot my treasure book and my basketball!"

"Hurry, please!" Annabelle called after him, but her nephew was already gone, his feet pounding up the steps.

"Girls, leave your dishes in the sink and run out to the car, buckle yourselves in. Wes, sorry, but we have to leave now."

She suddenly realized she felt flustered, not only by the

prospect of being late for work, but by the fact that Wes looked just as good this morning as he had last night. He looked even bigger today, if that was possible. Maybe because instead of that leather jacket, he wore that white tee that clearly revealed those sculpted biceps.

Good Lord, he really could have been a beefcake model in a commercial.

But this man was no pretty-boy model. The man standing in her kitchen looked like he could handle anything that came along. Cyclones or motorcycle gangs. Drug dealers, blizzards, or escaped murderers.

Rough and tough were understatements when it came to him. He wasn't just insanely handsome; he looked . . . edgy.

Dangerous.

Sexy as hell.

Even if she was interested in going out with a man—which she wasn't—he was so out of her league.

Not that it mattered. He certainly wasn't interested.

She couldn't read anything in his expression other than patience as the girls streamed past him with their dance bags hitched over their shoulders. The kitchen screen door slammed behind them.

"I'll get out of your hair. Just wanted to let you know I've made a list of repairs. Going to town for supplies soon and I'll get started today."

"Sounds like a plan." She started shoving dishes in the dishwasher as fast as she could, and speaking just as rapidly.

"Hope everything was good in the cabin last night. Did you have what you needed? No, don't tell me now; we'll discuss later. I've got to get to the community center. I'm teaching almost a full morning of dance classes and working in the office all afternoon. But I'll be home after that."

"No problem. Catch you later—"

But he broke off, stopping in his tracks. He stared across the kitchen, and Annabelle followed his gaze.

He'd spotted the half-full coffeepot and the strawberry pie sitting on the counter.

"You know, I'm not quite ready to face my whole family for breakfast this early in the morning," he admitted, then shot her a grin. "Don't have even a crumb of food in the cabin yet. Any chance I can steal a cup of coffee and a slice of that pie?"

"What . . . Oh. Sure." Slamming the old dishwasher closed—the only way to get it to latch properly—she thrust a cobalt blue mug at him. Hurriedly she grabbed a plate and slid a wedge of pie onto it. "You'll have to take it with you. We need to leave right now—"

"Ready!" Ethan yelled, racing back into the kitchen, his treasure book sticking out of his backpack and a basketball clutched within one skinny ten-year-old arm.

Suddenly, though, he skidded to a stop as he saw Wes holding the plate of pie.

"Aunt Annabelle, you said no pie for breakfast!" Ethan spun toward her, his eyes sharp with accusation. "That's not fair."

"You can have pie when we get home later, Ethan. Right now, Mr. McPhee is our guest. And we have to go."

"But it's not fair!"

"Why can't the kid have a piece of pie?" Wes asked her.

"No pie for breakfast. That goes for you, too." She grabbed the plate away from him even as he raised the fork toward his mouth. Scooping up a muffin from the basket on the table, she tossed it to him.

"Here, take this—and your coffee. And go. Ethan, get in the car and buckle up. Now."

"But—"

"Ethan!"

The boy shot her a frustrated glance and raced out the door.

Wes shook his head. "Bossy," he muttered. "Maybe I don't want to work for you, after all."

Her mouth dropped open before she saw the glint of humor in his eyes.

"You've already slept in my cabin and accepted the job, so you can't chicken out now."

Snatching up her purse and her own dance bag, she slung both over her shoulder and flew toward the door. "Just keep a list of whatever you need and how much it costs and slip it under the door."

He followed her, taking a bite of the muffin.

Since he gripped the steaming mug in one hand and the muffin in the other, she held the door for him, then closed it firmly behind them both.

"I might want to rework our arrangement," he said.

The words stopped her in her tracks. She whirled to face him.

"What does that mean?"

"Any way we can agree on room and board? This muffin's great. So's the coffee. How about including breakfast? I can come by every morning, pick it up, take it back to the cabin, and get to work."

"Done. So long as you don't expect a five-course buffet." Darting to her Jeep and tugging open the driver's side door, she wondered why she still felt flustered, and resolved not to let him see it. "I'll leave it on the porch for you if you're not here when we have to take off."

"That'll work."

Nodding, she slid into the Jeep, refusing to allow herself to peek into the rearview mirror as she roared away up the lane.

"Who was that man?" Michelle asked.

"He's kind of scary looking," Megan declared.

"Why were you going to give him some pie?" Ethan demanded.

"Calm down, guys. You know Sophie Tanner from A Bun in the Oven? That's her brother. He's visiting Lonesome Way and he's staying in our cabin for a few weeks."

"That place? It's a mess!" Ethan looked startled. "You won't even let us play in there."

"He's going to fix it up for us in exchange for free rent. And breakfast," she added, making the turn onto Squirrel Road. "Then we can try to rent it out."

"If we rent it out, we'll have extra money, right?" Megan was beaming.

"Some extra." Annabelle slowed as a deer and two of the tiniest fawns she'd ever seen strolled across the road.

"Enough money to get a horse?" Megan asked.

"Two horses?" Michelle chimed in hopefully. "I really wish I could have my very own."

In the rearview mirror, Annabelle saw the twins' eager smiles and her stomach twisted a little.

"I don't know if we'll have enough for horses, but there should be enough to buy all of you some new school clothes for the fall." She knew their dad had promised them a few years ago that he was saving up to build a new barn and to get them a couple of horses so they could ride regularly. But that wasn't going to be possible now.

Her own salary and savings didn't include building a barn or the upkeep of two horses.

"If Jimmy and me find the treasure, I'll buy us a whole barnful of horses," Ethan announced.

"Well, that sounds great." Annabelle managed to hold back a laugh. But something tore at her heart. Her sister's kids had lost their parents, and if she could give them the world—horses, barns, treasure—she would. Let Ethan have his dreams. And let the twins have theirs.

Her dream was to raise them the way Trish would have wanted them raised. Loved, safe, healthy.

Instead of two parents, they now had one measly aunt. An aunt who knew more about pliés and arabesques and an awful marriage than she did about homework, rules, and schedules. But she was learning. Adjusting. One step at a time.

"Everyone out. Hurry."

Annabelle rolled into a parking spot in the lot flanking the community center at exactly two minutes before nine. The kids raced for the building, and she started to follow.

She was just breaking into a run herself when suddenly a green SUV roared into the lot like a tank and nearly mowed her down, swerving at the last second. Her heart skittered in a hundred different directions. Shaken, she watched the driver slide into a parking spot and spring out of the car.

Her chest tightened. Clay Johnson.

She should have known.

The scumbag who'd ruined her reputation in high school for sheer sport was in his mid-thirties now, a divorced father, but from what she'd seen and heard since she'd come back to Lonesome Way, all the arrogance of the rangy blond captain of the wrestling team was still intact. And the boy who'd lied about her and boasted how easily he'd supposedly gotten her naked in the back of his truck out at Cougar Rock still lived on in the man.

She spun away and kept walking, focused on getting to the community center gym where eleven little girls were waiting for their first day of summer dance class.

"You need to look where you're going, Annabelle," Clay called out, his voice every bit as smug as she remembered.

"You need to slow down behind the wheel." She spoke crisply without glancing backward but felt her spine stiffen.

Ignore him, she ordered herself. That was what she usually did when she ran into Clay. He'd become one of the wealthiest men in Lonesome Way after taking over his father's string of automobile dealerships across Montana and Wyoming, and he was on the town's planning board, tight with the mayor, and a big donor to the upcoming Fourth of July fund-raiser, which was intended to raise enough money to add an indoor basketball court and track to the community center.

Since she always had the urge to punch him in the stomach—or kick him squarely in the balls—she tried to avoid running into him. But avoiding a power player like Clay wasn't easy in Lonesome Way.

His son, Connor, a year younger than Ethan, was on Ethan's basketball team this summer. He was small for his age, with a sallow, subdued face, and looked the exact opposite of his strapping, broad-shouldered father. The boy had also climbed out of the car, and now stood uncertainly beside the SUV.

"Go on inside, Bear. You don't need me to walk you in. I have a meeting at city hall with the mayor," Clay said dismissively, waving the boy away.

Bear. The most unlikely name for the small, timid-looking boy, but then, Clay no doubt nicknamed him that because that was what he wanted his son to be. A bear. Big, bold, mean.

Like him.

Annabelle smiled at the boy who trotted past her, eyes downcast, then ignored the man behind her, until he suddenly lengthened his stride and deliberately blocked her path the moment his son disappeared ahead of her inside the one-story brick community center.

"What do you think you're doing?" Halting, she stared at him through narrowed eyes. "Get out of my way. Now."

"Every time I see you, you're always in a hurry."

"You're right. In a hurry to get away from you." She veered around him, half expecting him to try to cut her off, or follow, but instead she heard his low, curt laughter trailing after her, the same laughter that had followed her in the halls of Lonesome Way High when he and his buddies were trading lies about her, calling her an easy lay. A slut.

Don't stop, don't look back, don't pay any attention to him, she told herself, but she couldn't keep her heart from thumping with a combination of anger and wariness.

The man was a bully. Always had been, always would be. And Annabelle detested bullies. She felt sorry for his son, who was only in town for the summer. Patty Ann Benson, who worked at her father's drugstore on Main Street, had mentioned at one of the parade committee meetings that Clay's ex-wife moved to Helena after their divorce. Though she had full custody of the boy throughout the school year, he spent the summer months with Clay.

Poor kid.

Annabelle knew a thing or two about bullies. Zack was a bully, too—not that she'd realized it before she married him. All smiles and charm on the outside, but beneath the veneer he was jealous and suspicious. He'd begun shoving her around early in their marriage if she even spoke to another man—belittling her, bullying her, trying to control her.

Oh yeah, I know how to pick 'em, she thought, bursting into the community center. Good thing she'd sworn off men even before she moved back to Lonesome Way.

Glancing at the clock on the wall, she sprinted down the hall to the gym.

"We'll start with a warm-up first," she told the class of young girls lining up along the barre. Michelle was already there, shifting into first position as Annabelle punched on the warm-up music.

"First position," she called breathlessly, and kicked off her sandals, then stripped down to her leotard. "This will be our starting point every day."

Pulling on her ballet slippers, she darted toward the barre.

"Like this, ladies." She raised her arms in a graceful arc. "Arms bent at the elbow, feet turned out. Chin up, everyone. Now hold. That's it. Tummies in, girls, backs straight, heads up. Stand tall, as tall as you can. Keep those feet turned out. Beautiful! Moving on now. Second position . . ."

The tense rush of the morning slipped away. She gave herself up to the joy of teaching dance.

Years ago, in a tiny Livingston dance studio, she and Trish had been just like these young girls, their eager faces tight with concentration, as they fulfilled their own need and longing to dance. Now it was her turn to teach little ones with eyes full of stars how to leap and spin and fly.

Chapter Five

～

"Tell me the truth. Isn't this the most beautiful thing you've ever seen?"

Charlotte was seated beside Annabelle at a table in A Bun in the Oven, holding her engagement ring finger up to the afternoon light.

The square-cut diamond on a slender silver band sparkled like a summer star. With her dark brunette hair pulled up into a long smooth ponytail, and her eyes alight, Charlotte gazed at her ring, clearly enraptured by the diamond glittering with cold fire on her finger.

"It's gorgeous, Char. Tim did good." Annabelle broke off a chunk of a cinnamon bun and popped it into her mouth.

"It's downright perfect—that's what it is," Tess added. Her own left hand rested on her baby bump, while the other held a forkful of warm apple crisp in midair. Tess was the picture of maternal contentment in loose jeans and a bright yellow maternity top, her shoulder-length, burnished red hair curled gently around her lightly freckled, girl-next-door pretty face.

"Oooh." Suddenly gasping, she set her fork down with a clatter. Then a huge smile spread across her face. "Wow. That one was something. Anyone want to feel this mini linebacker or ballerina kick?"

"I do!" Annabelle and Charlotte spoke in unison and reached out at once.

"That is so . . . awesome." Annabelle spoke in a whisper as she felt the rolling motion beneath her fingers. Her heart filled at her friend's rapturous expression. Tess had been pregnant before, a little more than a year and a half ago. But she'd lost the baby late in the pregnancy.

She and John had been devastated, barely getting through each day for months after. Though Annabelle saw hope and excitement in her friend's eyes today, she knew Tess was worried, nearly as anxious as she'd been back in seventh grade when her parents decided to divorce. She hid it well, but Tess wouldn't truly relax until her baby was delivered, alive and healthy and snug in her arms.

"I can't believe you don't want to know if it's a boy or girl," Charlotte teased.

"I like surprises. *Good* surprises," Tess amended quickly, a shadow of unease flitting over her face, then vanishing. "It'll make everything even more exciting when the time comes."

"You know, don't you, that you're going to be humongous when you walk down the aisle at my wedding?" Charlotte mused; then, as Tess and Annabelle both stared at her, brows raised, she clapped a hand to her mouth.

"Sorry—how rude am I? I'm sure it's good luck to have a hugely pregnant woman at your wedding, right? Let me look that up on my phone. There has to be some good karma there—"

Annabelle laughed as Charlotte's dainty thumbs danced across the buttons of her cell phone.

"You understand there's always a chance he or she will make an appearance before the wedding," Tess pointed out, then shot Charlotte a puzzled glance. "I don't understand why you're getting married in late July anyway. The planning will be so rushed. And if you push it back just a month or so, say to late August or September, I might even be back to my normal size and won't have to wear a tent down the aisle. Not that I'm telling you what to do or anything."

"Forget it. It's bad luck to postpone a wedding." Charlotte's mouth was set with determination. "And it's very good luck to get married on the night of the full moon, so that's the date I chose. Besides, I'm not giving Tim any chance to chicken out. Exactly two weeks and five days after the Fourth, I'm dragging that man down the aisle."

"Something tells me there won't be a whole lot of dragging involved." Annabelle popped another gooey chunk of cinnamon bun into her mouth. "I mean, have you seen the way he looks at you?"

She'd seen the way Tim looked at Charlotte. With love, with longing, with a kind of softness in his eyes. Sometimes she couldn't help feeling a tiny twinge of envy.

She had two best friends whom she'd known since the first grade. One of them was glowing and pregnant, the other glowing and newly engaged. She was so happy for both of them. They'd found good, solid, wonderful men. Men who loved and admired them.

She, on the other hand, had let herself be deceived by a man with all the charm of Dr. Jekyll and Mr. Hyde.

Her thoughts broke off as she noticed Charlotte studying her thoughtfully.

"Something good's going to happen soon to you, too, Annabelle. I have a feeling."

"Oh, man. Again with the feelings?" Tess grinned.

Charlotte was into horoscopes, good-luck charms, Ouija boards, and "feelings." She had been since the sixth grade. Only she frequently called them "intuitions."

"You better believe it. I read Annabelle's horoscope the other day and according to what it said, a new man is coming into her life. And soon. Then everything will change for the better."

"Romantically speaking, it can't get much worse." Calmly, Annabelle took a sip of her coffee.

"I'm serious here. I see you with someone . . . not someone like your dipshit of an ex, but someone good—"

"Like my grandson?" a voice chirped out of nowhere. Actually, it came from the back of the bakery.

Annabelle froze. Twisting in her chair, she saw Wes's grandmother, Ava Louise Todd, seated at a table at the back of the room. Annabelle had been so excited to see Charlotte's ring after her last dance class ended that she hadn't even noticed anyone else in the place, but there were about a half dozen other customers at various tables and booths, enjoying fresh coffee, baked goods, salads, and sandwiches. Now she realized that across from Ava Louise Todd sat Ava's daughter, Diana.

Wes's mother.

Her stomach lurched. Then her glance shifted to another table.

Marissa Fields and Darby Kenton sat there, nibbling on salads.

Marissa had been Wes's eighth-grade girlfriend at Lonesome Way Middle School. Though their "relationship" had lasted only a few weeks, typical for a couple of thirteen-year-old kids, Marissa had later dated Wes in high school for the last five months of senior year.

And back then, five months had been a record for Wes McPhee to be with just one girl.

He and Marissa had even gone to prom together.

Both Darby and Marissa were paying no attention at all to their untouched glasses of iced tea and had apparently been listening to every word.

"Mom, please . . ." Diana spoke quietly to her mother, but Ava Louise Todd seemed not to have heard.

"You could do worse than our Wes, you know," the tiny white-haired woman called out to Annabelle, her soft but commanding voice carrying through the bakery. Her arm was in a cast at her side, and a wedge of blueberry pie sat on the plate before her—forgotten.

Her expression was as imperious as if she were the Queen of England.

She raised her voice. "I believe my grandson is staying in the cabin on your property, isn't he, Annabelle? That's what he told Sophie when he stopped by at lunchtime. He's a fine-looking man; don't you agree?"

"Gran. Stop, please." Sophie's expression was stern as she darted from the kitchen carrying plates of lemon meringue pie. She set them down in front of two women drinking coffee at a booth, then whirled back to her grandmother. "Please, Gran. Not another word."

"Well, why not?" Ava dimpled. "Aside from your Rafe and those good-looking Tanner brothers of his, our Wes is the handsomest cowboy in this town. In any town, come to think of it. Don't you girls agree? Tess, Charlotte, Annabelle, be honest. You must have noticed, my dears."

"Wes is . . . very handsome," Annabelle managed to squeak out.

"Of course he is. And sexy to boot!"

"But some of us are already taken, Mrs. Todd." Tess intervened quickly as Annabelle sat frozen, fighting the temptation to slide beneath the table. "And"—Tess glanced at Annabelle curiously—"some of us didn't even know that Wes was back in town."

"Not to mention staying at your cabin," Charlotte murmured, her expressive eyes pinned to Annabelle's face. "Why didn't you tell us?"

"I . . . didn't have a chance. Besides, it's no big deal. He needed someplace to stay—"

"Because he wants to be here while I'm recovering," Ava announced proudly. "He promised me he'd stay until the Fourth of July. So it occurred to me that perhaps one of our lovely young single ladies in this town might draw his eye and convince him to stay on permanently."

She peered carefully around the bakery, her gaze pausing momentarily on Darby and Marissa.

"That's what I'm *hoping*, at least. And if anyone can convince him to stay here, I'd be in their debt."

Then her twinkling eyes shifted to Annabelle once more. And softened.

"Did you hear what I said, Annabelle?"

"Please don't look at me, Mrs. Todd. I have my hands full and I'm definitely not in the market for a man."

"Even one as handsome and smart and wonderful as my grandson?"

"Gran!" Sophie choked out the word, then drew a breath. "Wes will take off like a shot if he hears you talking like this. We'll never see him again."

"But he's not here, dear. This is just girl talk. I'm getting the word out there, as people say. It's not like I'm going on some online dating site and putting up a profile for him."

Diana Hartigan jumped up from her chair. "Mom, let's take our pie with us and get you home. This is your first day out since your accident. You need to rest. I think your concussion is speaking."

"Nonsense. My concussion is gone. But I do want to stop by the Cuttin' Loose and say hello to Martha, and everyone getting their hair done." Ava allowed her daughter to help her to her feet as Sophie exchanged speaking glances with her mother and hurried to get them carryout boxes for their leftover pie.

"You girls have a nice afternoon, now—and don't forget to spread the word," Ava instructed anyone listening as Diana bit her lip, her shoulders tense as she tried to hustle her mother out of the bakery without jostling the arm in the cast.

The moment they were gone, Sophie sank down into a chair beside Annabelle. Her eyes were wide with dismay.

"I'm so sorry about that! She gets worse with age. I swear, Gran, Martha Davies, and Dorothy Winston think they're everyone's fairy godmothers. Now you know why I call them Bippity, Boppity, and Boo."

The other patrons in the bakery had been listening in on the entire discussion, and a wave of chuckles ran through the room.

"Honestly, it's no big deal." Annabelle tried to ignore the flush she felt heating her cheeks, and hoped everyone else would do the same. "Your grandmother's as cute as can be, Sophie."

"She's a handful! Please don't ever tell Wes about this, okay? My brother might take off for parts unknown even sooner than he already plans to. We hardly ever see him as it is."

"Lips sealed," Annabelle murmured.

Sophie shot her a grateful smile and returned to the bakery counter as a noisy group of preteen girls crowded into the shop, followed by a couple of older kids in shorts and tees. All of the kids knew exactly what they wanted—the fresh-baked brownies and peanut butter cookies in the bakery case.

Darby and Marissa strolled over to the table, their faces alight with interest.

"So give us the scoop. How *is* Wes?" Darby asked Annabelle.

She'd been married to Stan Hadley, the assistant principal

at the middle school, for the past three years, but she was obviously still curious to hear about her friend's eighth-grade crush. After Annabelle replied that Wes seemed fine, though she hadn't really spent any time with him, Marissa broke in.

"What I want to know is this—is he still in a relationship with that woman?"

Annabelle stared at her blankly. "What woman?"

"Last time he was in town—maybe three years ago—I ran into him at the Tumbleweed and he told me there was someone in his life, some woman he worked with. Cara something. It sounded semi-serious."

Marissa was petite, with a fluff of short, toffee-colored hair. She was also divorced, supersmart, knew how to apply makeup perfectly, and worked as a stenographer at the courthouse.

"I . . . have no idea," Annabelle said truthfully.

"No biggie." Darby shrugged, moving off toward the bakery counter. "I'm sure we'll find out all the deets before long. This is Lonesome Way, after all."

Marissa lingered, her gaze thoughtful. "Was he wearing a wedding ring?"

"I don't think so." Annabelle felt like the most unobservant person on the planet. She hadn't even looked at Wes's hand to see whether he wore a ring. She'd been too caught up in that rugged, handsome face, that longish hair, that chest. . . .

"I'm sorry, Riss, I'm not exactly a fount of information, am I?"

"No problem." The other woman's lips curved upward in a confident smile. "By tomorrow or the next day we'll likely know everything. Every girl we went to high school with who's still single will be checking him out at the Double Cross and the Tumbleweed—you wait and see."

The moment the two women left, Annabelle realized that both of her best friends were staring at her curiously.

"What? Do I have crumbs on my face?"

"Wes McPhee, you idiot," Tess murmured. "Why didn't you tell us he was staying in your cabin?"

Charlotte leaned forward, her eyes dancing. "Dish. Is he as handsome as he was in high school?"

"Give me a break—not you, too." But a smile curved her lips. "Okay, fine. If you really want to know, he's even more handsome. But that has nothing to do with me. He's just a boarder who's going to fix up Big Jed's cabin in lieu of paying rent."

"Uh-huh." Charlotte shot her a piercing glance. "Annabelle, what's wrong with you? I mean, I know you're gun-shy after what happened with Zack, but that doesn't mean you can't move on. Are you going to let Zack Craig control the rest of your life?"

"Zack has nothing to do with my life anymore."

"So why don't you think about dating again?"

"I have dated. I've dated . . . several men since I came back to Lonesome Way."

"Um, that would be two. Two men." Tess snorted. "That's hardly several. And you only went out with each of them once. There are plenty more single men in this town—"

"Yep. But in case you haven't noticed, I have my hands pretty full with three children and a job." Annabelle laughed, then swallowed the last bite of her cinnamon bun and reached for her coffee.

"Doesn't mean you can't have any fun—and, you know, get *out* there a bit more." Charlotte sent her a look that was part challenge and part smile. "Come out with us tonight. Tim and I want to celebrate our engagement. Let's all go to the Double Cross."

"Yes!" Tess leaned forward. "John and I are in! I've been craving pizza all week!"

She leaned back suddenly, her hand moving to her belly, resting there. Annabelle guessed the baby was kicking again. Tess's wide smile confirmed it.

She suddenly wondered with a hint of wistfulness what it would feel like to have a new life growing inside her. A miracle . . . a baby of her own . . . with a man she loved . . .

"I'll be the one drinking herbal tea," Tess said, "but John can toast you guys with a beer or two." She turned to Annabelle. "So . . . say you're coming, too! You have to!"

"I'd need to find a last-minute sitter for the kids—"

"Very doable," Charlotte pointed out.

Annabelle bit her lip. "He thinks I'm bossy," she muttered.

"What? Who thinks you're bossy? Wes?"

"No one. Forget it."

As her friends exchanged raised brows and amused smiles, Annabelle stood quickly, scooping up her purse. "I'll make a few calls and see what I can do about a sitter."

"Seven thirty," Charlotte said. "First one there gets a table for five."

"*If* I can get a sitter."

When Annabelle walked over to the counter to pay her bill, Sophie glanced at her, sympathy and amusement brimming in her eyes. "I couldn't help overhearing. You need a sitter. And I thought you'd like to know that Ivy hopes to do a lot of babysitting this summer. She wants to go on an international high school trip next year and is saving up money for it. Now that school's out, she's working her tail off for Jake. She's putting in long hours at his retreat almost every day. As a matter of fact, Rafe and I hardly see her," she added with a rueful laugh.

Annabelle knew that Jake Tanner, the youngest of the three Tanner brothers, had turned his cabin and land on Blackbird Lake into a retreat for bullied kids and their families. Groups of kids from all over the country had the opportunity to come to Montana, learn to ride horses, to fish, and enjoy the outdoors over the summer and during winter vacation, too. The rest of the year, Jake rented out the cabins and main lodge he'd built to hunters, hikers, fishermen, and tourists.

"So I suppose Ivy has a regular babysitting job at night?" Annabelle asked.

"No regular job. She babysits here and there, but not every night. I happen to know she had a little tiff with her boyfriend and is free tonight, so if you want to go out, give her a call."

Sophie's stepdaughter, Ivy, was fifteen, very pretty, very responsible, and had babysat for Megan, Michelle, and Ethan several times, although not in the last few months. "I'll do that. Thanks, Sophie."

She was fairly certain Sophie had overheard the rest of the conversation, too. The part about her brother. She gritted her teeth as she headed out of the bakery.

There were definitely advantages to living in the big city, whether it was Philadelphia or LA. There, everyone didn't know everything about your life, your business. Your dating habits and social life.

Or lack thereof.

The truth was, she was nowhere near ready to even think about dating again. She'd gone out only a couple of times, and only because her friends kept pestering her.

"You have to get your feet wet again before you relearn how to swim," Charlotte always said, trying to be helpful.

But dating didn't seem like swimming. More like diving off the high board with your hands tied behind your back.

Even her closest friends didn't get that she really was unlucky in love. It was practically a family tradition.

Of course, according to the family stories, her grandparents had been happy together at first—living at the ranch her grandfather built on Sunflower Lane, running cattle on eight hundred acres that Big Jed Cooper—her grandfather's bank-robbing father—had purchased in the late 1800s, supposedly with what was left of his stolen loot after the bulk of it disappeared.

Grandpa Joe and Grandma Lillie had been very much in love and were thrilled when their first daughter, Lorelei, was born. Life had been good on Sunflower Lane.

But a few years later, on the very night that Annabelle's mother, Meg, came into the world, Grandpa Joe had gone out to the barn one more time to check on his horses and had been killed instantly by lightning.

Everything changed in that moment. Her grandmother's joy at the birth of a second daughter turned to devastation. Grandma Lillie had tumbled into a dark, fathomless depression, and though she dutifully went through the motions of caring for her newborn, she could barely stand to look at her, much less delight in her coos and smiles and tiny accomplishments. So Annabelle's mother had not only grown up without ever having a chance to know her own father; her own mother never bonded with her.

While Lorelei's birthday continued to be a day of celebration, of parties and cake and gifts, Meg's birthday had always been regarded by Grandma Lillie as a day of sadness and gloom. A day she stayed in bed, and stared out her window. Mourning.

On the day Annabelle's mother married, she'd written in her diary that she looked forward to being married to Sam Harper forever. But Annabelle's father abandoned her and his two daughters when Trish was twelve and Annabelle only nine. He'd run off with a divorced cocktail waitress named Lainie Durant who'd worked at a run-down little bar halfway up Eagle Mountain.

Aside from a birthday card or two the first few years after he left, neither of the sisters had heard from their father again.

Fortunately, Trish and Ron had been blissfully happy together in their marriage. They'd built a wonderful life on

Sunflower Lane. They had three great kids, and Ron was making good money. They were planning a trip for the entire family to Disneyland.

Until the plane crash.

Annabelle's own experiences with the opposite sex hadn't exactly given her confidence in the dating and mating arena. First, she'd been lied about in high school, thanks to Clay and his pals, and then . . . then there had been Zack.

Zack, the perfect man. Cute, fun, joking. Successful.

And a complete ass.

Who for way too long hadn't had the decency to give up and stay out of her life.

Men were far more trouble than they were worth. Most men, anyway. Charlotte's Tim was sweet and earnest, and utterly devoted to her. Tess's husband, John, was solid as a boulder, honest, and so caring about her and the baby. All three of the Tanner brothers were happily married to women they adored and cherished and treated with love and respect.

But some families aren't lucky that way, she often reminded herself.

And the last thing she'd ever want to do was mess up her young nieces and nephew by bringing some unreliable man into their lives.

They'd already had enough loss and upheaval.

So had she.

Stay focused on the kids, she told herself. *They need you. And they need stability.* But when she happened to see Ivy Tanner eating ice cream in the park with some friends as she was driving home, she pulled over and asked the teenager about babysitting that evening.

Ivy was available and eager for the job.

Deal with it, Annabelle ordered herself. *You'll have fun with Tess and John, Charlotte and Tim.*

She decided, though, that she'd drive herself so she could leave whenever she wanted to.

It might be good to get out a little bit for one evening. As long as no one asked her to dance and tried to put his hand on her butt—or wanted to buy her a drink in expectation that she'd hook up with him.

It wasn't going to be that kind of a night.

It was just a simple girls' night out, really. A girls' night out, with two guys tagging along. A soon-to-be married man and a soon-to-be father.

Wow, my social life totally rocks. She grinned to herself as she headed home to Sunflower Lane.

Chapter Six

Wes discovered a grimy old tape measure, along with a rusty hammer and hunting knife, in a bucket under the cabin's kitchen sink, and measured the broken windows first—right after polishing off his coffee, and that incredible muffin Annabelle had tossed at him. After making a note of the windows' dimensions, he stepped back and took a good hard tour around every inch of the cabin, then walked through it again, taking an exact inventory of all the repairs necessary to get the old place in shape.

The place was dim, musty, and thick with dust, but he saw nothing that couldn't be repaired with several weeks of hard work and elbow grease.

He stuffed the list of supplies he'd need into his jeans pocket, then headed to town and Merck's Hardware store.

As he steered his truck along the rough dirt road and past the Harper house, he thought back to that big mouthwatering slice of strawberry pie he'd had right in his hands. The one

Annabelle Harper had snatched away from him. A reluctant smile tugged at his lips.

She was very different from what he'd expected—from that gorgeous, feisty high school girl he remembered from all those years ago, a girl with a slutty reputation and a pretty little chin she liked to stick up in the air when she walked down the halls. She was still gorgeous, all right. Man, maybe even more so, he reflected, thinking of that elegant profile, the lush lips that were naturally pink without a trace of any lip goo, and a mass of dazzling blond hair caught up in a tortoiseshell clip this morning, making him want to pull that clip away and watch all that wavy golden hair spill down past her shoulders. But now she was somehow elusive, a little bit aloof, closed off. Her golden brown eyes had studied him warily when he talked about staying in the cabin.

She really hadn't wanted to let him—what was that all about?

Wes considered himself pretty solid at reading people—hell, if he hadn't learned how to do that, he wouldn't have lived this long—and he saw a wariness in Annabelle that puzzled him.

She didn't want anyone living close by. She wanted her space. Private and secure. Maybe because of her sister's death, of all the responsibility that had been thrust on her so suddenly. Maybe for other reasons as well.

She'd looked different than he'd expected, too. Softer, maybe.

But his guess was she was one tough female. Not physically tough like Cara had been—Annabelle didn't have the cool glitter he'd seen so often in Cara's eyes. Or the ability to blow a man's head off in less than a second, as he'd seen her do on more than one occasion, and then toss back a scotch an hour later and rake through every detail of the mission, pacing and running her hands through her hair, analyzing what had gone wrong and what had gone right.

But Annabelle Harper's devotion to those kids was clear as the Montana sky. She'd taken charge of them—and of him—in that kitchen with the determination of a commanding officer or two he'd encountered over the years.

A woman who looked soft as an angel and took charge like a CO.

Intriguing.

Wes liked strong women, but not necessarily bossy ones, he reminded himself. So why was he even thinking about her?

Annabelle might be a mouthwatering beauty, but she's still off-limits, he reminded himself. *She lost her sister, she's raising three kids, and I'm outta here right after the Fourth of July.*

So . . .

Nothing's going to happen.

Even if she wanted it to, which she clearly didn't.

She'd been all business with him. And a lot more interested in her nieces and nephew. Which was the way it should be.

Besides, a woman in his hometown, friends with his sister? Way too dangerous. Even for him.

Stick to the plan, he reminded himself as he turned off Squirrel Road and headed toward Main Street. *Get all the repairs done, visit Gran, bunk in the cabin—alone—and get out of Dodge on the fifth of July.*

Period, he told himself. A few minutes later he swung into a parking space across the street from Merck's Hardware, erased the delicate beauty of Annabelle Harper from his brain, and sprang out of the truck.

⁓

"Hey, Wes. Heard you were back in town."

Glancing up from the checkout counter as the teenaged clerk rang up his purchases, Wes saw Jake Tanner coming toward him, his hand extended.

He hadn't seen Jake since high school—aside from spotting him on TV a couple of times in one of those beer or shaving cream commercials the former rodeo champ now starred in. Back in the day, they'd been teammates on the high school wrestling team, though Jake had been a few years behind him in school.

"Good to see you, Jake." They pumped hands. "Unlike you, though, I'm not staying long." Wes grinned. "Heard you went and got married—threw in the towel on the rodeo life."

"You better believe it. For something a whole lot better."

He spoke so emphatically, Wes felt a twinge of surprise. Jake looked like the happiest cowboy in Montana.

"I've got myself a family now. Two little girls and a woman I wouldn't trade for every trophy on the circuit."

"Good, I'm happy for you. So what are you doing with yourself now that you're retired?"

"Hell, I'm not retired." Jake shook his head. "I'm working harder than ever. Still making some personal appearances at rodeos—and filming a few commercials now and then to help fund my new project. It's keeping me plenty busy. Did Sophie tell you about my retreat?"

Wes shook his head. "Not yet. At dinner last night we mostly talked about where I was going to stay while I'm here and debating how long," he said drily.

"Well, you should come out and take a look at my place sometime. We call it Lonesome Way Rodeo Camp. It's a retreat for bullied kids and their families—" He broke off. "Just had an idea, Wes. Maybe you'd be willing to come by and talk to these kids sometime while you're here. Antidrug stuff. Or empowerment, confidence building. Whatever you want."

"Sure. I never heard of anything like this, with whole families. Sounds like a great idea, though."

"These kids come from all around the country. Usually

when a kid is bullied, it rocks the entire family. They all need help, support. So I have different groups of families come and stay for a week or so over Christmas and spring breaks, or a week at a time throughout the summer months. We give 'em horseback riding lessons, go hiking and fishing. I've been bringing in counselors and role models, like athletes or artists who volunteer to speak, and to work with the kids, just trying to give them and their families a positive break, some support and coping mechanisms. It's going better than I even dreamed."

Wes was surprised. And impressed. "Sounds great," he said, and meant it.

"We're doing up a big barbecue this weekend. Burgers and hot dogs, a bonfire, s'mores, and even some entertainment. Madison Hodge and her band will be performing, and leading a sing-along. And next week there'll be an overnight camping trip in the mountains. Let me know if you want to come in sometime, give a talk about drugs, maybe even teach these kids some self-defense moves."

"Be happy to," Wes said instantly, liking what he was hearing.

"The self-defense stuff would be more about giving them confidence than promoting violence. Man, when I hear some of the stories about what these kids have gone through . . ." He shook his head. "Whatever we can do to build them up, make them stronger on the inside, can make a huge difference."

"Sure. I'm glad to help out—any way I can." After his years working at the DEA, Wes knew better than anyone the kind of irreparable harm drugs and violence had on young and old alike. "Just so you know, I'm heading out after July Fourth, so let's set up a couple of dates real soon."

"Tell you what, how about I buy you a beer tonight at the Double Cross and we'll work out the details? Carly has some friends coming over later for a little quilting party, so I'm on my own. They're all making squares for a friendship quilt to sell at the Fourth of July celebration. All the proceeds go to updating the community center. Want to meet around eight?"

"That'll work. Actually, I'd like to pick your brain some, too." Wes hefted his bags of supplies and turned toward the door. "There's a little project of my own I've been thinking about, and I'm ready to get it off the ground. It's different from yours, and won't be based in Lonesome Way, but maybe you can give me some tips."

"You got it. Whatever I can do."

Wes frowned as he realized that the hardware store's young clerk was listening intently to their conversation. He wasn't ready for his plans—his not-yet-completely-formalized plans—to spread around the town like wildfire.

"I'll fill you in tonight. Look forward to your input." He shook hands again with Jake and swung out the door.

Chapter Seven

It was right after he finished loading his supplies in the truck that Wes spotted the dog.

Pausing in the pale spring sunlight, he stared at the white-and-black-speckled mutt wandering through the park. There wasn't anyone near the animal, and the dog ignored the kids laughing and shouting on the swings and the slide. He was all alone, nosing around the wastebasket near the picnic tables. Searching for food, Wes realized with a frown.

The animal was skin and bones.

He's got a little bit of pit bull in him. Maybe mixed in with some Lab. And God knows what else.

The mutt's coat was dirty, his body scarred in a lot of places, and he looked weak. Grimacing, Wes strode toward him.

He watched the dog sniff around the grass beneath the picnic tables and find a crust of bread, which he gobbled up even as Wes approached.

No collar, Wes noticed. His gut tightened as the dog cowered when he drew near, then started to veer away.

"Hey, buddy. It's all right. Nobody's going to hurt you. Sure as hell not me."

The dog didn't seem to believe him and turned to run, but Wes spoke with authority.

"*Sit*."

The animal glanced back at him, looking confused—half alarmed and half intrigued.

"Sit," Wes repeated.

The dog sat.

"So you *were* somebody's pet once." Wes approached slowly so as not to scare him. The mutt didn't appear to be sick—or mean. But he was plenty weak, and more than a little apprehensive.

Pity and anger churned through Wes.

Pity for the animal. Anger at whoever had inflicted some of those scars on the dog's scruffy coat.

"You don't have a home, do you, buddy?" Though he was speaking more to himself than to the dog, the mutt's ears lifted hopefully.

Sophie and Rafe might want another dog. They already had Tidbit and Starbucks, but still. . . .

His eyes narrowed as the mutt's scraggly excuse for a tail started to wag.

"I'm going to help you, pal, but I'm not going to keep you," he added, feeling the need for some full disclosure. "First off, we'll get you checked out by the vet."

Kneeling beside the dog, he felt the lick of a dry tongue.

"Bet you'd love a steak right about now, wouldn't you, buddy?"

The dog offered him a paw.

"Tough guy, huh?" Wes chuckled as he stroked behind the dog's ears. Hell, the repairs could wait.

From the corner of his eye, he saw two boys running

across the park toward him. One of them was Annabelle Harper's nephew. The fair-haired kid slid to a stop a few feet away, causing the dog's ears to shoot up warily. Then the second boy dropped onto the grass alongside Ethan.

"This your dog?" Ethan asked eagerly.

"Nope, just happened to come across him. We're headed over to the vet to check him out. Maybe you want to keep him?"

"Yeah! I wish! But my sister Megan's scared of dogs, so we can't get one. But I sure wish we could!"

The other boy spoke up. "We've got a dog and two cats. My mom keeps saying that's enough for one house."

As he spoke, the mutt took a tentative step toward the two boys. They both reached out to pet him.

"He's so skinny," Ethan whispered.

"And look at all his scars." The other boy gently stroked the dog's back.

"Yeah, that's why I want the vet to see him."

The dog leaned his head tentatively toward the boys, and his droopy tail began to wag. Wes watched Ethan rub behind the dog's ears. The mutt immediately huddled in closer, sitting right between the two boys, suddenly looking very much at home.

Ethan's face lit. "I just had an idea. We should name him Treasure!" He glanced excitedly at his friend, who grinned widely. The boy was all teeth and freckles.

"Yeah. That's perfect!"

As Wes raised an eyebrow, Ethan explained, "This is Jimmy. His great-grandfather and my great-grandfather were both part of the old Barnum gang—they were train robbers and bank robbers! They hid all their treasure somewhere near Lonesome Way and we're going to find it!"

His enthusiasm made Wes grin. "Awesome."

"All the members of the gang shot one another to death," Jimmy added with relish, "and the gold could be buried anywhere. A lot of people think it's up in the mountains near Coyote Pass. We read this book that says there's a hidden map somewhere that shows the exact spot. We're going to find it."

"Great. Happy hunting." Wes couldn't hold back a smile at their enthusiasm. He stood to his full height, glancing down again at the mutt. "See you later, guys. I'd better get him over to the vet, and see he gets some food and water in him."

"Jimmy! Ethan!" A woman's voice rang out from across the park. "Come on, boys. Time to go home!" A fortyish female in jeans and a tucked-in white shirt was motioning for the boys to join her.

"That's my mom." Jimmy sighed. "We gotta go. See ya." He took off running toward his mother, and Ethan raced after him.

"Bye, Treasure," he called over his shoulder. "Bye, Mr. McPhee."

Wes bent and lifted the dog into his arms. The mutt licked his chin.

"No slobbering," he ordered as he headed for the vet's office.

The dog merely licked him again.

"No getting attached, either."

It was the way he lived his own life. Not everyone's style. But it suited him. It had for the past twelve years. Hell, in the DEA, you'd better not get too attached to anyone because everyone you knew, everyone you worked with and socialized with, could be dead in an instant. And often were.

It had worked for him. He'd absorbed the losses the way he'd absorbed all the other blows in his life. His father's stinging criticism, sharp reprimands, and brutal sarcasm. He hadn't minded so much what Hoot said to him. But when he'd started in on his mother and on Sophie—even when Sophie was still just a little kid . . .

Wes had been filled with anger. Swift, hard, ugly anger.

And then, one time, when Sophie had run sobbing up to

her room, and his mother was in town buying groceries, he'd had it out with the old man. Told Hoot if he ever caught him tearing into Sophie that way again, he'd knock his teeth out.

The words of an angry, frustrated eighteen-year-old trying to protect his sister had ignited a white-hot rage in Hoot that burned like rocket fuel on takeoff. His father had hit him in the face, sending him crashing into the armchair in the living room. Before he could get up, Hoot had come after him again and tried to kick him, but Wes grabbed his foot and yanked.

Hoot went down, and Wes surged to his feet.

What happened after that was ugly. Not as ugly as some of the fights for his life Wes had engaged in during his career, fights against drug lords and mob bosses and thugs of all ilk and nationality and color.

But ugly because the man was his father. Up until that day.

The day after, Wes decided he had no father. And no place anymore in Lonesome Way. He'd packed up, struck out on his own, found work on a construction crew, and put himself through college and law school without a dime from home.

It had taken him eight years. Eight years of scraping by, eating peanut butter sandwiches and potato chips for supper, wearing his jeans until they were falling apart, only going out for a beer with the guys every other week. Studying and working nonstop.

And it had been worth it never to have to see Hoot again. Never to be beholden to him.

He'd wanted to come back and beat the crap out of him again when he heard that his father had been cheating on his mother, having affairs with several women in Lonesome Way—including Lorelei Hardin, the mayor's wife.

But then he learned that Diana had thrown him out of the house, off the ranch that her grandfather had built, and wanted nothing more to do with him.

And Wes had forced himself to be satisfied with that. If he'd come home and confronted Hoot again at that point, given all the hell the bastard had put everyone through over the years, including his mother and Sophie, not to mention Wes himself—Wes just might have killed him.

That was what he was afraid of.

So he'd stayed away. Focused on the life and career he'd begun building for himself. He hadn't come home, even for Hoot's funeral.

He had to admit, the town felt different now that Hoot was gone.

It had always been a friendly town—Wes had almost forgotten that—but even as he walked to the vet's office, people smiled at him, some reached out to pat the dog's head as he passed, and just as he reached the building, his old girlfriend Marissa walked out of the drugstore and immediately came toward him.

"Made a new friend, I see." She smiled—that slightly mysterious, suggestive little smile he remembered from high school. Marissa was still as pretty as she'd been in the twelfth grade. And apparently she wasn't furious at him anymore for breaking up with her and leaving town without a word the day before the big senior blowout party following graduation.

"You want him?" he offered as she reached out to stroke the dog's head.

"I have a cat; sorry. That's all the responsibility I can handle right now. But you and me . . ." Her head tilted to one side. "We should catch up."

"Yeah, well . . ." The dog was wriggling in his arms, and Wes set him down, saying, "Stay." He looked at Marissa. "I'm not hanging around for too long."

"Funny, I heard you'll be in town until the Fourth of July. Darby and I got all the scoop at A Bun in the Oven a little while ago."

"Always knew there was a reason I didn't like small towns."

"We're not so bad. And . . . it's good to see you, Wes."

"You, too, Riss."

"Darby and I are headed over to the Double Cross tonight. If you're not busy, stop by, have a drink with us. We'll catch up."

"So happens I'll be there, but it's for a business meeting."

"Perfect. Come on over and hang out when you're done. But just so you know, Big Billy still doesn't allow dogs." She smiled, catlike, over her shoulder as she sauntered past him toward Spring Street.

"By tonight he'll be someone else's problem," Wes assured her.

She glanced back at him, still smiling. "Then I'll see you later."

He watched her walk away. Oh yeah, he remembered that walk. It had turned him on back then, and now it still did, a little.

But an image of Annabelle Harper from this morning, looking luscious and rushed and in charge, her tocnails painted hot pink, riotous blond curls swinging over her shoulders, a faint trace of freckles on her delicate nose as she rustled those kids out of the house, suddenly popped into his head, extinguishing Marissa from his brain. Annabelle was hot and gorgeous without even trying. There was something unaffected, determined, and honest about her that was very different from the deliberately sensual vibe he'd always picked up from Riss.

With Annabelle, there was no hidden agenda, no subtle come-on. The only thing Annabelle Harper was focused on doing was taking care of her nieces and nephew.

Refreshing, he thought, then deliberately pushed away the memory of how her wildly sexy curves filled out her jeans and T-shirt. Of how those golden brown eyes had warily searched his face.

Steer clear, if you know what's good for you, he reminded himself grimly as he herded the dog into the vet's office. *That way trouble lies.*

⌒

The animal trembled like an autumn leaf caught in a gale storm during Doc Weatherby's quick once-over.

Weatherby checked for a microchip, but found none. Fortunately the mutt didn't have fleas or ticks or anything else that might pose a problem. On the other hand, he was nervous, underweight, and shaking.

"He seems pretty hungry and scared," Wes said after the exam. "You'll feed him soon, won't you?"

"Oh, I can't keep him here, Wes. You'll have to take him over to the shelter. They'll see to him."

"Shelter?"

"It's a new one. Real nice facility, modern, clean, and good people run it," the vet said. "Don't feel bad about taking him there."

"I don't." Wes glanced at the dog, who stared beseechingly into his eyes. "But I may just keep him for tonight, so I see he gets a good meal. Tomorrow I'll bring him in for a full exam—shots, whatever he needs. Then he can go to the shelter."

"I have surgeries scheduled at nine A.M. and ten A.M. Bring him in at eleven thirty and I'll perform a thorough exam. Angie from the shelter will be here assisting me tomorrow, so she can always take him over there afterward, if you don't want to stick around. Thanks for bringing him in, Wes. We'll take good care of him."

Wes shook the vet's hand, then strode to the door. The dog bounded after him like a shot. *He can't wait to get out of here, poor guy.*

Wes couldn't blame him.

"Okay, here's the deal. I'm bringing you home for one night," he told the mutt as they headed toward his truck. "One night only, then you go to the shelter. Got it? But we'll pick up some burgers at the drive-through first." He glanced down at the dog trotting eagerly at his side. "Don't get any ideas, though. It's only because I'm hungry, too."

Chapter Eight

～

"Okay, you two. It's time to make a decision."

Annabelle regarded her friends over the giant dessert menu at the Double Cross Bar and Grill. "What's it going to be?"

She was seated at a big square table across from Charlotte and Tess, enveloped by the blast of lively country music, rowdy laughter, and the incessant click of pool cues.

Tess was still peering at the menu. She finally looked up and took a sip of her decaf iced tea before answering. "First we need to narrow it down to the top three."

"That works for me." Annabelle glanced at the menu again. There were too many tantalizing choices, but she finally made a decision.

"My picks are the double-fudge marshmallow cake, the fresh peach cobbler, and a peanut butter sundae." Her eyes danced with anticipation. "All in favor, speak now."

The three women had polished off a large salad and a pizza, while the guys had devoured steaks and double-baked potatoes. As usual, the Double Cross was packed, nearly every seat taken, the cavernous room alive with laughter and chatter, accentuated by the excellent sound system and Jason Aldean's voice crooning from the jukebox.

"Help me out here, guys," Annabelle demanded over the music. "I refuse to make such a big decision all on my own."

"All of those sound awesome. Let's split them three ways." Tess's dark auburn hair glowed in the bright light of the bar as she glanced at Charlotte for confirmation.

But Charlotte bit her lip. "Sorry to be a downer, but I vote no on the sundae. Let's split the cake and the cobbler between us and call it a night."

"What? No sundae?" Tess questioned, her eyebrows shooting up.

"Not for me. Tomorrow I'm shopping for a wedding gown with my mom. I need to cut back—*way back*—on desserts, on everything—at least until after I walk down the aisle."

"That's so not fair," Tess protested. "*I'm* eating for two."

"That means you get to order as many desserts as you want," Annabelle said soothingly. "And chances are, the guys will want some, too."

Her gaze flitted to Tim and John, still totally immersed in shooting pool.

"Oh, never mind them." Tess waved a dismissive hand toward her husband's broad back. "By the time they drag themselves away from that pool table and come over here for dessert, I'll be ready for seconds."

It was a good thing Big Billy—the Double Cross's owner and bartender—had a huge space here, complete with a dartboard and plenty of pool tables, along with a big dance floor, because nearly every inch of the place was packed. The giant, noisy bar was a sea of men in cowboy hats, jeans, and boots, and an ocean of women wearing short skirts and skimpy tops, or jeans with glittery tees or silk blouses, and boots or high heels.

Annabelle sipped her wine, taking in the tourists swarming around the long, curving mahogany bar. Lonesome Way had become an increasingly popular destination for tourists over the past few years, and her gaze swept from an obvious Easterner wearing stiff new designer jeans and a polo shirt to a woman with a haircut that looked way too sophisticated for the Cuttin' Loose Salon.

She also caught sight of Darby and Marissa on the opposite side of the dance floor, seated on barstools at a tall table, and surrounded by local ranch hands—guys they'd all gone to school with. Some of them were men Annabelle had gone out with when she'd returned to Lonesome Way—her "one-timers," as Charlotte called them.

Annabelle had gone out on a date only one time with each of them. Though they'd all asked her for a second date, she'd said no, explaining that it wasn't easy getting a sitter, and she didn't like leaving the kids too often at night.

Especially so soon after their parents' deaths.

Of course, if she'd met someone who knocked her socks off, things might have been different. But she hadn't.

And that was a good thing, she'd told herself more than once. Because the last man who'd knocked her socks off was Zack—and he'd also knocked her into a wall when she gave directions to a lost tourist in Philly—a young man simply trying to find the Liberty Bell Museum.

Zack, who'd been looking out the window of their apartment, happened to see her talking to the man—smiling, standing close to him as she gave him directions.

And he'd flipped out.

When she'd come up to their loft, he'd thrown her against the foyer wall. Hard. Pinned her there, shouted in her face . . .

She swallowed now, closed her eyes a moment.

No more men. No more mistakes.

She hadn't gone out on a second date with any man in

Lonesome Way. Her friends knew everything that had happened with Zack, but they simply didn't believe she was serious about being done with men.

Oh, they were sympathetic. They were horrified by what she'd gone through. And protective.

But they hadn't been there. Not in the loft where she and Zack had lived, or in the building's elevator, when he'd accused her of flirting with the new tenant on the sixth floor. They hadn't been in the hotel, either, the time she and Zack had gone to Atlantic City, when the doorman had complimented her new silk dress as she passed by.

They hadn't felt the fear, the pain, the shock of Zack's hands crushing her wrists, of his fist slamming into the bones of her face the moment they reached their room.

Men weren't worth the trouble, the letdown, or the heartache.

Sounds like a country song, she thought to herself, even as her glance skimmed past Dick Tyson, owner of a ranch on Mule Road, who'd taken her out to a fancy dinner in Livingston. He was nice enough, but he had beer breath, and talked endlessly about his ex-wife, who'd cheated on him with a stockman from Laramie.

She didn't need a man. She had three young children to care for, and friends to celebrate good times with, and a cabin she might be able to rent out soon. . . .

And maybe, just maybe, a little chocolate business that she might get going one of these days . . .

I'll make dark chocolate truffles for Charlotte's bridal shower favors, she decided, her heart lightening. *And maybe caramel chews and milk chocolate mint hearts—plus some mini chocolate wedding bells. Wrap them in delicate little gilt bags tied with silver ribbon and . . .*

At that moment, the door of the Double Cross opened and Wes McPhee strode in, all six foot four inches of magnificent, hunky male.

Oh God, give me a break. Her pulse pumped faster at the sight of him. Honestly, why did he have to look so . . . so . . .

Hot.

There was just no other word for it.

Those sharp green eyes swept the entire place in the space of an instant, sizing up the room like a boxer sizing up any opponent who could possibly step into the ring.

When he saw her, he gave a brief nod of acknowledgment, a slight quirk of his lips, then nonchalantly strode toward the rows of tables and booths on the opposite side of the dance floor. Annabelle didn't want to do it, but she couldn't help herself from craning her neck to see where he was headed.

A flicker of surprise rippled through her when she saw him shake hands with Jake Tanner, then slide into a chair opposite him at a small table.

Now, what's that all about?

Not that it was any of her business. Nothing about her temporary new tenant was her business.

"Wow, can you feel it?" Charlotte murmured in awe.

"Feel what?" Annabelle asked.

"The electricity."

Tess grinned, and waved her hand over her face as if she was fanning herself. "Oh, yeah. I think every single woman in the place is tingling right now. And a few married ones. Even me. But don't tell John," she added quickly, with a blush.

"Honestly, Annabelle, your life is going to be so interesting, what with Wes living so close by. Right down the lane, really," Charlotte murmured. She studied Annabelle from beneath her dark lashes. "I can tell you, if I wasn't engaged and madly in love—"

"Not another word, either one of you."

Thankfully, their waitress, Christy, a mother of four, interrupted, skidding up to the table to take their dessert orders. As soon as Christy strode off, Annabelle changed the subject.

"Let's talk about something important. Like your wedding shower."

That got Charlotte's full attention, and she trained her gaze on her friends, apparently forgetting all about Wes.

"Tess and I need to start planning ASAP," Annabelle continued. "You should go dance with Tim while we work out a few preliminary details."

"But—here's the thing." Charlotte drew a breath. "Don't be mad, but . . . I . . . I still don't even know if I want a wedding shower. First I have to do a little more research and make sure it isn't bad luck—"

Suddenly, though, she broke off, her eyes brightening as her gaze fell upon her fiancé, slapping high fives at the close of a game of pool. "Well, all right," she declared, pushing back her chair. "If you insist, I'll go dance with that handsome man over there. Talk amongst yourselves."

Tess leaned forward after Charlotte rushed toward Tim and pulled him to the dance floor.

"So, Charlotte's aunt Susie called me this afternoon. She offered to have the shower at her house. Charlotte's mom will help with everything. Susie suggested ordering cupcakes from A Bun in the Oven, and she'll make finger sandwiches—tuna salad, chicken salad, and cucumber–cream cheese bites, along with fruit and a veggie platter. I'll bake a lemon chiffon pie and deviled egg casserole. Can you make your mom's strawberry pie and her macaroni salad? And maybe some chocolates?"

"Way ahead of you." Annabelle's eyes sparkled. "I'm thinking chocolate hearts, bells, and tiny chocolate wedding cakes. And truffles. The pie, too, of course."

"Love it!"

"We'll need two or three party games and flowers for the

tables," Annabelle mused, but she broke off as John appeared suddenly and leaned down to kiss Tess on the cheek.

"Hear that?" he asked with a grin.

Randy Houser's "Runnin' Outta Moonlight" boomed from the jukebox. "Playin' our song, honey. How about a dance?"

"Go on—dance with the man," Annabelle ordered, as Tess glanced at her, hesitating. "I'll guard your sundae when it gets here. Won't even take a teensy taste, I promise. Go on." She touched Tess's arm. "Once that baby comes, you two might not get out much together for a while."

After watching John put a protective arm around Tess's waist and lead her to the dance floor, she found herself fighting off the urge to glance again at the table where Wes and Jake were seated. Finally, she allowed herself a quick peek across the room. They were deep in conversation. What could they be talking about?

And why do you care? she asked herself crossly. Pushing Wes from her mind, she watched Christy set down a huge slice of gooey marshmallow fudge cake, along with the peach cobbler, two scoops of vanilla ice cream, and Tess's peanut butter sundae.

Yum. But even all that scrumptious deliciousness didn't distract her for long. A moment later, she couldn't resist glancing again toward the two men. Or rather, toward Wes, who was speaking steadily to Jake. He wore his jeans and boots well, she couldn't help noting, and with the sleeves of his navy shirt rolled up, revealing darkly tanned, muscular forearms, he looked better than any dessert on the Double Cross menu.

He's bad for you, she told herself as she tore her gaze away. *All men are bad for you. And don't forget it.*

Chapter Nine

❧

"Survival camp?" Jake Tanner's eyes lit up. "Man, that's a great idea. Especially in these parts. Damn, I wish I'd thought of it."

Wes took a chug of his beer. "Struck me it could be useful. Too many folks think they know what they're doing. Figure they've got a backpack, a compass, a cell phone, and they're good to go."

"They're the ones who get into trouble." Jake nodded. "There was a lone hiker up on Storm Mountain a few weeks ago, headed to Coyote Pass. You hear about that? A young guy from back East—he told Lem over at Benson's Drugstore he was a student, doing research on the Old West. He was planning to follow the old Beacon Trail to Coyote Pass, all alone. Next night, a storm blew up, a bad one—and he never made it back. Sheriff Hodge sent out search parties, the whole town organized volunteers—and no one's found a trace of him, or any of his stuff. Didn't see any traces of blood or clothing, either—the rain must have washed it all away. His sister from back East came out, offered a reward. More people searched."

Jake sighed. "People think they're smart and prepared, and that they know what they're doing, but stuff happens out in the wilderness, stuff no one expects."

Wes leaned forward. "That's why I'm thinking a course that prepares them for every contingency might be valuable. It could save lives. I figure all the daredevils and adventurers out there might like it, too—a way to challenge themselves on a whole other level. I've got a buddy in Wyoming—former FBI guy, Scott Murray. He's married now, got his family there—mentioned he might want to go in on it with me."

"Wes, once this thing gets started, I bet you could even franchise it out. Could be a big market for this across the entire western United States—and in some places back East, too."

"I'm not planning that big—or that far ahead, Jake. Not yet. Just thinking I'll make a start somewhere—maybe Wyoming with my buddy, or if we decide to open two at once, I'd start mine at the same time in Colorado. I've read about a whole lot of people who're used to camping someplace flatter, tamer—country not so far from civilization. And then they think the mountainous regions in the West are a challenge, but maybe not so different from what they're used to. Some of 'em get hurt when they try it, and some—like your hiker—don't make it back."

"Why not start right here? Livingston and Big Timber are only a stone's throw away. They attract thousands of campers and hikers each year. More and more have been passing through Lonesome Way, too, these past few years. We've got a bunch of great trails practically right in our own backyard, and some of them are pretty damned tough. The Cottonwood Lake Trail in the Crazies, the Trespass Trail. A lot of folks come for the views of the Absarokas and the Bridger Mountains. Pretty steep hiking up that way. Folks don't realize how quick bad weather can blow up. Then they get stranded, can't get back down to the campgrounds."

Wes drained his beer. "Yeah. The idea really came into focus while I was driving here from Denver. Heard about a family that got stranded in the Rockies. They were rescued after three days, just when their rations were running out. The father had a broken leg—no one in the family knew how to set it. They had no meds, no cell phone service, and their shelter blew the hell away in the storm. Seems like there's a need for some training, considering all the people into hiking, fishing, and just plain exploring. Too many don't have a clue how to survive out there if the weather turns nasty on a dime, or if something else goes wrong."

"You know," Jake said thoughtfully, signaling to the waitress for another round, "if you want to kick things off here, I'd love to incorporate a class or two into my program for the kids. Nothing too complicated, just basic survival stuff. I bet they'd enjoy it, and it could come in handy some day. I realize this is small stuff compared to the course you have in mind, but—"

"Let's do it." Wes looked him squarely in the eyes. "I like what you're offering for those kids and their families. It's a great thing you're doing, Jake. And it would be easy for me to tailor some tips for them. Basic survival skills can add a lot to a kid's confidence level. I can start with that while I plan out the full course and explore my options. My buddy in Wyoming found an old lodge near the mountains he thinks could be used as a headquarters. I haven't checked it out yet, but in the meantime—"

He broke off abruptly in mid-sentence.

Not that he'd been paying attention, but Annabelle had been sitting at a table across the room with her friends, and suddenly he noted she was alone. Sipping wine and watching Tess and Charlotte dancing with John and Tim.

It seemed like a damn shame to see such a breathtaking

woman sitting there all by herself. Not that she appeared to mind. She watched her friends with a smile on her face, looking relaxed and at ease. And more luminous than any other female in the place.

Kelly Clarkson's latest hit blared through the bar. Laughter and music and the hum of the crowd filled the room up to the rafters. He saw Annabelle lift a fork and take a delicate bite of the cake on the table before her. He felt something heat up and tighten inside him.

Jake was speaking to him, but he didn't catch the words as he noticed Tobe Flynn beating a path straight toward her.

Flynn. That guy had always been a hanger-on. He'd been one of Clay Johnson's closest friends way back as far as grade school—a run-of-the-mill jock on both the football team and the wrestling team, but he'd had no interest in school except scraping by enough to graduate. He'd been one of those who'd joked endlessly with Clay about Annabelle in the locker room, going on and on about how easy she was. How she'd not only given it up for him on the first date, but had begged him for more. Again. And again.

As Flynn beat a path toward her, Wes tried to refocus his attention on what Jake was saying—something about how he'd like to schedule two one-hour classroom survival sessions for the group of kids arriving in ten days' time.

"Sure, I can do that," he replied automatically, then felt a light hand on his shoulder.

Glancing up, he saw Marissa standing beside his chair, looking sleek as a cat in a white halter top and tight jeans. Beside her was Darby Kenton, and another girl from high school whose name he didn't remember.

"So what did you do with the dog?" Marissa's pink-glossed lips curved into a wide smile.

Wes stood, and offered her his chair. "Dog's hanging at my place. Tomorrow he goes to the shelter."

It struck him that there was a time when he would've

been caught up in how good Marissa looked in that tight halter top, and how good she smelled—some pretty, light floral perfume clinging to her skin—and by how eager she seemed to reconnect—but instead, he was focused only on Annabelle, noticing from the corner of his eye that she was headed to the dance floor with Flynn's beefy arm wrapped around her waist.

He forced his attention back to his own little corner of the bar as Jake pushed to his feet to greet the women, then tossed a few bills down and announced he was headed home to his family.

"We'll talk more tomorrow," he told Wes before he made his way to the door.

Automatically pulling up chairs for the women and one for himself, Wes remembered his manners enough to ask what they'd like to drink.

"Mojito," Marissa said instantly, sliding into a chair with catlike grace, while the other two women debated a moment between wine and cocktails.

Jake signaled for the waitress, but before she could make her way through the throng surrounding the pool tables, he saw something that made his eyes narrow.

He shoved back his chair. "Excuse me a moment."

Without a glance at any of the three women, he took off across the room.

 ⌒

Oh, crap.

Annabelle's heart had sunk the moment she saw Tobe Flynn rise off a barstool and amble straight toward her.

Great. Tobe was one of her one-timers. A stocky, average guy who thought he was God's gift to women. He'd spent the first half of their one and only date informing her how he was the highest paid, most in-demand ranch foreman in the county, and then ran through every detail of what he did to make the Circle O ranch profitable. Next he spent the second half of their date trying to convince her that they were going to end up having mind-blowing sex in the bed of his truck one of these days, so why not start right away?

She'd been ignoring his calls ever since, and fortunately hadn't run into him in town—until now.

"Annabelle. How's it going? I got the impression lately you don't want to talk to me much, since you haven't returned any of my calls. But we don't have to talk while we're dancing, now, do we?"

Before she could answer, he reached for her hand and tugged her out of her chair.

"Tobe, I'm not really in the mood to dance. Sorry I didn't call you back. I've been busy with the kids and work and—"

"And you don't want to go out with me again? Hurts my feelings, you know."

He grinned and drew her toward the dance floor, one lean arm snaking casually around her waist as all around them couples melted into each other, swaying to the music. "Just tell me what I did wrong, Annabelle honey, and I'll fix it."

Where do I start? she wondered. *Too much phony charm and way too sure of yourself.* And tonight, she realized suddenly, he'd had too much liquor. Tobe hadn't been drunk the night they went to the movies in Livingston, but he was definitely drunk now. His face was flushed, his eyes overly bright.

"The truth is, I just don't have time to date anyone, Tobe. Or even to go out much. I'm too busy taking care of my nieces and nephew and it's going to be that way for a while—"

"You know what they say about too much work and no play. What you need is someone to teach you how to have some fun."

"I know how to have fun."

"I'll just bet you do. But I can teach you new ways."

"That's what I'm afraid of."

He laughed loudly. His thick hand strayed from her waist to her bottom and gave a hard squeeze. Annabelle reached behind her and shoved his fingers away.

"We're dancing here, not groping. Learn the difference."

On the words, she tried to pull away, but he tugged her back and held on tight.

"I like you, Annabelle. You've got spunk." Chuckling, he let his gaze dip down from her outraged face to her breasts. He appeared fascinated by her floaty pink silk top that reached just to the waistband of her jeans. "Know what? I think you like me back; you just don't want to admit it."

Planting her feet, she tried again to pull free, but he grinned and swung her back, right up against his chest.

"Got news for you, Tobe. I don't like you nearly as much now as I did ten minutes ago. That's enough. Let me go."

She was about to kick him in the shins—or the balls; she couldn't decide which—and was strongly considering a side kick to the knee when another voice came from right beside her.

"You heard the lady." Charlotte's fiancé, Tim, stood beside her.

"Back off, Flynn. Now." Tess's husband, John, was there, too, staring hard into Tobe's face.

"Thanks, guys, it's okay, really," she said quickly. Her heart sank as she looked beyond them and saw everyone in the bar turning to stare. A scowling Big Billy thundered around the bar with quick, heavy steps to break things up before any trouble erupted. Charlotte and Tess suddenly slid to either side of her and other people were lining up, glaring at Tobe.

"Holy crap." Letting go of her arm, he peered around uneasily, a frown darkening his broad face. He hiccupped.

"Fine. Suit yourself. You're not worth it, you know that? Clay said you put out for every guy in high school, but now you act like you're too good for everyone. Or maybe you just think you're too good for me. Is that it? Don't you know you're nothing but a cheap little skank not good enough to—"

That was as far as he got. Annabelle kneed him in the balls and he sank with a scream to the floor.

He crouched there, groaning, his face twisted with pain, until suddenly a ranch hand from the Circle O pushed through the crowd and hauled him to his feet.

"Let's get you outta here, boss," the ranch hand muttered, but Tobe jerked away and rounded on Annabelle again.

"You damned dirty little slut—"

A fist shot out like a cannonball and sent him spinning downward. He crumpled to the floor and lay there, dazed and moaning.

Wes stood over him, his face dark with anger, his huge fist still clenched even as a gasp of shock circled through the room.

"You okay?" His expression grim, Wes glanced at Annabelle.

She couldn't speak. She was shaking too hard. She felt like she was going to throw up.

Those words. Those lies. They lived on. Still.

Clay was still bad-mouthing her, telling everyone those bald-faced lies . . . repeating those ugly words.

Skank. Slut.

She'd thought she'd left them all behind. All those names she'd been called. The whispers in the hallway she'd hoped had withered into silence, like barbed arrows buried in dust.

"Annabelle?" Suddenly Charlotte was hugging her.

"Honey, are you all right?" Tess's face was pale. "Don't let him get to you. Come on back to the table and let's all have dessert."

"Char, Tess . . . I can't. I'm sorry. . . ." She felt shaky. Sick. Forcing herself to look at her friends, she drew a couple of deep breaths, noting the anger in Tess's normally gentle blue eyes, the tension in Charlotte's face.

"Annabelle, honey, it's over now." Tim tried to calm her with his gentle smile. "Let's all go back and sit down awhile."

She shook her head, choked with fury, shame, disgust, and a sickening sense of déjà vu.

For a moment all the whispers and laughter and snide locker room glances from long ago collided in her brain again. Then a deep, lone voice broke through the ugly swirl of memories.

"Annabelle. You want to stay—or go home?"

It was Wes. Speaking quietly.

All of the other voices and words seemed to fade into a void.

Except for his.

Her gaze fastened on his face. "Home," she whispered.

She needed to get away from here. As she met his eyes, she realized there was no hint of anger in his face now—only something that might have been concern.

"Sure, let's go."

Charlotte dashed back to the table and snagged Annabelle's handbag. "Are you sure you're all right?" she asked, rushing back to Annabelle and studying her worriedly.

"Positive. But I need to get out of here now. I need to be with the kids. Char, Tess, I'll talk to you both tomorrow."

Tess squeezed her hand, her usually gentle eyes flashing with anger. "He's a jerk, honey. Don't let him get to you!"

"He didn't. Not so much. Hey, don't be upset. It's not good for the baby."

Tess's cheeks were pale and she looked a little shaky, even with John's arm snug around her waist.

"Go sit down," Annabelle ordered. "Don't worry about me. I'll be fine. I just need to go . . . home."

Big Billy, who always looked so fierce but had the soul of a gentle giant, took a big step forward. "Sorry about the trouble, Annabelle. Next time you come in, your meal's on the house. The kids' meals, too, if you want to bring 'em."

"Thank you."

And then Wes's strong hand was at her waist, guiding her to the door.

Outside, in the glow of a luminous June moon, he turned toward her.

"You look kind of shaky. How about you let me drive your car home? I can always get a lift back to town tomorrow for my truck."

Still in a haze of anger and mortification, she handed over her keys without protest, aware that her hands were trembling. Silently, she slid into the passenger seat of her Jeep.

Wes didn't speak as they left the lights of the Double Cross parking lot behind—or even after the darkened shops on Main Street receded into faint blurs in the rearview mirror. Not until he turned onto Squirrel Road did he glance over at her.

Annabelle was staring straight ahead. He couldn't see any tears on her cheeks, but he was pretty sure she was holding herself together by a few slender threads.

"Don't pay any attention to what that asshole said. Any man who goes down from one punch and doesn't get back up isn't much of a man at all."

"He's a worm. And so's Clay. Lower than a worm. Whatever that makes him. Them."

"Amoeba, maybe."

"Amoeba works."

"Didn't we study amoeba in biology that year?"

All she remembered about biology was how Wes had performed the frog dissection by himself. She knew he was trying to lighten the mood, distract her, but her heart felt like it was clamped in a bear trap.

Wes tried again. "You handled yourself pretty well back there."

"Thanks. I've had a little practice. Though right now I wish I'd taken him out with a knife hand to the side of his neck."

In surprise, he glanced at her. "You've had training."

"Some. Enough to do some damage and get away from an attacker if necessary."

"Training for fun—or out of necessity?"

She looked straight ahead. Her voice was low. "Necessity. My ex-husband had a violent streak. He was the jealous type. When I finally left him, I knew I needed to learn how to protect myself in case he ever showed up."

Wes scowled in the darkness. Driving down the deserted country road, he took in the enormity of what she'd just told him. "Sorry to hear that," he muttered at last. "How long were you married to the bastard?"

"Less than a year. Eight months, maybe. The insane jealousy didn't show up until a month after we got back from our honeymoon. Up until then, I didn't have a clue."

Shit, he hated to think of her with someone like that. He'd come across that type on the job, screwed-up bastards with sociopathic tendencies who wanted to own and control women.

"Has he given you any trouble since the divorce?"

"Some phone calls, the occasional threat. Especially if he was drinking. He showed up at my apartment once or twice when I still lived in Philly, before . . . before Trish and Ron had the accident and I moved back here. Luckily he's still on the East Coast, and I'm not."

"So, are you saying you feel safe?" He glanced over at her, and as she met his eyes, he read the mixed emotions there.

"Pretty much. Phone calls and text messages are easy to delete. And they stopped a while ago. So that's good."

Wes was an expert at reading body movements and voices. Despite her attempt at a casual tone, the tension in her shoulders was obvious and the undercurrent of pain in her voice unmistakable.

Steering around a jackrabbit crouching two feet into the road, he spoke quietly. "Did he ever threaten to come after you?"

"Not in so many words." She hesitated. "He implied it once or twice. I think he's bluffing, but after his last call about a month ago, I decided it wouldn't hurt to take some shooting lessons down the road. I've been meaning to get on that, not just because of him, but because we do live a fair distance from town, and we don't even have any neighbors close by."

"I'd be happy to give you some pointers."

She turned to stare at him in surprise. "Th-thanks. I appreciate the offer. But . . . you're doing enough. And I know you want time to visit your family, especially your grandmother. I'll find someone to teach me—all I need to know is how to hit what I aim at. The trouble is, I'm a little nervous about having a gun in the house with the kids," she admitted.

Wes wished he could get his hands on that ex of hers for about thirty seconds. She spoke calmly enough about what she'd gone through, but he knew that beneath her calm, steady exterior, there was an uneasiness that probably rippled just under the surface pretty much day in and day out.

Annabelle was plenty smart, and she had to know damned well that if that asshole ever showed up, she might have to protect those kids as well as herself.

"Sometime when the twins and Ethan are all busy at a friend's house, I could give you a few lessons. Some target practice, if you're interested. Of course, since we have a business arrangement, I'd want something in exchange."

Her gaze flew to his face and she studied him warily. "What would that be?"

"Strawberry pie. A whole one."

Her quick laughter warmed the darkness.

"That's it?" she asked, sounding more relaxed than she had since they left the Double Cross.

"To help out a friend—you bet."

A friend, she thought. *Yes. That's what we are . . . or are becoming, perhaps. Friends.*

Silence ticked between them for a minute and then he spoke quietly. "I'll have a word with Tobe when he's sobered up. And I promise you he won't bother you again."

"That's not necessary, Wes," she said quickly. "It's my problem. I don't want him trying to cause any trouble for you."

In the darkness she saw his grim smile. "I kinda hope he does."

"Men." She muttered the single word under her breath.

"Listen, Annabelle, Tobe's not exactly the brightest bulb in town, but he was drunk tonight. Chances are he'll be ashamed of himself by tomorrow. I doubt he's going to try to cause trouble for either one of us. But what the hell is the deal with Clay? Maybe I should kick his ass. He still trash-talking you?"

She stared straight ahead at the dark curving road, illuminated by a silver moon.

"You know all about me and Clay. You two were friends."

"You mean way back when?" There was a wry note in his voice. "I didn't actually *have* friends back then. I wasn't too interested in friendship in those days, didn't really get what it was. I kept to myself, in case you didn't notice."

"Of course I noticed, but . . . you two hung out together. You were both on the wrestling team. A lot of the guys used to talk about me and I thought—"

She broke off. Had she ever seen Wes pointing or grinning at her in a group of guys? She couldn't remember.

"I heard rumors," he acknowledged, glancing at a fox lurking in the shadows beneath a tree. But his mind was on the past, those days in high school when he'd never had any close friendships. Those friendships hadn't come until much later, until the DEA, when the bonds he forged with other agents in the field—life-or-death bonds, where partners and teams depended on one another, trusted one another, had one another's backs—had taken hold.

But in high school, he and Clay had hung out frequently, drinking and partying and looking for girls to pick up. They'd watched football games together, gone fishing in Sage Creek now and then with a couple of other guys, traded stories about girls they thought were hot.

And yeah, Clay had talked about Annabelle. He'd talked a lot of trash about her. And he wasn't the only one. Annabelle Harper was easy—so most everyone said. She'd supposedly had random sex with Clay and Tobe and Matt, and oh yeah, Scooter—all on first dates. And with a couple of other guys, too, according to several who'd bragged in the locker room. You didn't even have to take her to a movie, or buy her an ice cream cone at Lickety Split; all you had to do was get her alone, drive up to Cougar Rock or over to the drive-in, wait until the movie ended and the other cars were gone, and she'd get down and dirty in the backseat of a car or the bed of a truck in under a minute.

He'd never known whether everything or anything those guys said was true, but he hadn't doubted much of it. Hadn't really thought about it, either—it was just Annabelle's reputation. And since he'd been dating Marissa steadily most of his senior year, Annabelle, with her long-legged, graceful beauty, slutty reputation, and lame attempts to keep up in biology class, hadn't strayed very often into his thoughts.

"I didn't pay a lot of attention back then to what Clay or anyone else said," he admitted slowly. "I was sort of wrapped up in my own problems."

There was silence for a moment before she spoke. "You mean your father?"

When he nodded, she felt her way along. "I knew there were issues. I heard some things about . . . all of that."

His eyes were trained on the lonely road that had begun twisting upward at a steep angle as they neared the turnoff to Sunflower Lane. "I can guess. That the two of us didn't get along, that Hoot was hard on me, demanding, that he threw me out—"

"No. That you beat the crap out of him one night and then left home and didn't come back."

"Yeah. There was that." Wes's smile was grim. He shot her a quick glance. "Trust me, he had it coming."

He sounded so cool, so calmly unrepentant. Her thoughts flashed to her aunt.

Aunt Lorelei's affair with Hoot McPhee had finally been revealed years later and resulted in the destruction of both of their marriages. The mayor had filed for divorce from his cheating spouse and Diana McPhee had thrown her husband out of the family home.

Hoot had toughed it out and stayed on in Lonesome Way, while Aunt Lorelei had fled all the way to the East Coast, as far from Montana as she could get. But it wasn't long before everyone in town learned that Lorelei Hardin wasn't the only woman Hoot had been seeing.

There was a long list of others—both in and around town. And within a thirty-mile radius.

As Wes turned the Jeep onto Sunflower Lane, he had to ease up on the gas as the wheels bumped over the rough road. Through the Jeep's half-open windows, Annabelle caught the scent of daffodils and larkspur from her garden, mingled with the scent of sage drifting down from the hills.

A night-light gleamed softly in the twins' bedroom. Ethan's room—once her mother's sewing room—looked out over the back, with a view of the mountains, and she couldn't see whether there was a light on there, but the lamp in the living room glowed.

Ivy Tanner was probably stretched out on the sofa, watching a movie or texting on her phone.

Everything was normal here, quiet. She drew a long breath, knowing she needed to compose herself before going into the house. The mad spinning of her thoughts had eased, at least, and her heart had stopped racing.

Something about being here on Sunflower Lane always steadied her.

Megan, Michelle, and Ethan needed her. She was the only one left to care for them and she had to be strong for them. They were the focus of her life. She couldn't let Clay Johnson or Tobe or anyone else distract her from being the best she could be for Trish's kids.

Suddenly she noticed something, though—something hidden initially by the darkness.

An old banged-up Silverado was parked in the shadows beside Ivy's car.

Annabelle froze.

Does Ivy have company?

The sudden clench of worry in her chest had her springing out of the Jeep almost before it came to a full stop.

"No one's supposed to be here when I'm gone. Those are the rules," she said breathlessly as she strode toward the porch.

Wes had noticed the two vehicles an instant before she did. He easily beat her to the steps and held the screen door open as she shoved her key into the lock.

She went in first, but he was right behind her.

Chapter Ten

❦

"Ivy?" Rushing into the hallway, Annabelle kept her voice low, trying to control her panic.

In the same instant, the babysitter jumped up from the sofa, startled. "I'm sorry, Ms. Harper. I can explain!"

A boy came quickly to his feet beside Ivy Tanner. A handsome, lanky teenaged boy, no more than sixteen years old, wearing ripped jeans and a black T-shirt. He had shaggy brown hair, an athletic build, and a guilty look on his face. He stood motionless as Ivy dashed forward, her eyes round and scared, but the moment she spotted Wes, she stopped dead in her tracks and looked like she wanted to run like a jackrabbit in the opposite direction.

"Uncle . . . Wes," she gulped. Pink color flooded her cheeks, matching the bright color of her jeans. "Wh-what are you doing here?"

"What's up, Ivy?" He kept his tone easy. His sister's step-daughter looked like she was about to pass out with shame, but he'd already taken in the fact that she and the kid in the black T-shirt were both fully dressed.

That was a relief.

He didn't see any joints, or smell anything funny, and there were no liquor bottles anywhere in sight.

Annabelle seemed to have noticed this, too, because he saw her visibly relax.

"Ivy." She spoke very quietly, but there was a sliver of steel in her tone that Wes liked. "I thought I made it clear. No friends, no boys, no one else in the house without my permission while I'm gone."

"I know, Ms. Harper, I'm sorry, but Nate—um, this is Nate—Nate Miles—" She cast him a quick glance, her eyes glowing. "He's my boyfriend—well, he was, and now he is again." She flushed. "We had a fight and sort of broke up, but he found out from my friend Shannon I was babysitting tonight and he called me and wanted to talk. That's all we did—we just talked! I swear, nothing else happened. And Megan and Michelle were already asleep when he got here. Ethan was still up reading his treasure book but he didn't come down here or anything and . . . I'm sure he's asleep by now. I'm . . . sorry."

"It's all my fault, Ms. Harper." Nate took a step forward. "I kind of needed to see Ivy right away. I had to apologize to her for being a jerk and making a big mistake. But we just talked, I swear. She didn't want me to come, but I drove over here anyway. I was just on my way out."

Annabelle's anger melted as she saw tears glimmering in the babysitter's eyes. She let out her breath. "Listen, I understand. I don't mind, Ivy, this time. As long as it never happens again. If you're even thinking about having company while you babysit, call me and run it by me next time. Okay? And if I say no—"

"Then it's no," the girl finished for her. "I promise!"

She spun toward her uncle, worry etched in her young face. "Uncle Wes . . . are you going to tell Sophie and my dad?"

"The way I see it, not much to tell, honey. But whatever there is—you might want to tell them yourself."

"Yeah, well, maybe I don't." She grimaced. "You can't believe how strict my dad's gotten ever since I turned sixteen. But I might tell Sophie. She'll understand."

As soon as Annabelle pulled some bills from her purse and handed them to Ivy, the two teenagers practically raced outside. Nate stopped short on the porch and turned around, closing the door quietly behind him.

"I didn't expect any of that!" Sinking down on the sofa with a sigh, Annabelle pushed her wild blond curls back from her eyes. "Sorry. I'm not strict usually, but I need whoever's babysitting to focus on the kids."

"Can't say I blame you. You've taken on a big responsibility here."

"You have no idea." Skimming her fingers in frustration through her hair, she turned those golden brown eyes to him. "Three kids. Ages seven to ten. Depending just on me. *Me*. The free spirit of the family." She groaned.

"The dancer who left this town for the big city, wanting nothing more than to dance, and pursue my dreams of . . . perfection, I guess. No matter how many hours a dancer practices, technique can always be improved upon. I was really searching for the impossible dream. Trish used to call and tell me whenever she had a problem with the kids, or when she wasn't sure how to handle something—like Michelle wanting to take her blankie everywhere when she was three, and Ethan getting out of bed ten times a night when he first had a big boy's bed. But Trish knew what she was doing. I was only a sounding board. Now . . ." She swallowed and leaned her head back against the sofa.

"Now it's up to me to make all the decisions. To keep

them safe, and on track, away from drugs, and from kids who do drugs, and who drink, and all that other stuff. I mean," she added, "Megan and Michelle are too young for that, and Ethan's only ten, but still . . ." She drew in a long breath. Then her eyes met his.

"I never had to make rules for anyone before, or think five steps ahead as to what they might do or what might happen."

"Hey. It's okay. Take it easy." He joined her on the sofa and slipped a reassuring arm around her shoulder. "You're doing just fine, Annabelle. Actually, I think you're doing great."

"I wouldn't go *that* far." But she found herself relaxing against him, struck by his innate kindness. Not to mention his tall frame, which was so solid. So deliciously strong. She felt like she could sit here for hours, drawing comfort just from his wonderful hunky nearness. But she couldn't do that, couldn't give in to need, or let herself start depending on someone else to help with her problems.

"I'm sorry." She straightened. *Get a grip.* "I promise . . . no more venting. I'm sure the last thing you need is a hysterical woman unloading on you right now."

"You're hardly hysterical. Matter of fact, you sound pretty damned rational to me. From what I saw this morning at breakfast time, you're doing a terrific job. You're doing everything right."

"Thanks, though I doubt that." She laughed. Then her voice took on a wistful note. "I just wish Trish was back for one day—so I could ask her a million questions and she could give me some of her tips. She and Ron were such fantastic parents and I'm trying to do what they would have—"

Breaking off, she gave her head a shake. "Okay, don't mind me. I'm rambling."

"You're not. You just miss your sister."

Wes froze at the sudden sheen of tears in her eyes. She

nodded mutely at him. *Shit.* He'd faced down thugs, knives, guns, bombs, and fire, but a woman's tears made him want to turn tail and run. He searched his brain for something soothing to say.

In the end, he reached instinctively toward her again and pulled her close against him.

"It's all right to miss her, Annabelle. Trish was your sister. And a great one at that, I gather."

"The b-best."

Annabelle sniffed. For a moment she just leaned against him, going limp in his arms, her head resting against his chest.

She felt like a wimp, but . . . it felt so good to be held. A man hadn't held her in a very long time. Of course, she hadn't gotten close enough to let that happen. She'd been too scared. She should be scared of Wes, too. He was probably the strongest, most physically tough man she'd ever met—much bigger and taller and deadlier than Zack, and she was terrified of *him*—but here she was, melting into Wes, relaxing, letting her eyes drift closed as, for just a moment, she felt . . .

Safe.

Safe? What was she thinking? She wasn't safe.

Her eyes flew open, and common sense rushed back. Every semblance of safety vanished.

Wes might not be Zack, but he was a man—was he ever—and though she knew he'd never hurt her physically, she also knew men were no good for her. She'd figured that much out, at least.

She was about to pull away . . . except his arms felt so good around her, his body taut, rugged, and deliciously strong. Every inch of him packed with muscle.

Her resolve wavered. Lifting her head, she looked up into those intense green eyes and studied them.

Well, how much can it hurt? she asked herself. *To stay*

right here enjoying being close to him just a little longer?
Looking into his eyes . . . such beautiful eyes . . .

A wave of heat sizzled through her. She knew she was dancing on the edge.

But as she watched his gaze grow warm, then drift lower, settling on her mouth, her knees went weak.

Stop being an idiot. Move away from the hunk.

But she didn't. She didn't move an inch—and then it was too late because her hands lifted suddenly and encircled his neck, and at the same instant she leaned toward him, Wes tugged her onto his lap. His strong arms banded around her waist.

"That's better. Much better, isn't it, honey?" With a surprisingly gentle smile, he brushed his mouth against hers.

Fire shot through her. Instant, red-hot fire.

You're doomed, she thought.

And kissed him back.

They didn't seem to know how to stop kissing. Annabelle found her senses whirling like a merry-go-round as his warm lips tasted hers slowly, gently, before eventually traveling down her throat to nibble at her collarbone. When she moaned with pleasure, he returned his attention to her mouth, kissing her deeply, and then deeper still, like a starving man who couldn't get enough.

Neither could she.

He wasn't just tasting her; he was savoring her. And she was savoring him right back.

She stopped thinking then, the words to describe it dissolving into bits of nothingness as her train of thought floated away. Fire sparked through her as he took each kiss deeper, hiking the intensity in slow degrees, making her blazingly aware of everything about him at once: the strength of those iron muscled arms around her, the dark male taste of him, the possessive way his warm mouth claimed hers.

She could barely breathe, but she didn't care. No one had ever kissed her like this. Wes kissed her as if he couldn't get enough of her, of her taste, her scent, her very soul.

He must have an advanced degree in French kissing, as well as a black belt, she thought faintly as her hands slid to the warmth of his broad chest and she kissed him with a desperate, single-minded passion that made her forget who she was, where she was, everything.

Everything but him.

The two of them seemed to become one, devouring each other with an out-of-control need that deepened with each lick and taste. Their tongues danced a slow, sexy tango; then his hand slid up beneath her pink top to brush her breast. Annabelle gasped in pleasure. She didn't want even an inch of space between her and Wes. She only wanted to melt into him, to kiss him forever . . . and then . . . what? She couldn't think beyond that. She didn't care. . . .

Whatever happened next, happened. Breathlessly, she shifted on his lap so her legs were straddling him. If the next step felt half as good as this, she thought, stroking her fingers through the thickness of his hair as his mouth devoured her, she was all for it. . . .

Wait, wait. This is crazy. This isn't in the game plan. You swore off men. All men. And now you're kissing perhaps the most dangerous man of all . . . a man who's killed people, though probably for a good reason, if there is such a thing as a good reason . . . and he's also leaving in a matter of weeks. . . .

But that could be a good thing, too. A temporary thing . . . a little kiss or two to tide her over. It had been so long since she'd even thought about kissing a man. . . . Maybe she needed this . . . needed him . . . not forever, but for just right now. . . .

He was pulling off her silky pink top and she was reaching for his shirt when suddenly a sound broke through the pleasure and the heat. A creak in the floor, coming from above . . .

"Aunt Annabelle?"

She froze as the small voice floated down from the upstairs hall.

Instantly Wes's hands dropped to his sides. She caught the slight lifting of his eyebrows as she yanked her top down, jumped up from his lap, and spun toward the stairs. Her nephew was stumbling toward the second-floor landing.

"I had a bad dream," Ethan muttered, rubbing his eyes. *Oh God. Did he see anything?*

Panic rushed through her. But no, he couldn't have seen them—the poor kid appeared only half-awake. Maybe a quarter awake. He looked small and innocent and tired in his navy blue pajamas dotted with brown horses.

"You're okay, Ethan. Everything's okay." Still feeling dazed from Wes's kisses, and a little bit breathless, she hurried up the steps and met her nephew halfway. They both sat down, sharing a step as she slipped her arm around his shoulders.

Wes stayed downstairs in the hallway. He stood at ease, watching, but aside from one quick glance at him, Annabelle pinned her gaze firmly on her nephew.

"I can't stop thinking about the treasure." The boy leaned against her. "I dreamed that a bad man found it. But I need to find it first. I know it has to be here somewhere."

"Oh, honey, you don't really know that. I've told you—"

"It's true, Aunt Annabelle. I read a lot more of the book before I went to bed and it says that Big Jed told a woman in the town of Fork's Peak that he'd buried a clue to the treasure near Coyote Pass. In a place only he would know, and that if anything ever happened to him, no one would ever find it."

She hugged him tight, her pulse finally slowing from the heat of Wes's kisses. "Well, the clue hasn't been found, not in all these years. It could be anywhere on that mountain—if the story's even true. And Big Jed could have moved the treasure someplace else after that—if he ever really had it. There's no proof that there even *was* a treasure, Ethan, or that one of his partners didn't take it and hide it someplace else. It could be up in the Crazies or the Absarokas or at the bottom of Blackbird Lake for all we know."

Ethan struggled to smother a yawn. "Naw. I'm sure it's somewhere near Coyote Pass," he insisted sleepily.

Hugging him again, she smoothed her fingers through the unruly cowlick of his hair. "We'll talk about it more tomorrow. You need to get some sleep. No more reading until morning, promise?"

By the time she tucked him back into bed, and left his door half-ajar, Wes was no longer downstairs in the living room. She realized that he'd let himself out the door and was standing on the porch, one big hand resting on the railing as he stared out into the night full of stars.

She joined him, quietly closing the screen door behind her. Fields full of crickets hummed and sang in the darkness, but she paid no attention. She was focused on how broad his shoulders were, how darkly handsome he looked silhouetted against the inky sky. And remembering with a wonderful shiver how his mouth had felt as it intimately explored hers, how his eyes had softened when he pulled her closer, so close that the more he kissed her, the more they felt like one . . . joined by their mouths so close together, by the delicious heat and tension of her body pressed up against his, by something elusive she couldn't quite put her finger on. . . .

She walked toward him as he turned to face her.

"Ethan all right?"

With a smile, she wrapped her arms around herself as a sudden cold gust blew down from the mountains and her silky top fluttered. "Aside from being treasure-hunting crazy, Ethan's fine."

A grin touched his lips. At the same time, a wolf gave a far-off howl in the darkness—a wild, lonely sound—reminding her how far she was from town, how isolated. Much closer to prairie and mountains than to Lonesome Way.

"All little boys dream of finding treasure." Reaching out, he stroked his fingers through her curls. For a moment those green eyes lingered on her face; then his gaze dropped to her mouth, and a shiver of electricity spiked through her.

She thought he might kiss her again. She hoped he would. But his hand dropped to his side.

"You'll need to be up early tomorrow. I should say good night."

Disappointment pinged through her. Some part of her wished he would stay. The foolhardy part.

"Thanks for . . . what you did back there." She shook the vestiges of Tobe's ugly words and contemptuous sneer away. "I appreciate your defending my honor," she said as lightly as she could.

"Anytime, Annabelle. You know where to find me." His slow smile lit something wild and yearning inside her. Something she didn't know was still there.

When he touched her cheek as if it was the most natural thing in the world to do, another slow wave of heat trembled through her.

She tried to focus. "Can I . . . give you a lift back to town in the morning? We're headed to the community center again, same time as today—"

Before he could answer, she heard another sound, one far less familiar way out here than the call of a wolf. She broke off, head tilted, listening as it came again.

"That sounds like . . . a barking dog." Her brows knit as she peered toward the sound. "We don't have any close neighbors . . . much less one with a dog. . . ."

"Sorry—guess I forgot to mention it. Came across a stray in town—a mutt—and brought him back to the cabin. Just for the night. Hope that's okay—I plan to take him to the vet tomorrow for a thorough exam and shots, and then drop him at the shelter. That is . . ." He smiled into her eyes. "Unless you tell me you and those kids want him?"

Annabelle loved dogs, but she was forced to shake her head. "Megan's afraid of dogs. Even little tiny ones. I'd like to change that, but until I do, I really can't bring one into the house. She'd absolutely freak out. Sorry."

"Maybe there's a way to get her past that."

"I wish, but I'm not so sure. I suppose we could try. . . ." Her voice was soft with doubt.

Wes lingered on the porch another moment. His gaze locked with hers. "About that lift—I'm planning to get some work done in the cabin first thing tomorrow morning. I'll find a ride to town later."

She nodded, and he took the steps two at a time, then suddenly turned and sprang back up onto the porch, right in front of her.

"Just wondering—what's for breakfast tomorrow?"

"Scrambled eggs and biscuits." A quick smile curved her lips. "You're welcome to come inside and join us if you'd like so your eggs don't get cold."

"Nah, don't want to cause you any extra work. Biscuits and coffee left on the porch will do fine."

Yet still he lingered, gazing down at her as if reluctant for this crazy evening to end. For a moment she thought he might kiss her again, and for an even crazier moment she thought about raising up on her tiptoes and kissing him first, but then it was too late, because he brushed a thumb gently down her cheek, turned, and ambled down the steps.

He set off along the dark rocky path to the cabin without another word. And without looking back.

She watched him go, a sense of disappointment filling her. He walked swiftly, making little sound in the night, which was astonishing for such a big man. She waited until he disappeared over the ridge that sloped down toward the cabin. It was too dark to even make out the shape of the cabin beyond the ridge or to hear any sound except the crickets chirping up a storm. Even the dog had stopped barking. The night was silent.

She might have been alone in the world.

But she didn't feel alone.

Stepping inside, she locked the door. To her surprise, she didn't think at all about Clay or Tobe or anything that had happened in the Double Cross Bar and Grill. She ran up the stairs and thought about how Wes had touched her, kissed her, looked at her, and again felt that electric shiver of heat.

You know better, she told herself as she kicked off her shoes, pulled on a peach-colored cotton sleep tee, and glanced at herself in the mirror. *Things with men never work out. Not for you. Pretend it didn't happen and try not to want it to happen again.*

But she did want it to happen again. She loved the way Wes kissed her, the way he made her heart race. She loved the way he tasted and the easy way he moved, and the feel of his hard body pressed close to hers.

And the way he'd stood up for her . . .

She wasn't used to anyone but her girlfriends doing that.

She tried to talk herself out of it as she opened her bedroom window a few inches, letting the fresh, nippy breeze slip in. Sinking into bed, she did her best not to think about Wes.

She noticed that the dog hadn't barked again. Peace had settled into the darkness. But she didn't feel particularly peaceful.

He'd been back in town only a few days, but she wanted to feel Wes McPhee's arms around her again. Wanted his hot, searching mouth on her lips, and his tongue doing that sexy dance with hers.

She wanted . . . Oh, no, she wanted way too many things,

all of them involving wild, endless sex with Wes. But that wasn't a good idea. Not at all.

Punching her pillow, she turned over, the blankets twisting as she stared at the ceiling. Whatever attraction there was between them, no matter how searing hot it might seem, she had to fight it. She could do that. And she would.

But as an owl hooted at the stars overhead, and the old bones of the house creaked pleasantly around her, she fell asleep still trying to come up with a battle plan that would save her from herself.

Chapter Eleven

❦

"Run out to the car, guys—quickly. I'll be there in a minute!"

Annabelle had pushed herself out of bed fifteen minutes earlier today and woke the kids up a little earlier, too, so they wouldn't be so rushed. Somehow, though, she was still racing the clock and trying not to be late for class.

Today the girls started their art program at the community center and Ethan had basketball camp, and she was teaching teen and adult ballet and contemporary dance all morning. She had to get going, but she really wanted to load the breakfast dishes into the dishwasher and clean the table where Michelle had spilled some blackberry jam. She'd thought of sending Ethan down the dirt road to make sure Wes hadn't changed his mind and wanted a ride to town to get his truck, but in the hustle and bustle of getting everyone up and moving, she hadn't remembered to do it.

"Buckle yourselves in," she called as the girls—in matching pink shorts and white T-shirts with a single pink heart in the center—rushed past her out the door. "I'll be right there."

Ethan bounded out behind them, apparently determined to reach the car first.

The screen door had barely slammed behind him before she heard a high-pitched scream that made her spin away from the counter and dart outside.

Her heart flew into her throat as a million dangers crowded into her mind. She thought of coyotes and foxes and snakes . . . of that wolf she'd heard last night somehow wandering down their lane . . .

But she skidded to a stop, her eyes widening as she saw . . .

A dog.

An excited, medium-sized black and white dog whose tail was wagging furiously as Ethan and Michelle knelt on the ground petting him.

"Hi, Treasure!" Ethan nuzzled the dog happily, and Michelle kissed the top of his scruffy head. But Megan stood frozen on the garden path, the bones of her small face clenched with fear and her brown eyes wide as pansies.

Oh God. Annabelle sprinted toward her. "Megan, honey, don't be scared. It's okay."

Dropping to her knees, she clasped the little girl's hand. "This dog is friendly. See? Look how nice he is—he's giving Michelle and Ethan lots of kisses—look."

But Megan clutched her hand tightly, refusing to look at the dog who was licking her brother and sister repeatedly, as if they were long-lost friends.

"Aunt Annabelle, I wanna go back inside."

"Megan, I know you're scared. But let's just get you in the car, okay? Then I'll finish up in the kitchen for one minute and we'll be off to class."

"If I move, he'll chase me," the girl whispered. She clutched Annabelle's hand more tightly. Her terrified gaze locked on the dog, who was happily jumping all around Ethan and Michelle, silly and eager to play.

"He won't hurt you. He's friendly—don't you see?"

Her little tomboy niece, the girl who was fearless when it came to climbing to the tops of trees and jungle gyms, who loved catching lightning bugs, and wanted more than anything to sign up for softball in the fall, was trembling, and though Annabelle had never been afraid of dogs, she knew Megan's fear was all too real.

Something we'll have to work on soon, she realized, making a mental note. But right now, she was pretty sure she'd left the water running in the kitchen sink and they were almost certainly going to be late for class. Again.

Luckily the director of the community center happened to be her best friend. If it was anyone but Charlotte, she might be out on her butt. . . .

The dog suddenly became aware of the two of them, and raced eagerly over, his stump of a tail wagging furiously, tongue hanging out. Megan screamed, shrinking against Annabelle. Even as Annabelle scooped the seven-year-old into her arms, she heard a long, low whistle.

Then Wes's calm, authoritative voice.

"Hey, boy. Over here. Got a treat for you."

The mutt stopped in its tracks, skidding like a cartoon dog, and the next thing Annabelle knew, the animal was loping joyously toward Wes, who happened to look insanely sexy today. His long legs were encased in snug, faded Levi's and his black polo shirt clearly revealed the bulge of rock-hard biceps.

Annabelle tore her gaze from him, focusing instead on the mutt, who almost daintily closed his mouth around the dog biscuit Wes fed him, being very careful not to bite.

Still, Megan clung to Annabelle's neck, shaking with fear and pleading. "I want to go inside. Aunt Annabelle, take me inside!"

"Sorry about this." Wes's concerned gaze flicked to the little girl in the ball cap. "He ran off while I was getting the ladder set up to check the roof. Guess I should've had him on a lead."

And then he strode toward Megan, speaking in the gentlest, calmest tone Annabelle had ever heard from him. "I'm real sorry he got loose and scared you, honey. He's a friendly dog, though—he won't hurt you. This big guy wouldn't bite a flea, much less a ladybug."

He frowned as she buried her face in Annabelle's shoulder.

"I don't want to be out here near that dog," Megan whispered, her voice breaking.

"That's okay, Megan; you don't have to be." Annabelle carried her to the Jeep, calling out to the other kids to get in and buckle up.

Slamming the door so the mutt wouldn't be able to jump into the backseat with them, she sprinted back toward the house, past both Wes and the dog. Turned off the water in the sink, glanced around at the breakfast dishes, took ten seconds to scrub the blackberry jam from the table.

The rest of the cleanup would have to wait. They were already much too late.

Rushing back outside, she found Wes on the porch and the dog wandering excitedly around the front yard, sniffing and investigating.

"There's some poppy seed muffins and coffee over there," she told him quickly, pointing to the small patio table in the corner with a covered wicker basket, a small coffeepot, and a very big mug sitting atop it.

"Thanks. Sorry again he got loose. I'll put him on a lead next time."

"You're keeping him?" She stopped short at the bottom of the steps.

"Not planning to, but . . ." He eyed the dog, still

unhealthily gaunt, despite the bowl of dog food he'd gobbled down last night and another this morning. "He thinks he adopted me yesterday in town, and I don't want to dump him in a shelter without first trying to find him a home. Is that a problem?"

"No . . . I guess not. Not if you keep him by the cabin." She started toward the car, trying her best not to think about all the kissing they'd done last night. "I love dogs and Ethan begs me all the time to let him get one, but Megan had a bad experience once. A friend's puppy nipped her on the chin and she's terrified of being bitten again. I just don't want her to be afraid to go outside the house."

"I promise, he won't be around for more than another day or two, max."

Even distracted by everything about him and in a hurry, Annabelle realized that the idea of taking the dog to a shelter was a last resort for big, tough Wes McPhee.

"That should be okay. I hope you find someone to take him." She paused a moment to smile at him before climbing into the car, then found herself flushing absurdly as all the memories of Wes holding her and kissing her last night flooded back. She felt warm all over and it sure wasn't from the tepid morning sun.

"Gotta go," she called lamely through the open window, and put the car into gear.

You're a dork, she told herself. *A dork who's dangerously close to getting hung up on another man. The wrong man. A man who'll be gone before the summer is half-done.*

He lifted a hand, his quick, unexpected grin lighting his face in an impossibly attractive way. "Catch you later."

Driving up Sunflower Lane, she peered back through her rearview mirror, pondering what those last words meant. Did he mean he'd see her later, or did he mean he'd catch her later, as if he was going to catch her in his arms again? Maybe even kiss her?

Her heart gave a crazy little jump. What was wrong with her? This wasn't a good idea. She shouldn't even be thinking about getting involved with him on any level other than landlord and tenant.

Unless it's something totally casual and I don't make too much of it, she thought instantly. But it had never been in her nature to have casual flings with men, or the kind of breezy short-term relationships some of her friends had managed with ease back in Philly.

But a man like Wes could tempt a woman to change her ways.

No strings, no heartbreak. Wasn't that how those things were supposed to work?

As she neared the end of the drive, she glanced in the rearview mirror again and saw him pluck a muffin from the basket. He took a bite, then broke off some more, feeding it to the dog.

For a tough guy, Wes McPhee definitely had a soft heart.

She had only that one brief glimpse of him before she turned the corner, but it was definitely enough to whet her appetite.

For him? For . . . what? She didn't know exactly.

It was like a dance not yet choreographed. You make up the steps as you go along, try them out . . . see what happens . . .

In all her years of training she'd learned she was good at choreography. Good at chassés, pliés, and grand jetés.

But up until now, she'd never been good at keeping her heart in check.

Something told her it was time to improvise.

Chapter Twelve

Wes spent the remainder of the morning setting the new windows in their frames, measuring and cutting replacements for the sagging floorboards, doing a thorough check of the roof. The old place could use a brand-new roof, but he'd have to settle for patching it. Putting in a new one would take longer to complete and cost Annabelle a lot more money. He didn't want to start something he couldn't be sure of finishing in time. The patches would be good for a while if Annabelle wanted to rent out the cabin for a year or two before investing in a new roof.

As he carried the ladder to the narrow shed behind the cabin, he remembered how pretty she'd looked this morning. All that amazing fairy-princess blond hair twisted again into a long ponytail, making him wonder what it would look like if she let it all come tumbling down past her shoulders. She'd been wearing cut-off jeans and a lavender tee that hugged her curves. He tried not to think about those curves.

Or those long and shapely dancer's legs.

Or those crazy-hot kisses last night.

But his mind kept going back to it, all of it.

Annabelle had kissed him like no other woman he'd ever met. She kissed like it mattered. Like she never wanted to stop. It had stunned him a little. He'd thought she'd taste good, but hell, she'd tasted amazing. Sweet as a peach pie in July. Everything about her was amazing. That casual, natural beauty—he was pretty damned certain he'd find himself thinking about that long after he took off for parts unknown.

Her skin smelled like sunshine and soft new rose petals—and there was no question she had a killer body. But the thing was, she'd just felt so . . . so good, so kind of right, in his arms.

Hey, so have a lot of other women, he reminded himself, shoving the ladder into the gloomy back corner of the shed and trying to derail the track of his thoughts.

But he kept coming back to the idea that there was something special about her. Something sweet, spiced with a kind of determined toughness. Something honest and down-to-earth, he reflected, yet casually sophisticated all at the same time.

Something that made him want to know more . . .

And taste more . . . and touch more . . . a whole lot more.

But he sensed she wasn't the type of woman to do short-term bed hops. Not with three kids under her roof and a sense of responsibility as big as the entire state of Montana.

Annabelle didn't roll that way, despite the two of them getting a little carried away last night. He should steer clear.

Leaving the darkness of the shed for the sunshine, he strode to the porch and lowered his tall frame into the battered old rocker, wondering whether it would support his weight. It did, and before he knew what had happened, Treasure was there, curled up at his feet.

"Don't get attached, fella. I'm moving on shortly and I'm not much for having company in my passenger seat."

The dog ignored him, but that was okay because his cell phone rang. He looked at it and frowned.

Walt Carruthers? What the hell . . .

His first partner and former boss at the DEA was now on a fast track, set to lead the biggest division of the agency. The last time he'd talked to Walt, they'd been at a dusty airport in Colombia as rain hammered down, bribing and bullying their way out of the country on a battered old excuse for an airplane.

"Shit," he said when Walt finished talking. "Is this intel credible? Kramer's *sure* he saw Rivers?"

"Kramer positively ID'd Cal Rivers three days ago in El Salvador—the same day our man Carlos Arroyo turned up dead in an alley two miles away. Arroyo had been shot five times, then drowned."

Wes gritted his teeth. Grief shook through him. Carlos Arroyo had been his friend throughout his years in the DEA, and was his third in command on the DEA mission that killed Diego Rodriguez's son.

Shit, had Diego's longtime hit man Cal Rivers killed him all on his own? Or was the old drug lord still alive and giving the orders? Perhaps ordering hits in revenge for his son's death . . .

Wes's gut told him Diego was behind this. But there was no proof.

"Kramer's looking into it and we're hunting for Rivers. Could be he's setting up shop now for Diego—or for himself to go solo, taking over the operation. I know you're out of it these days, Wes, but I thought you should know."

"Thanks, Walt. Keep me posted." Scowling into the distance, Wes saw not the stark beauty of the Crazies rising into the clouds, but a scene of blood and carnage from his past—the night Manuel Rodriguez had been killed.

"Will do. But . . . best you keep a lookout, Wes. If Rivers is on a payback mission, he could come for you or Rick Sutton next. You both were there when Diego's son was killed. Who knows your location?"

"Me, my family, and everyone in this little town. And an old buddy from the FBI."

"You didn't tell anyone else where you were headed?"

"What do you think?"

Walt grunted. "Well, I know you're retired, but I needed to make sure you haven't lost your edge. Rivers and Diego—if that old bastard did survive and is running the show—will probably keep a low profile for now, but they'll resurface as soon as they feel it's safe. You could be next on their list."

Cal Rivers is still at the top of mine, Wes thought, but kept it to himself.

A click in his ear—and his old boss was gone.

At his feet, Treasure looked up at him and wagged his tail.

"It sure is quiet out here," Wes muttered, and absently stroked the dog's head.

Things needed to stay quiet. Which meant, right after the Fourth, and not a day longer, he'd be on his way. And make a little noise when he reached his next stop, wherever that might be.

If Rivers wanted to come after him, that was fine with him. As long as it was nowhere near Lonesome Way—or the ranch house on Sunflower Lane.

As the dog rested his head on Wes's boot, he stared down at the stray. What the hell was he going to do about this dog?

Sophie might take him, he thought hopefully.

His sister and Rafe had a couple of dogs already. Hell, they probably wouldn't even notice one more. Or else he might be able to get his mom and Doug Hartigan to take him in.

Wes couldn't accept the thought of a shelter. Treasure would have to be locked up there. And Wes had been locked up a couple of times himself. In cages, in rooms bolted shut with steel rods, in underground jails, in tiny, filthy cells where he was left for days without food, and where people had only come back to kill him.

He'd managed to kill them instead.

But he didn't want Treasure locked up like that. There had to be someone in this town who'd give the mutt a real home. . . .

Too bad Megan was scared of dogs. If she could get over the fear, she'd be a lot better off. And then Treasure could live right on Sunflower Lane with those three kids. And with Annabelle.

He decided he'd feel a whole lot better about leaving here if Annabelle and those kids had a dog to look out for them.

Maybe, he thought, scratching the top of Treasure's head, *there's still a way to make that happen.*

Chapter Thirteen

A few weeks later, Wes drove over to the Good Luck Ranch house and spent the better part of a morning visiting with his grandmother.

He brought her an early-morning breakfast of cinnamon buns, banana nut muffins, and a fruit salad from A Bun in the Oven, and sat at the kitchen table beside her, drinking coffee and listening good-naturedly to all of the latest town gossip she'd gleaned from her friends, who stopped by daily to visit her.

He'd been coming by every few days to hold her good hand and listen to her stories, relishing her tales of her days as a renowned horsewoman who had her pick of a dozen suitors from miles around.

And every time, she'd squeeze his hand, peer into his eyes, and make him reaffirm his promise to stay until at least the day after the Fourth of July. He had to hand it to Gran—she was indefatigable. And Wes loved her for it.

Today when Martha Davies and Dorothy Winston arrived for lunch and an arranged meeting regarding the agenda and marching order for the big parade, he took advantage of the opportunity to cut and run. Gran had walked him out to the porch, and waved to her friends as they arrived. But after he tipped his hat to the ladies and headed past them down the driveway to his truck, he couldn't help hearing Martha's excited voice carrying across the clear morning air.

"Ava, you won't believe who rolled into town this morning. Guess! No, you'll never guess, not in a million years, not if I gave you a thousand hints!"

"It's Ben. *Your* Ben. Ben Adkins!" Dorothy interrupted impatiently. "What do you think of *that*?"

There was silence. Total silence. When his grandmother didn't answer, Wes turned and glanced back. She was seated on the porch swing, a startled expression frozen on her face. Her penetrating eyes stared into the distance with a look of shock that made him pause.

"Did you hear me, Ava?" Dorothy settled into a chair beside her.

"Of course she heard you," Martha said, also taking a seat. "She has a broken wrist, Dorothy. She's not deaf."

"I heard you." Ava spoke at last. "And I'm supposed to care why?" she asked crisply.

Ben Adkins. Wes didn't know the name. But he'd definitely caught an odd note in his grandmother's voice, despite the fact that her sweet, still-beautiful face was now serene, and that she hadn't moved a muscle.

As he stepped into his truck and accelerated down the lane, he glanced in his rearview mirror and saw her sitting in the sunshine with her friends, everything appearing normal.

But something about the exchange stuck in his head and left him wondering just who this Ben Adkins was.

⌒

"No need to get prickly about it," Martha said after a prolonged silence.

"Who's prickly?" Ava shot back.

"We just thought you'd want to know." Dorothy bit her lip, concern settling into the lines of her face. "You don't still have feelings for him after all these years, do you?"

"What do you think?" Ava's expression was haughty. Then she smiled. "I barely remember the boy."

"Well, he's a man now. And still as good-looking—not to mention very successful! You know that chain of office supply stores—Office Super Plus?" Dorothy savored every word she spoke. "Ben just stepped down as CEO. Yep, a month ago. He retired, turned over the reins of his company to his grandson. I heard it myself from Winny Pruitt."

"How nice for him." Ava spoke airily. "It's certainly no concern of mine."

"Don't you even want to know why he's back in town?" Martha stared at her suspiciously.

"Why should I?" Ava's brows lifted, and her green eyes rested indifferently on her friend's face.

"Because . . . because . . . he was your first kiss!" Dorothy exclaimed. "I remember specifically. You told us all about it. It was in sixth grade and you couldn't stop talking about him. Dreaming about him. Everyone remembers their first kiss! Mine was Pete Miller. And Martha's was Jack Carpenter. And yours was Ben Adkins."

Martha chimed in. "He kissed you in the playground, at the bottom of the slide after school let out—when everyone else had gone home. You told us every detail and said you were going to marry Ben Adkins one day—"

"And you still were in love with him in tenth grade. And eleventh grade and twelfth—" Dorothy continued. "Until he left town without so much as a *so long* to you or anyone—and never came back."

"Nonsense. I was in love with my husband. We were married for forty-nine years. I barely remember Ben what's-his-name."

The two other women exchanged glances.

"If you say so," Martha muttered.

Dorothy still looked perplexed. "Of course you were in love with Clyde Todd, Ava; we all know that, but you didn't meet him until you were twenty. That was two years after Ben took off. Before he did, you had the biggest crush on him I've ever seen. You wrote pages and pages in your diary about him every afternoon when you weren't out riding across the pastures—or on a date with another beau. You sometimes read them to us—"

"Oh, goodness, who remembers?" Ava stood. "It's getting quite warm out here. I'd like a glass of iced tea. Can I get you some?"

Martha and Dorothy exchanged glances again.

"Tea would be nice." Dorothy followed her old friend into the Good Luck Ranch house. She held the door for Martha, right behind her. The owner of the Cuttin' Loose Salon stepped inside with a slight frown.

"Well, if you don't care that Ben is back in town, I can tell you a dozen women from our high school graduating class who do. There'd be more, I'm sure, but some of them aren't with us anymore." Martha carefully watched her friend's face for a reaction, but Ava appeared totally indifferent.

Putting on the teakettle, Ava changed the subject without commenting.

"My daughter and I are headed to Big Timber today to buy a shower gift for Charlotte Delaney. Would you both like to come along? We're stopping by A Bun in the Oven for pie on the way home."

Her friends agreed eagerly. Martha had already bought

a shower gift online, but she enjoyed shopping in Big Timber. Dorothy needed a gift before Saturday.

The subject of Ben Adkins and his unexpected return to town dropped away, as Ava hoped it would.

But his name burned in her mind. She suddenly wished her friends would go away for an hour and leave her alone, as dear as they were to her, just so that she could absorb the news of Ben's return privately.

It sliced her like a scythe.

Even after all these years, she reflected hollowly. Now, how could that be?

He was your first love, she reminded herself. Her first heartbreak.

He'd broken every promise he'd made to her. . . .

I'm not leaving without you.

That was what he'd said. He'd talked to her often about his urge to see the world, to go to New York, the business capital of the world, attend college, be somebody. Ava had made it clear she didn't want to live anywhere but Lonesome Way.

She straightened her shoulders and poured tea for Martha and Dorothy.

None of it mattered now. Curious as she was, she didn't want to see Ben again. She didn't want to allow all of those silly memories and feelings to come sneaking back.

But Lonesome Way being Lonesome Way, what were the odds she wouldn't run into him the very next time she went to town? This afternoon, even, at A Bun in the Oven . . .

What on earth is he doing here? Ava wondered, feeling a crack through a small piece of her heart. *How does he still have the power to do this to me?*

She'd wanted to ask Martha and Dorothy more questions, to learn everything, but even more than that, she hadn't wanted to reveal how much she wanted to know.

They'd said he was still good-looking. Not that it

mattered. He'd broken his word—and her heart—and left her feeling like a fool.

Good looks were no substitute for character.

She, Ava Louise, the most sought-after young woman in town, had pined for him too long after he left her—until she met Clyde and fell in love with him, of course.

But she'd still thought now and then of Ben, and how he'd kissed her when she'd careened to the bottom of the slide. Her very first kiss—with a spatter of spring rain pinging down. She'd rocketed to the bottom and into his arms with a screech of laughter, stood up, and his arms had gone around her. They were twelve years old, on the verge of thirteen, and he'd been only a half inch taller than her.

"Go ahead," she'd dared, knowing what he wanted to do. Wanting to feel his lips on hers. Eager for her very first kiss.

It was the one to which she'd always compared the rest.

He was so handsome and funny, with his crooked, mischievous smile. She'd wanted him to be the first boy to kiss her—and he had been. It had been a soft, sweet first kiss that held a promise of more. That was what he'd given her when they were in sixth grade.

But the next kiss hadn't come until much later. When all the boys came calling on her, Ben had come around, too. He was the one she never got tired of, the one she always wanted to see at her door.

He'd sworn one day in the barn when her parents had gone to town, and they'd climbed into the hayloft, that he was going to marry her on the day she turned eighteen. They'd come *this close* to making love in the hay, with her dear horse Country Boy snoozing in the far stall.

But the day after graduation, Ben had left town. He'd run off and married Margie Forrester and they'd settled in Spokane, where her mother's family lived.

That was the story that whipped through Lonesome Way.

Everyone whispered that Margie was pregnant. Nobody knew for sure.

Ben hadn't even bothered to say good-bye. Ava hadn't ever heard from him again.

She'd tried not to think about him.

And she hadn't given her heart away for a long time after that—not until she met Clyde.

She didn't believe she cared to see Ben Adkins again. But if she did, she reminded herself, it didn't matter.

He was nothing to her now.

Chapter Fourteen

Wes made one stop before heading home to get some work done on the cabin. He took a detour to the Lonesome Way library and hit the shelves until he found just what he was looking for.

Afterward, driving back down Sunflower Lane, he was surprised to spot Annabelle at home, working in her garden. He braked alongside her and her pretty, winding rows of flower beds.

"Didn't expect to see you here. No classes today?"

Peering up, she smiled at him, and stood with a grace that knocked him for a loop. He felt something like a punch to the stomach—but in a good way.

Then she brushed her hands on her denim shorts. Her sage green tee had specks of dirt on it, but they didn't detract from the pretty picture she made, with her long legs and those delectable curves. He sprang out of the truck and strode toward her, no longer in a hurry to get to the cabin.

"Everything was canceled," she told him. "Some kind of power outage in the building—all the kids were sent home."

"Home? You sure? It's awfully quiet around here."

A small laugh burst from her. Wes realized it was a sound he liked. A lot.

"The kids are plenty busy; don't worry—they're just not *here*. Ethan's spending the day with Jimmy—searching for the treasure again, of course. This time near Sage Creek. Jimmy's older brother, Corey, was bribed into supervising—and Ethan's going to sleep over there, too, so I dropped off a packed bag for him a little while ago. The same for the twins. They're having movie night at Kaley Mattson's house—*E.T.* and *Frozen*. It'll be my turn to host the sleepover next week." She shook her head. "Little girls do love their sleepover parties."

"I'm fond of them myself."

He liked the easy way she laughed at him and turned those soft honey eyes on his face.

"No surprise there. Never met a man who wasn't."

Especially when a man gets within ten feet of a woman like you, he thought, but aloud he said, "The cabin's coming along great. Still a ways to go, but—want to walk down and see what I've done with the place so far?"

"I'd like that." The smile she flashed him was warm, but then she hesitated. "I have a few things to do first. Come in for a minute? There's coffee."

"Sounds good."

Wes tried not to stare like a fourteen-year-old kid at the sway of her hips as she moved ahead of him into the house. He realized, not for the first time, how much he liked everything about her. Not only the way she looked, which was incredibly sexy, even with her hair haphazardly tied up in a messy braid, even in sneakers and shorts. But he liked how she took care of her sister's kids, with equal parts energy and patience every day, and he respected the hell out of the way she'd upended her entire life to be there for them.

Since that night he'd kissed her, Wes had avoided being alone with her. He was too damned attracted to her, and he'd be damned if he'd act on that fierce attraction again. It wasn't a smart move. And it didn't make sense to start something here he couldn't finish. She was staying put in Lonesome Way and he was leaving.

Soon.

More than that, he didn't want to take the chance of hurting her. Annabelle had gone through plenty in her life without him adding any more complications.

Best to keep things simple. Businesslike. Which meant keeping his distance. And not starting anything that could end badly.

He'd be gone before long and if he ever wanted to come back and see his grandmother and his family again, he didn't need any messy loose ends or hard feelings waiting for him.

Entering the kitchen, Wes stopped short. She was scrubbing the dirt from her hands at the sink, but he stared around him at the old oak counters. They were full of chocolates.

The place smelled like Willy Wonka's Chocolate Factory. Round balls of chocolates rested on wax paper and baking sheets everywhere he looked.

Drying her hands on a brightly striped kitchen towel, she caught him staring and a smile curved her lips.

"Chocolate truffles. For Charlotte's bridal shower on Saturday. I had some time this morning with the kids gone and busy, so . . ." She shrugged. "I need to wait and put them in the fridge in about . . ." She glanced at the old sunburst clock on the wall. "Ten minutes."

"You made all these?"

"And lots more. Look." She opened the refrigerator door and he peered inside. The shelves were filled with brightly colored storage containers with various chocolate candies packed inside. Some were heart-shaped; others looked like miniature wedding bells and bridal cakes.

"Seems to be you could open your very own candy shop. Looks like a lot of hard work, though."

"It's fun. It takes time and patience, but it's not too difficult. I love making chocolate—I've been doing it since my college days. I used to make them for my friends' bridal showers, and later for baby showers. I made them for Trish's shower, too, before she and Ron got married."

"I don't suppose you have a few to spare?" He was joking, but she immediately reached into the fridge and pulled out one of the containers.

"These are some I put aside for the kids. Help yourself," she offered, opening it and revealing an array of dainty chocolate hearts, roses, and wedding bells.

He plucked a wedding bell out—hoping that didn't mean he was doomed to walk down the aisle someday—and popped it in his mouth. Immediately his eyes warmed.

"I knew you were a woman of many talents."

She shook her head, eyes sparkling with amusement. "Only two talents, I'm afraid. Dance and candy making. I'm not good at crossword puzzles or bowling, and I'm awful at poker. Terrible at—"

She never finished the sentence because Wes closed the distance between them in the space of two seconds. When she caught the warm gleam in his eyes, her mind went completely blank. Any words on the tip of her tongue vanished—what she'd been about to tell him disappeared into thin air.

He stood right in front of her and slowly, firmly, pulled her close. A second passed where he just looked at her and she looked at him. She looked right into those amazing green eyes, with her heart slamming in her chest. She was certain she couldn't move, but then he did.

He leaned down, cupped her face in his hands, and kissed her.

"I've been wanting to do that for weeks. Ever since . . . that night," he said by way of explanation.

Then he kissed her again, more slowly this time. More deeply. Intoxicatingly.

And without a second thought, she kissed him back, aching with hunger for him, a hunger that had been building since the night he'd brought her home from the Double Cross.

You're an idiot, a voice inside her screamed. She ignored it. She gave herself up completely to the kiss. When he deepened the angle, drawing her in even more, tasting her slowly, deeply, she gave a willing sigh, and nestled into his arms.

And then she thought of nothing but how wonderful it felt to kiss him, how her heart was pounding—and so was his.

When he lifted his head to gaze into her eyes, he still held her close.

"You're good at kissing, Annabelle. Actually, you're fantastic. Add it to your list."

"That's reassuring—since . . . until that other night . . . I . . . hadn't exactly had a lot of practice lately."

"We can fix that."

"We can, but . . ." She tried to think through the dazing effect his kisses had on her. "Should we?"

"Definitely. One hundred percent." He stroked a big hand gently through her hair. His eyes, dark and amused, were locked on hers.

Oh God, her pulse was racing way too fast. She leaned into him more closely, thinking of nothing but the sensations firing through her as he ran those strong hands down her back and caught her lips with his again.

Her mind went blank. All she knew was the strength of that rock-hard body pressed against her, and the way his mouth was tasting her slowly. She made a mewing sound as his tongue teased and stroked against hers.

This time it was a longer kiss . . . a series of kisses, really. Hot, soft, ever-deepening kisses, the kind that made her melt. She lost herself in him, kissing him with an abandon that had him suddenly tangling his hands in her hair and groaning.

She didn't know how long they stood like that in the middle of the kitchen, kissing and touching, surrounded by chocolates as the old clock on the wall ticked, and . . .

She froze and jerked back suddenly. "My truffles! What time is it . . . Oh, crap." She pushed him away and whirled toward the trays of chocolates.

Eleven minutes had passed! Grabbing yet more storage containers from the lower shelf of a cupboard, she began loading the truffles in neat rows.

"You distracted me. Good thing I realized in time—"

"Gotta say, I didn't distract you for very long. Must be losing my touch."

"Trust me, you're not losing anything." Her fingers flew, plopping the truffles into their boxes.

"I'd like to take your word for it, but I think we need to test that out some more."

She laughed, her cheeks flushing. No way. Any more "testing" would be purely crazy.

She did her best to muster both her common sense and her composure as she stuffed the truffles into the refrigerator, between a tray of heart-shaped chocolates and a jar of homemade spaghetti sauce. She needed to put a stop to this . . . whatever *this* was . . . right now.

Wes McPhee was so out of her league. And no good for her. But his way of kissing blocked her brain from working properly. When he held her, or stood close to her, all of her instincts for self-preservation against men seemed to implode.

Failing her when she needed them most.

If she wanted to get back in the kissing game with a man, she needed to pick one who was harmless—a man who wouldn't make her heart shake when he touched her, and who didn't spark lightning-like flames through every inch of her skin.

But she couldn't stop craving the feel of his mouth on her. Or wondering what that incredible, hard-muscled bod looked like beneath his shirt and jeans.

Or what it would be like to have Wes touch her. Kiss her. *Everywhere.*

A deep shiver trembled through her.

"Ready?" He moved closer as she closed the refrigerator door, and wrapped his arms around her again, drawing her back to him.

"That depends. For what?" Her lips curved up into a smile at the same time she knew she should be running in the opposite direction. But Wes didn't take the bait. He just grinned, a relaxed cowboy grin, and gently threaded his fingers through her hair.

Oh, she liked the way he touched her way too much. Heat fired through her at that oddly gentle stroking of her hair and at the easy, steady glint in his eyes.

"To take a look at what I've done with your cabin," he said at last.

It's better than seeing what you're doing to me, she thought, knowing she needed to put a stop to this before she did something wild, something totally unlike herself. Before she broke all her own careful, sensible rules.

"The problem is, I don't have a lot of time—not right now. Maybe tomorrow. I'd love to see the cabin, Wes, to see everything, but I need to—"

She broke off. Her mind was blank. Utterly blank. She was sure there was something she had to do. . . .

She groped through the fog of what used to be her quite adequate brain and finally came up with it.

"I need to finish my planting. And do laundry."

"Uh-huh. Planting and laundry. I get it." Wes shook his head. "Annabelle, you really do know how to hurt a guy."

"No . . . it's not that—I'm just . . . busy. Very busy. With a million things . . ." Her voice trailed off, and then she saw his face change. The amusement vanished and he looked . . . accepting. Understanding.

"No problem. I get it."

Her stomach dropped.

Really? He understands? That meant . . .

He was backing off, too.

That was a good thing, right? He realized, too, that they were heading down a path that would only lead to complications.

Still, more than a twinge of disappointment pinged through her as for a brief moment she wondered what had happened to the brave, confident girl who'd gone off to Philadelphia to study dance.

The girl who'd worked and supported herself and yes, auditioned for *So You Think You Can Dance*—and had almost made it. The girl who'd dated and laughed and compared notes with her girlfriends, who'd enjoyed the company of men and felt confident being alone with them.

She'd had courage back then; she'd believed in herself. In her talent and her judgment and her ability to make good decisions and . . .

With a start she realized that thanks to some bad choices where men were concerned, she was now living only half a life. And a cautious life at that.

Even now, this minute, when the hottest, most handsome and easygoing man she'd ever met was standing right in front of her in her kitchen, close enough to kiss . . .

"Um, changed my mind. Let's go down to the cabin. I think I really do need to see how things are coming along."

"You sure?" His gaze pinned her.

Nodding, she started toward the door, reminding herself that the cabin would be a great source of income once the renovations were complete. That it was important to supervise what Wes was doing. He was leaving soon and she'd have a tenant—a new source of much-needed income. This had nothing to do with the way she felt when he kissed her, and it didn't even mean that he would ever kiss her again. . . .

But I want him to.

The thought came unbidden and she pushed it away, to deal with later.

"As your landlord, it's my solemn responsibility. Don't you think?" She managed a light tone and smiled in response to his quick grin.

They started up the rough track together, surrounded on both sides by flowing streams of sunflowers and wild grasses. A mild sun sparkled overhead. But then the barking started.

Fast, loud barking.

She stopped short.

"Is that what I think it is? You still have that dog!"

"Yep. Temporarily." For once Wes McPhee, Mr. Smooth and Calm, sounded slightly embarrassed. "He hears our voices, that's all. He doesn't usually bark that much."

"You didn't have the heart to bring him to the shelter, did you?"

"I know what it's like to be locked in a cage. He's a good dog. Someone will come along who wants him."

She glanced at him. "It sounds to me like *you* do," she said quietly.

There was silence for a moment. Then his voice took on a hard note. "I don't have room for a dog in my life. I travel alone."

Point taken. A warning light switched on again in her head. He was warning her not to get too involved. No matter what happened between them, Wes wasn't about to be locked up in a cage again.

A cage-like marriage. Or perhaps even the cage of a relationship. Then another thought struck her.

Did he mean he'd been locked in a cage literally?

Her heart skipped a beat.

She couldn't imagine his life when he worked for the DEA. He never talked about it. He must have seen and lived through some terrible things, things she couldn't stand to even think about.

"Maybe if we can get Megan used to him somehow, we might be able to keep him," she said cautiously, as the barking grew louder, more excited, the closer they got to the cabin. "But . . . that's a big IF."

"People can and do overcome their fears." He sounded very sure. "It might take time, though. I spent some time reading up on the fear of dogs—and how to help someone overcome it. I was thinking . . . maybe if we work together, there's a way to help Megan get past this."

For a moment she was too surprised to speak. Then she said slowly, "Thank you for looking into it. I'm willing to try. It would be nice to have a dog around. If Megan is okay with it, I know Michelle and Ethan would be over the moon."

The cabin came into closer view then, and she had a glimpse of some of the changes. The broken windows were no more, and in their place were nice, clean new ones. The roof looked solid and smooth, the little porch was swept clean, and the weeds had been cleared away. It made the entire knoll where the cabin sat look wonderful, cared for, cozy.

When Wes opened the door and waited for her to precede him inside, the dog leaped toward both of them, his tail wagging furiously. After Annabelle paused to pet him, Wes tossed him a treat from a bowl on the kitchen counter, rubbed his head, then watched Annabelle stroll slowly through the living room.

All of the old furniture in the big sitting room had been pushed against the far wall of the cabin, and a number of rotting pine floorboards had been removed.

"Careful, there. Watch your step," Wes warned, coming

up behind her. "Once I replace those boards, I'm going to sand and stain all of it, match it up best I can. If you throw a rug over that section of the floor later, with the sofa behind it, no one would see if there's any slight color differences. Or, if you want, I can replace the entire floor, then sand and stain it."

"No, this looks amazing. Much better than I ever anticipated." She gazed around, delighted at how swept and clean the place looked. It was equipped with all modern plumbing but hadn't been lived in or updated for nearly twenty years. The old sofa sagged in several places, and the wood coffee table was full of nicks and chips.

She needed to buy some new furniture. A new tan or chocolate-colored sofa and maybe a storage ottoman. Some armchairs. Maybe a bronzed lamp on the side table.

She could drive to Livingston, try to find something not too expensive at a furniture store. Then replace the graying, faded curtains with something new and fresh.

Ideas spun through her mind.

She'd expected layers of dust, but of course, Wes had swept out the place and scoured it down. It made a world of difference from the last time she'd set foot in the cabin.

Wandering down the hall, she entered the large bedroom that had once slept two to four ranch hands in double bunks. When she was a girl, her mother had turned this place into a rental home, and leased it out to a pair of brothers who worked as ranch hands for a time at the Tanner horse ranch.

Later, when she was in high school, her mom had occasionally rented the cabin out to others passing through, but that was a long time ago.

Nothing much had been done with the place in all these intervening years, but now Annabelle began to see the possibilities for extra income become real before her eyes. Once the walls were painted and the kitchen updated, once there was a new granite vanity and modern shower added to the bathroom, it was entirely possible that both tourists and seasonal workers would want to stay here.

With a few nice extra touches, like throw pillows on the sofa, some artwork on the walls, she could make this cabin inviting and cozy in a snap.

Both beds were neatly made up and she had no idea which one Wes had been sleeping in. There was an old, badly scarred dresser that looked like a leftover from the 1800s—that would need to be replaced, too.

"I'll probably need new mattresses," she murmured, turning to Wes. "I'm almost afraid to ask—how bad is the one you've been using?"

"See for yourself." With a grin, he took her hand and led her to the double bed closest to the window.

When she sat down on the coverlet, intensely aware of him, he sat beside her.

"Not a very thick mattress. I'm sorry; I didn't even realize."

"It's deluxe compared to some places I've bedded down. I sleep like a log."

"Is that so?" She slanted him a smile.

Eyes alight, Wes leaned in closer. His gaze was steady on hers as he wrapped his arms around her. When she didn't protest, he brushed his thumb down her cheek. "You don't believe me? Maybe you should stay the night and sing me a lullaby."

"If I were to stay here, Wes McPhee, something tells me we wouldn't be doing a whole lot of singing."

"Damned straight." He laughed. His gaze was hot on hers as he tugged her closer. "Not when there's so many other things we could do. Like . . . *this*."

And he kissed her again, softly. Their mouths clung as if they'd both needed the touch, the brush of each other's lips and breath and closeness.

"I've fallen asleep thinking about you the past few nights." He traced a finger along the delicate line of her jaw, then touched it to her lips. Both of them were breathing faster, holding on tighter. "Thinking about what it would be like if you were here with me."

She felt almost too breathless to speak from the sweet heat of his kisses, but managed to murmur teasingly, "You're making that up."

"Wish I was. You're a skeptical woman, Annabelle Harper. Either that or you don't really understand how you affect a man. This man."

"What if I told you that you affect me, too?" she whispered. She pressed a kiss to his throat. Her lips lingered there, almost against her will, her heart racing, pinned up against the rock-hard wall of his chest.

It felt so good to be close to him.

"I'd think that was nice news. Real nice news."

Then pleasure flooded her as his hand slid beneath her T-shirt to cup her breast. Her heart tumbled in somersaults and her skin tingled where he touched. Gasping, she drew his head slowly down toward her, and kissed him.

The kiss was long, deep, and nearly stunned her breathless. It grew hotter, deeper, and more desperate the longer their lips clung together. As his hand slid beneath her bra and brushed her nipple, she couldn't hold back a moan of pleasure and soul-piercing hunger—and then they heard the dog barking fast and deep, and sounds of a car rumbling down the rough road.

"What the hell. Who's that?" Wes released her and looked up, suddenly alert. "You expecting anyone? I'm not." With a grimace, he pressed a quick kiss to the hollow of her throat that left her tingling. "I vote we ignore whoever that is."

Before she could respond, there was the sound of a car door slamming, the dog barked even more frantically, and a man's voice rang out.

"Wes!" There was pounding on the door. "Wes McPhee!"

Annabelle went completely still. She knew that voice. That smug, demanding, overly self-confident voice.

It belonged to Clay Johnson.

⌒

"Damn it." Wes pushed off the bed, frowning. "Don't move. I'll get rid of him."

But Annabelle was already scrambling up, straightening her bra and her tee.

"What's he doing here?"

"Beats me. Haven't seen him since I got back to town. And I don't want to see him now. Why don't you wait here—"

"McPhee!" Clay shouted again, and Wes's eyes hardened. He started toward the door, but after a minute, Annabelle tore after him.

"Damned if I'll hide from Clay Johnson at this stage of my life."

She was only a dozen feet behind him as Wes opened the front door of the cabin wide and the black and white mutt dodged out ahead of him.

"You have to help me, Wes." Clay stared at him, his expression taut, sweat beaded on his face as the dog barked frantically. "You were with the DEA—you know how to find people quicker than that useless, by-the-book sheriff. My kid—he ran away, the little bastard. My ex-wife is screaming bloody murder and this is gonna cause a shitload of trouble for me—"

He broke off as Annabelle stepped onto the porch.

"Holy crap—*you*?" He glared at her as if she were a fly in his ice cream sundae.

"Watch how you talk to the lady," Wes warned sharply.

"Hey man, it's your funeral, but this female here is no damned lady—"

Grabbing Clay by the front of his button-down shirt, Wes

yanked him forward hard, then shoved the other man back, pinning him against one of the posts on the porch.

"Think you'd better apologize to Annabelle, Clay. Right now, if you know what's good for you."

Purple color suffused the other man's face, but there was also sweat dripping from his blond buzz-cut hairline, and though he was big—a former football star—Wes was bigger and Clay couldn't shake free of Wes's grip.

The dog growled low in his throat.

"Back off! Damn it, Wes, let go. Sorry!"

Wes held him pinned a moment longer, then released him with a scowl. "How'd you find me?"

"This is Lonesome Way, man." Clay practically sneered the words. "Everyone knows you're back in town—and where you're staying. This is important, damn it! I've got to find my son and you need to help me. Sheriff Hodge is writing up a damned report, but he goes by the book and there's only him and his deputy looking for the boy. Don't you know how to track people fast? I'll pay you whatever it takes, anything you want, but you need to help me find Bear."

"Why did he run away?" Annabelle asked quickly. "Did he leave a note?"

"Yeah, he left a damned note," Clay spat out. "All it said was he was going home. That means back to his mother—in Helena. He must be walking . . . or hitching a ride, the little idiot. Paige called me, and damn near broke my eardrums—"

"Why would he run away?" Stepping off the porch, Wes positioned himself between Annabelle and the other man.

"How do I know? He's a kid. I yelled at him a couple of times. Wouldn't let him talk to his mother unless I was there, 'cause kids always complain about stupid stuff, you know? Are you going to help me find him or not? If I wait for Hodge and that deputy of his—the kid could get run over by a truck, or fall over and get hurt, or be dumb enough to get in a car with a stranger—and there's all kinds of perverts out there. I need help!"

"You have a photo of the boy? Do you remember what he was wearing?"

"Photo, yeah. Sure, I have a photo." Quickly, Clay yanked out his phone and thumbed through it, then thrust the phone toward Wes.

"He's seven, but puny for his age. Looks more like his mother than me. I don't remember what he was wearing this morning. I dropped him off at the park for a while—there was town hall business I needed to attend to. I was supposed to pick him up for lunch."

Wes studied the photo of a small fair-haired boy with a timid-looking smile, then passed the phone over to Annabelle, whose throat was tight with concern for the child.

Clay impatiently swiped a hand through his brush-cut hair. Sweat poured down his face.

"Your ex has full-time custody?" Wes asked.

"During the school year, yeah. Summers he comes to me. He should be here all the time, though, 'cause she's made a wuss out of him. I've just been trying to wean him from the apron strings and he doesn't like it much. But what difference does it make, Wes? I want to get my boy back and I want him safe!"

"So you called his mother and told her he ran away? Or did Sheriff Hodge?"

"Hell, I didn't call her. Neither did Hodge. The kid called her—borrowed some older kid's cell phone in Benson's Drugstore, and when Paige didn't pick up, he left her a voice mail saying he was on his way home—or something like that, according to her. Paige called me as soon as she heard it and nearly took my damned head off with all her yelling."

"What did you really do to him, Clay?" Annabelle handed him back his phone. She kept her voice calm, but she was boiling with anger and fear. She was angry with Clay Johnson, and afraid for his child.

If he was as big of a bully with Connor as he was with anyone else he thought was weaker than him—and based on what she'd seen, she suspected he was—that little boy must have been desperate to get away.

"Not a damned thing. You stay out of this, you nosy bitch—"

Wes's fist shot out with a punishing thwack that sent Clay spinning off the porch, landing facedown in the dirt. The dog growled again, ears up and alert as the man on the ground swore.

"Get out of here now, Clay." Wes spoke tautly. "One more word and I'll beat the crap out of you. I mean it."

"What'd she do to you? You're back a few weeks and you treat me like this? We were friends, Wes. All through school. I thought I could count on you, that you'd care more about a missing kid than this piece of ass—"

"Don't!" Annabelle grabbed Wes's arm as he was about to launch himself at Clay. "He's not worth it."

Wes froze. Going still for a moment, he forced himself to draw a deep breath.

He wanted to kick Johnson's ass from here to next Sunday, but Annabelle was talking to him, her tone low and urgent.

"Wes, we need to think about that little boy. His name isn't really Bear. It's Connor. Clay just calls him Bear because . . . Well, you know Clay. But Connor's a sweet boy—he plays basketball with Ethan at the community center. We need to help find him."

"We will. You're right."

She squeezed his hand, then stepped off the porch. As Clay managed to push himself unsteadily to his feet, she plopped her hands on her hips.

"You're on my land, and I want you off it. Now. We'll try to help find your son, but you need to leave. Go."

His eyes narrowed and for a moment she thought he was going to scream at her, or even rush at her, but instead he took one look at Wes's hard eyes and imposing presence, and spun around. Scowling, he strode back to his fancy black SUV.

"Fuck you. I'll find him myself."

The moment he roared away, back up Sunflower Lane and past her house, Annabelle rushed inside the cabin. Grabbing her cell phone, she speed-dialed Benson's Drugstore.

Lem, who worked the cash register, answered on the third ring.

She wasted no time asking him whether he'd seen Clay Johnson's son borrow a teenager's cell phone.

"Matter of fact, I did. The little boy was all upset. I asked him what the trouble was when he came back up front, but he just rushed out."

"Did you hear what he said on the phone?"

"No, but I bet Shannon Gordon did. She's the girl that gave him her phone. She was standing by him in aisle two, near the candy and school supplies—and it seemed like she was trying to talk to him after, but like I said, he didn't seem to say much. Kid was in a big hurry to leave."

"Got it. Thanks, Lem."

She turned to Wes. "Shannon Gordon is the one who loaned Connor her phone. Isn't she best friends with Ivy?"

"She is. And you're brilliant." He caught her to him and pressed a quick kiss to the top of her head. "She and Shannon are almost inseparable. Come on, I'm calling Sophie and Rafe, see if they can help us track Shannon down."

Fifteen minutes later, they were inside the Gordons' small gray frame house, talking to both Shannon and Ivy, while Shannon's mom, Kate, listened with a concerned frown.

Seated at the kitchen table, her daughter repeated the phone message Connor had left for his mother, telling her he was leaving, he couldn't stay anymore with his father, and she had to come get him.

"Did he say *where* she had to come get him?" Wes interrupted.

"No, I don't think so, not exactly. He said he couldn't stay in town because his father might find him. He said he was leaving and—I think he told her to pick him up somewhere . . . but he said it really quietly and I didn't quite catch it. I heard . . . something . . . but I'm not sure. . . ."

"Think, Shannon." Wes's tone was level. "Take your time. It's important."

The girl squeezed her eyes tightly shut. "I think he said something about a soldier. . . . No, no, he said a colonel. That's it. He said he was going to the colonel. That she should come there."

Annabelle and Wes stared at each other.

"Colonel who?" Annabelle muttered. "Who could that be? I don't know of any colonels living in Lonesome Way. Maybe it's someone in a nearby town. Do you—any of you—know?" She turned worried eyes to Kate and the girls.

"I don't know any colonel in these parts." Kate Gordon shook her head.

Ivy suddenly looked up. "Uncle Wes . . . this might sound dumb but . . ."

Her voice trailed off.

"Nothing's dumb, Ives. Tell me."

"There used to be a KFC a half mile out of Big Timber. By a big parking lot where they used to sell fireworks and touristy stuff at the edge of town. It closed a year or two ago, but . . . I don't know. If Connor said he was going to the colonel . . . maybe . . ." Her voice trailed off as her uncle studied her thoughtfully.

"You could be right, Ivy." Annabelle nodded. "It's

probably six or seven miles from the outskirts of Lonesome Way. Maybe Connor thought he could walk there."

"It's far enough from here that he might have figured his father wouldn't find him," Shannon suggested. Then she glanced over at her mother.

"The three of us walked it once. Me, Ivy, and Val, I mean."

Kate Gordon's mouth dropped open. Ivy winced, apparently wishing her friend hadn't mentioned that little fact.

"It was daytime—and summer—and we stayed a little ways off the road," Shannon continued in a rush. "There were three of us, Mom, and we were perfectly safe!"

Wes stood and strode to the door. "Thanks, girls. It's a start. We'll check it out."

"Good detective work, Ivy!" Annabelle shot a warm smile to the girl as she slung her purse over her shoulder.

"I used to read Nancy Drew when I was little. Now I watch *NCIS*." Ivy grinned. "I just hope you find him. Will you let me know, Uncle Wes?"

"I'll let you all know. Thanks, ladies." Wes held the screen door for Annabelle and then followed her into the late-afternoon wind, blowing down from the north.

"You're a pretty good detective yourself," he told her when they walked outside. "That was a good idea, finding out who lent him the phone."

"I read Nancy Drew, too. Let's just hope we're right about this colonel business. It'll start getting dark in a couple of hours. And cold. I hate to think of that little boy out there all alone on some country road. My God, if it was Ethan or Megan or Michelle—"

She broke off, trying to shake the fear knotting in her stomach at the thought of a child alone, in trouble.

"We'll find him, Annabelle." Wes glanced at her as he placed his hand over hers. The strength and warmth of his touch calmed her.

"Let's just hope we find him before Clay does," she said in a low tone.

"Yeah. Clay's on the verge of losing it."

"You know, I get that he's worried about the boy, but he's so angry with him, too. We have to hope we or his mother get to him first."

"Been hearing some rumors about Clay lately." Wes opened the passenger side door for her. "None too flattering."

"Why am I not surprised?" But she glanced at him, curiosity pricking through her as he sprang into the truck and backed out of the drive. "What sort of rumors?"

"A few people on the planning board have their noses out of joint," he said. "Clay's been rubbing folks the wrong way, pushing some zoning issues that would be good for the locations of his dealerships, but not as favorable to the downtown businesses."

"And how do you know all this after being in town only a few weeks?" She was stupefied. She hadn't heard a thing.

"Heard it on the down low. Sheriff Hodge and I had dinner together a couple of days ago. Professional courtesy, lawman to lawman. Seems the sheriff's wife, Joanie, is on the planning board, too, and mentioned the tension there. Speaking of the sheriff, why don't you call him and tell him our theory, see if he has any leads on the boy or if he wants to meet us at the old KFC site? The kid's mother could be there any minute, too. Let's hope she beats us there and is with him right now."

Annabelle vaguely remembered Clay's ex-wife. He and Paige had met in college, but the last time Annabelle had come home to spend Thanksgiving with Trish, Ron, and the kids, she'd heard that they were in the process of getting divorced. Charlotte had introduced her to Paige one time when they'd run into Clay's soon-to-be ex outside of Carly's Quilts on Spring Street.

She remembered Paige having pretty strawberry blond hair, and working as a school counselor. She'd seemed harried and stressed that day.

Of course, who wouldn't be harried and stressed having to deal with Clay through something as complicated and nasty as a divorce?

Annabelle kept an eye out for a small boy as they wove their way through the back roads. When they neared the outskirts of Big Timber, thick woods reared up on both sides of the road. Her heart jumped when she spotted the empty lot ahead on a deserted corner, just a couple miles from the main streets of the town.

But here on the fringes, there was only a barren lot where a boarded-up drugstore and a burned-out diner now stood alongside the remnants of a building that had once been an old KFC.

Annabelle didn't see any sign of Connor. She didn't see anyone.

Maybe they'd beaten him here . . . but they hadn't spotted him on any of the roads, either. . . .

She bit her lip, hoping hard that the child was here, perhaps hiding in the trees behind the lot, or in the brush alongside the road. Maybe he was waiting, alone and afraid and determined, watching for his mother.

She and Wes both jumped out of the truck and slammed their respective doors. Her hopes that the boy would hear and see them and perhaps emerge faded.

There was only silence. No little boy peeking out from behind a pile of broken lumber or the old skeleton of the chicken restaurant. No sign of movement from behind the tree stump at the far end of the lot, or in the thick mess of brush beyond both sides of the road.

"Call out to him." Wes spoke quietly. "He'd probably be more reassured by a woman's voice."

She unclenched her hands. "Connor?" She tried to sound calm, reassuring. "Connor, it's Annabelle Harper. I'm Ethan's aunt, remember? You and Ethan are in basketball camp together. I'm here to tell you that your mom is on her way to get you. And we'd like to wait with you until she gets here."

No sound. No movement. Not even the rustle of a breeze.

"Connor, please, are you here? Please come out. I'm with my friend Wes. He's sort of a police officer and he wants to help you get to your mother, too. You can call your mom on my cell phone and tell her where you are, and we'll wait with you until she comes."

Still there was nothing. Her heart fell.

Maybe he wasn't here, after all. Maybe he'd gotten hurt, or lost or . . . maybe there really was another "colonel" somewhere back in the vicinity of Lonesome Way? She didn't want to even think about the possibility that the boy might have climbed into a stranger's car. . . .

Her heart clenched as suddenly a small voice broke the silence.

"When's my mom coming?"

Then a small figure pushed his way through the thick brush behind the parking lot.

"Whew. Good work," Wes said under his breath.

Connor's face was pale and scared. Annabelle spoke softly, curbing the urge to race toward him in relief.

"Connor, she's on her way. I'm so glad you're okay."

But still the boy stayed where he was, his expression wary. "You're not taking me back to my dad. Are you? Promise!"

"No way, buddy." Wes leaned against the truck, relaxed and easy. The last thing he wanted was to spook the kid even more. His voice was smooth as caramel. "We'll help you get to your mom; that's it."

Connor trotted forward then, straight toward Annabelle. Close up, she saw that his face was streaked with tears.

"Can I call my mom now? Please? Before my dad finds me?"

She knelt instantly and handed him her phone, her throat thick with emotion.

"Sure you can, sweetie," she managed to gulp, even as she blinked back tears of relief. "You go ahead and call her right now."

Chapter Fifteen

With her hair still damp and curling wildly after her shower, Annabelle darted into her bedroom, fighting panic.

Dinner. She was going out to dinner. With Wes McPhee.

In fifteen minutes.

And she had nothing to wear. *Nothing.*

Oh, she had clothes, but as she stood in her pale peach thong and matching bra before her open closet and studied its contents, there didn't seem to be anything right for this occasion.

Not that it was an occasion, exactly—it was only dinner. Now that Connor was safely on his way back to Helena with his mother—after getting Sheriff Hodge's blessing—Wes had suggested they celebrate.

It's not really a date; it's just a celebration, she told herself. *A small boy helped to safety.*

What do you wear for something like that?

Her cell rang. Was that Wes? Canceling . . . ?

Scooping up the phone, she saw Charlotte's number.

"Char, I'm a little busy right now. Is it something important?"

"I'd say so. My bridal shower. I decided I want one!" Her friend laughed and rushed on before Annabelle could get in a word.

"I Googled everything about bridal showers and they're not bad luck, not at all, so we're on. Full steam ahead, for sure. I'm getting really excited now. You have to come to Livingston with me next week to help me find a dress—"

A dress. Reaching into her closet, Annabelle snatched a casual, flowy white lace dress she liked wearing over a sea green tank. Casual. Pretty. Perfect.

"Sure, you pick the day, but Charlotte, I have to go now. I'm running really late."

"Late for what?"

"For . . . um, dinner."

"With the kids? What, are they driving you crazy or something? Make some mac and cheese. Easy peesy," Charlotte said cheerfully. "It'll take five seconds—"

"No, not dinner with the kids. I'm . . . going out."

"Going *out*?" Charlotte sounded blank. As if Annabelle had spoken in an alien tongue. "You mean . . . you have a date? With who? Wait, don't tell me. Wes!"

"It's not what you think. It's just dinner. We're celebrating something good that happened today. Char, I swear, if you don't let me get off this phone, I'm still going to be naked when he gets here!"

"I bet he'd love that. Men are into naked. But yeah . . . go. And have fun! Don't forget to tuck that lucky dragonfly charm I got you last year into your purse."

Annabelle had lost that dragonfly charm somehow, and didn't believe in lucky amulets anyway, but she let that go as Charlotte rushed happily on.

"Tim and I are having a little date of our own as soon as he gets home." She giggled. "Naked, right here in bed."

"Can't get any luckier than that." Annabelle tossed the dress and the tank on her bed and scanned her closet for the right pair of shoes. "But, Charlotte, this isn't a date. It's just . . . Charlotte? Charlotte?"

But Charlotte was gone.

And Wes's truck would be rattling up that rough track any minute now.

Five minutes later she twirled in front of the mirror even as she heard a horn honk outside the house.

Not bad, she thought, grabbing up her cell and her purse. The tank made the dress look casual, but still cute. She wore low, nude-colored heels, and her hair was thankfully dry, and fell in loose sunny waves across her shoulders.

Small gold hoops in her ears—and she'd even dabbed on some pinky peach lip gloss.

An odd feeling came over her as she rushed down the stairs.

She sure felt like she was going on a date.

Wes was waiting on the porch when she opened the door. Her knees quivered and she almost dropped her purse. Why did he always have to look so damned sexy? Irresistibly, ruggedly, dangerously sexy.

He held a black cowboy hat in his hands, and in that steel gray button-down shirt, jeans, and boots, he looked relaxed, handsome, and good enough to lick all over.

At the thought, she felt herself spark with heat. "Hi," was all she could think to say. Only he had that effect on her.

"Hi yourself." He smiled, a slow, easy, heart-melting smile that a woman could get used to, then caught her hand in his. "Hope you're hungry, because I'm starved. We did good work today," he added as they walked to the truck and he opened the passenger side door, helped her in.

"I bet you say that to all your partners."

"Only the beautiful ones."

She thought about that as he put the truck in gear and they took off down Sunflower Lane.

"Have you had a lot of them? Women partners in the DEA, I mean."

"Sure," he answered without hesitation. "At least a dozen on various teams. There's not nearly as many women in the DEA yet as men, but the numbers are climbing. I've worked with some great female agents. The best." His voice sounded tight as he said those last two words, and she quickly glanced at him.

"But . . . something, someone . . . didn't work out so well?"

"Not in the way you think."

He was silent for so long, she wondered whether he was going to continue or if she should change the subject, but then he spoke abruptly, his eyes on the starlit road ahead.

"My teams included some of the bravest and toughest women on the planet. A few were ten times tougher than any of the male partners I've ever had, and they were all pretty damned tough. But the toughest of all—"

He paused, his mouth tightening.

Annabelle waited, hearing the pang in his voice, sensing sadness, even grief.

"Cara Matthews. She and I were teamed up on a bunch of missions. She was one of a kind. The most badass of the badasses. And the best of the best."

"What happened? Is she . . . Do you . . . still keep in touch?"

Wes stared at the road ahead and didn't answer for a moment. "I wish," he said at last, his voice tight. "Cara was killed in the line of duty."

"I'm sorry."

He let out a sigh. "I was halfway around the world when it happened. She was embedded with a good team, a solid bunch of agents, but things got fucked-up. She didn't make it back."

Annabelle closed her eyes a moment, her heart filling with horror for a woman she'd never met—and with sympathy for Wes, for the very idea of him losing someone so important to him. She was trying to imagine this woman—brave enough to plunge into an underground world of illegal drugs and drug lords, a woman that tough and smart and strong.

"It must have been terrible for you. How . . . how long ago did she die?"

"Been a little over two years now. She was only thirty-two. For a long time, I kept thinking that if I'd been there on the ground when things went to hell, maybe it would have turned out differently. But I'll never know. She was probably the best agent I've ever worked with—man or woman—and she—" He stopped abruptly, gritting his teeth.

"Sorry, Annabelle—I didn't mean to keep talking about Cara. I wanted this to be a celebration. Not a wake."

"I'm glad you told me about her. She was important to you, wasn't she?"

"Yeah. She was. Cara was something else." A brief smile flitted across his face. "She didn't have one warm, cuddly, sentimental bone in her body, but she was one hundred and thirty pounds of guts, strength, and determination."

Annabelle looked down, then stared straight ahead at the road before her. The summer darkness seemed to close in upon the trees like an ever-spreading, ever-thickening cloak.

Ask him. Just ask him.

She had to know.

"Were you in love with her?" Her voice was very quiet.

Wes looked startled. "No." He shook his head. "I'm not the *in love* type."

He glanced at her quickly then. Warningly, she thought.

"*In love* doesn't seem to be in my DNA. It was never like

that with Cara and me. We were friends, colleagues. Which isn't to say we weren't involved," he added.

Then Wes hit the brakes hard as a wolf suddenly skulked across the road.

"It just happened," he continued with a shrug when she remained silent. "We worked closely together, and we *got* each other, if you know what I mean. Hell, we made a great team. We knew what it was between us, though—and it wasn't love. Not for either one of us. It was attraction and friendship and respect—especially with all that adrenaline rushing like Niagara Falls while we were teamed up. Add that to the fact that we knew all the same people, faced all the same risks, and there you go. Cara was good at her job, damned good. I admired the hell out of her. Her drive, her smarts. But I never loved her." He glanced at Annabelle, his tone even.

"Cara's kid brother died of a drug overdose when he was fifteen, and after that, she was driven to get drugs off the street. One dealer, one crime lord, one gang at a time. Nothing held her back. Not fear, not danger—there was no hesitation no matter the situation. I admired that."

"She sounds incredibly brave." *Unlike me,* Annabelle thought. *I didn't even call the police on Zack the first half dozen times when he punched the wall right next to my head. Or that time he put his hands around my throat. I was too shocked, too stupid.*

But you got over that big-time, she reminded herself. *You left him and you learned to fight back. To steer clear and protect yourself, to be smart, careful.*

"Do you mind if I ask . . . how she died?"

His mouth twisted. "Firefight. With some low-life thugs, small fish in a bigger pond. I was a continent away, up to my neck in a different case."

"That's horrible. I'm sorry, Wes. Did they catch the men who killed her?"

"They sure as hell did."

They were driving past Carly's Quilts on Spring Street and Annabelle could see the lights of the Double Cross Bar and Grill up ahead.

"Cara's team went in—got them a week later," Wes told her with satisfaction. "Those boys weren't about to let the bastards get out alive. I only wish I was there with them when they took 'em down."

She closed her eyes a moment, stunned by the world of violence he spoke of so casually.

"Knowing that she got justice—did that . . . give you a sense of peace in the end?"

They were rolling down Main Street and the center of town now, passing Pepperoni's Pizza, which was packed inside and out, with people and their kids sitting at small tables outside, enjoying their pizzas and Cokes, the moon swimming bright overhead on this warm June night.

It seemed odd, she reflected, her throat dry, to talk about firefights and drugs and death while cruising along the peaceful streets of Lonesome Way. Here the biggest problems faced by Sheriff Hodge and Deputy Mueller seemed to be an occasional drunken fistfight, a shoplifting escapade, or some small-scale cattle rustling.

"Getting justice for Cara gave me satisfaction. Closure." Wes shrugged. "But peace? Not really."

He cut the wheel into the parking lot of the Lucky Punch Saloon, parked with swift efficiency in a spot near the entrance, and switched off the engine. "I'm not even real sure what that peace thing is." He shrugged. "Maybe I've gotten some measure of it working on the cabin. I did construction to put myself through college. I've always liked working with my hands. Guess there's just something deepdown satisfying in that."

Without thinking, she reached out to touch his hand. He was still gripping the steering wheel.

"I know what you mean, Wes. I think peace sometimes comes at unexpected times." She hesitated. "When Trish and Ron died, I hurt like hell. I thought I'd never stop grieving. But I felt a sense of peace the instant I reached home."

Suddenly she smiled into his eyes. "When I walked into our childhood house, moved through the familiar rooms, I was hit by all the memories. I was hurting like hell, but something quieted inside me." Her voice was very soft. "Especially when those kids ran into my arms. I knew what I had to do—I knew the only thing that mattered. And I knew I was exactly where I belonged."

She stopped then, shook her head. "Oh God, sorry. I don't know what's wrong with me. Too much talk about the past," she murmured, annoyed with herself for bringing up a subject that could only be described as a downer. Opening the door of the truck, she hopped down, certain that Wes would never want to take her out to dinner again.

But the next thing she knew he was already around to the passenger side, standing beside her. He slammed her door, then drew her close to him.

"One thing I've learned about the past, Annabelle. It's always with us. The good *and* the bad. There's no escaping it. But . . . to be truthful, when I talked about that bit of peace I found working on the cabin . . . Well, I don't just feel it then." He stroked a hand through her hair, loving the silky feel of it sliding through his fingers. He smiled.

"I happen to feel it when I'm with you."

She stared at him. "You do? *When?*"

He grinned. "For one thing, every time I take a bite of those amazing muffins you leave for me in the morning. And when I see you, anytime, anywhere—like today when I found you working in the garden—I just had to stop at the sight of you. I don't know why—I can't explain it exactly. And I didn't even have a clue about the chocolates then." He chuckled.

"Chocolates give you peace?" she teased.

"No. You do." His gaze was steady on hers. "When we went searching for Clay's kid today and helped him get safely to his mom—that felt a lot like peace to me, too. You know something? I'm beginning to think that being around you brings me the closest I've gotten in a while to any semblance of peace."

A rush of warmth flooded through her. And so did shock. For a moment she couldn't speak. Silence settled softly over them as they stood in the parking lot facing each other. Dusk finger-painted the sky, drifting down slowly to envelop the town.

"I'm glad," she heard herself say at last. "I . . . I feel that way when I'm with you, too."

Slowly, he pulled her into his arms. She couldn't help melting against him, and everything outside of the two of them floated away.

When he kissed her, the kiss seemed as deep and tender as the Montana night. She loved the feel of his brawny arms holding her close, and the way his warm mouth caressed hers as if they were the only two people in the world.

The kiss went on for a very long time. She breathed in his clean, outdoorsy scent, his warmth and dark male sexiness, as his tongue slipped through her parted lips and his hands slid down her body possessively. Intense pleasure flowed through her as the kiss grew hotter and need built, filling her until she thought she would burst.

He made her want more than a kiss. Much more. *He made her want all of him. . . .*

"Annabelle," he breathed. "You've got to know, I think you're amazing." Then he kissed her again, more fiercely.

His mouth sent licks of fire through her as her hands slid down his back, and then he deepened the kiss even more, taking her to a wild, sexy, need-filled place she'd never been before.

"Wes, I . . ." she began, her heart pounding, but suddenly

a car roared into the parking lot, its headlights shining, music blaring, and laughter exploding through open windows.

Annabelle jumped and Wes lifted his head. He frowned at the two couples—twenty-somethings—who piled out of the Ford pickup and with shouts of hilarity raced right past them toward the double doors of the Lucky Punch Saloon.

"Guess we'd better continue this later," he drawled. "Preferably some place a lot more private." His lips quirked into a smile as he caught her hand in his. He nodded toward the restaurant. "This place okay with you?"

"Of course. I love the Lucky Punch. This is where we came to celebrate the night Trish and Ron got engaged. It was the happiest evening. Those two were so in love you could feel it in the air. That night they had their whole lives ahead of them."

"Good memories, then." Wes squeezed her hand as they crossed the crowded parking lot. "The kind to hang on to."

"I remember everyone used to say that the steaks here were the best in town—and it seems a little quieter and more sedate than the Double Cross—but, maybe not, with *those* folks inside." Her eyes danced as she looked toward the two noisy couples who'd spilled into the restaurant ahead of them.

"According to my sister, they also have a better wine list here." Wes held the door for her.

"You . . . discussed our going out to dinner with your sister?"

"Sure. She called to invite me for supper tonight with the fam. When I told her I had other plans, of course she wanted to know what they were." He shook his head. "By now, my whole family and half the town probably know we're having dinner together."

She flinched. His whole family. She pictured Diana McPhee, elegant and controlled and dignified. And wondered what Wes's mother thought about this.

On the other hand, maybe she didn't want to know.

Wine, I need wine.

"Charlotte knows, too," she murmured. "So I'd lay odds the entire town is probably up to speed."

"Hey, all or nothing, right? Be prepared for gossip and questions. And more gossip." Wes grinned as he followed her inside.

⌒

Two hours later, after appetizers of mushroom bites and buffalo wings, after a shared bottle of wine, a couple of T-bone steaks, double-baked potatoes, and hot, buttery biscuits, they left the restaurant and drove leisurely back through the center of town.

It was quieter now, peaceful and shadowy, almost magical, Annabelle thought. The streets were mostly empty and silent, lit only by pale streetlights, soft as candlelight. The moon glowed in a deep amethyst sky.

To her surprise, Wes parked outside of the Lickety Split Ice Cream Parlor, just as it was about to close up for the night. The temperature hadn't yet dropped into the fifties and he strode inside and bought them a couple of ice cream cones. They ambled over to the park, deserted now, quiet and sheltered by trees and shrubs and gardens.

Past the empty picnic tables, past the swings and the slide, there was a low bench, and a garden surrounded by shadowy elm trees.

Sitting on the bench beside Wes in the darkness, Annabelle licked her ice cream cone and gave a sigh.

"Something wrong?"

"Just the opposite. Everything's right."

But Wes heard another tiny sigh.

"Out with it. I used the wrong fork with my steak, didn't I? Or stepped on your toes under the table? Tell me—I can take it."

She laughed at him. "Wes, this has been an absolutely perfect night."

"Good to hear. They don't come along too often."

And after everything that has happened today, it's a shock—a pleasant one—that the day turned out like this. Connor must be home by now, in Helena with his mother. Clay was out of luck, having only narrowly escaped cooling his heels in a jail cell after losing his temper and shouting obscenities at Sheriff Hodge—not to mention taking an ill-advised swing at Deputy Mueller.

And she and Wes were . . . *here.*

Here alone in this little park on a summer evening, sitting close together in the darkness. And for one moment in time, all seemed peaceful and right with the world.

"This evening is a small miracle," she murmured.

"Actually, it's a pretty big miracle—one you had a lot to do with." Leaning back on the bench, he watched her, enjoying the delicate, sexy way she licked her ice cream cone, and wondering with a surge of lust how it would feel to have her tongue and those warm, crazy-lush lips trailing over every inch of his body.

Pure heat and need surged through him. He forced his attention back to the conversation with a supreme effort.

"Today could have ended very differently if you hadn't thought of tracking down Shannon Gordon."

"And if you hadn't been there to explain the situation to Hodge when he showed up," she pointed out, "it definitely would have ended badly. Especially for Connor. Luckily, Hodge respects you. He listened to you."

"He's a solid cop. Good thing he listened to Paige, too, when she finally got there, and he saw how scared the boy was and how happy he was to see his mom."

Despite several enraged phone calls from Clay Johnson during the course of the search, Sheriff Hodge had arrived outside the closed-down chicken restaurant in time to speak with Clay's ex-wife when she came roaring up the road look-ing for her son. He'd listened to Wes's quick summary of the situation without interrupting, had observed for himself how desperately the young boy clung to his mother's waist, and noted how, despite the lines of worry and tension in her face, she had clearly and calmly explained that she had full custody of the boy, including an agreement from the court that he was allowed to visit his father twice a year, subject to her wishes and best judgment.

Clay had no right to keep Connor in Lonesome Way if Paige wanted him to come back home—and she'd guaran-teed the sheriff that she'd fax him all of the relevant court documents to prove it in the morning.

Hodge, taking into account the boy running away from his father, then calling his mother in desperation, had deter-mined that he had no real jurisdiction to force the boy to go back to Clay, and that Paige was fully within her parental rights to take him home.

There was no doubt Clay would fight that to the teeth, but he'd have to fight it in court, and that was his problem.

"All in all, today turned into a pretty awesome day." Annabelle shot Wes a smile as she polished off her ice cream cone. "Because of you."

"Don't like to argue with a lady, but I'm pretty sure it was because of you."

This time when he pulled her close, his kiss was long, slow, and hot as a stoked bonfire. Her heart somersaulted the moment his arms went around her, and then again when he drew her onto his lap. As he took the kiss deeper, his tongue caressing hers, she let out a moan of sheer pleasure. She edged even closer against him as one kiss followed another. She needed to be near him . . . as close as she could get. . . .

"Maybe we should . . ." Wes broke off after trailing warm

kisses down her neck. "Head back to my place. There's . . . a helluva lot more privacy there."

"How . . . long will it take . . . to get there?" she gasped as her senses swam and his warm lips scorched the hollow of her throat.

"Too long." His voice was rough with need. He nibbled her lower lip. "Warn me when those kids are coming home—will that be first thing in the morning?"

"N-no, I packed . . . everything they need . . . and . . . Megan and Michelle are going straight to the community center with . . . Kaley. Mmm . . ." She tangled her hands in his hair and parted her lips as he kissed her like there was no tonight, no tomorrow, just *now*.

"Jimmy's mom will f-feed the boys breakfast and then drop them at the community center," she whispered as she traced her fingers lightly down his shirt.

"Now, that sounds like a plan. What the hell are we waiting for?" Grabbing her by the hand, he tugged her off that bench. "I just remembered something I forgot to show you earlier at the cabin."

"Etchings?"

"Something much better."

They ran, laughing, like a couple of teenagers toward the spot where he'd parked the truck. Soft night air blew through Annabelle's hair, and the moon—a world away—looked huge and close enough to touch.

"Why . . . are we running?" she gasped at last. She felt like a schoolgirl, young and carefree and alive—more alive than she'd felt in a long time.

"You'll see. There actually *was* something I planned to show you this afternoon before we got interrupted." When they reached the truck, he opened the door for her. His eyes gleamed into hers.

"Tonight, honey—no interruptions. I promise."

She plopped onto the passenger seat and turned to him with a big smile. "Cowboy, I'm going to hold you to that."

After the black truck rumbled away from Main Street, a man stepped out of the darkened alley beside the ice cream parlor.

He was tall and lanky slim, in his late forties. He wore jeans and a red-and-black-plaid shirt. He looked no different from most of the other men in town, but he didn't hail from this puny little nothing of a dump. He wasn't even from Montana.

He was originally from South Dakota, but he was a citizen of the world. A fugitive with no home, no boundaries, no allegiances—except to the man who paid him. He lived and worked and slept in the shadows.

Blending into them now, he walked swiftly toward a black Silverado and vaulted inside. Keeping a safe distance between his vehicle and the truck he was following, he pulled out a cell phone and placed a call to the man who'd hired him.

"Got him. Nailed everything I need to know. And you'll like this. Seems he's got him a woman—she lives down the road from where he's holed up. Seen them together a few times—yep, they look real cozy."

He listened a moment, and smiled thinly. "Thought you'd say that. I can take care of them both—you sure you want to trouble yourself coming here? I can always send pictures of what's left when I'm done."

He said nothing as the old man on the other end of the line spewed out a dozen epithets that made his intentions clearer than clear. The man in the plaid shirt didn't flinch.

"All right, then, I'll wait for you to come. I guarantee you'll enjoy the show. Got some real special plans for the two of them. When do you think you'll get here?"

A moment later, when the old man bit out his reply and

disconnected, the stranger pocketed the cell phone. It didn't bother him that the boss wanted to watch. He did some of his best work in front of an audience. Putting the Silverado in gear, he hit the accelerator and zoomed forward into the Montana darkness.

Chapter Sixteen

⌒

Treasure's barking pierced the night when they approached the cabin. The ruckus didn't abate until Wes unlocked the front door. Immediately the dog began jumping around in greeting, leaping back and forth between Annabelle and Wes like a crazed beast.

"Here you go, mutt." As Wes held the door wide, the dog bounded happily out.

"He won't run away?"

"He's way too smart for that. Treasure knows when he's got it good. He actually loves to sleep on the porch. Me, on the other hand—" His grin widened. "I've slept on the floor or in a foxhole enough, I like sleeping in a bed. Especially when there's a beautiful woman there with me."

"Oh, so we're going to sleep, are we?" Stepping toward him, she tilted her head up, and slanted him a teasing smile.

"We might sleep. Eventually." Wes caught her to him and

breathed her in. She smelled like the most delicate of flowers. Slowly kissing her lips to seal the deal, his palms cupped her curvy bottom.

Damn, if she wasn't the sexiest woman he'd ever met. He kissed her again, a hot, tender, explosive kiss, and felt his blood surge as she trembled in his arms.

"We'll sleep some—just not quite yet," he promised against her lips.

With that, he scooped her up and carried her down the hall toward the bedroom, then paused on the threshold, holding her easily.

"Forgetting my manners. Would you like some wine?" His eyes glinted into hers.

"No wine. Only you—us—now." Annabelle couldn't tear her gaze from him. She didn't know what in the world she was doing, but she sure as hell wasn't about to stop.

Pulling his head down, she kissed him again, a long, yearning kiss, breathing in the scent and taste of him. She'd never felt this way before. She couldn't get enough of him.

"There's beer . . . and whiskey," he muttered huskily against her lips. "I suppose I could rustle up a tea bag somewhere—"

"Just shut up and kiss me," she begged as he crossed the threshold of the bedroom with her in his arms. Laughing, Wes plunked her down on the nearest of the two beds made up with plain red-and-brown-patterned quilts.

"Oh, believe me. I'm planning to do just that. And a hell of a lot more."

His eyes burned into hers as she reached for him, and suddenly they were both lost—immersed in a world of wanting, a world that was dark and hot and simmering with need.

A world with space for no one else.

They began kissing and stripping off each other's clothes with an urgency that made each breath come quick and fast.

Wes's chest was tight as he yanked off his boots, but she was the one to reach for his belt the moment she stepped out of her heels.

He grinned as she unbuckled it slowly, her gaze rapt on his. Then she unsnapped his jeans and with single-minded determination went after the buttons of his shirt.

They kissed some more, fast, urgent kisses, before her hand slid down, desperately tugging at his zipper. He heard her draw in her breath at the size of him, and grinned as she managed to work the zipper down.

Fair was fair. The moment his jeans came off, he got her out of that lacy white dress in about five seconds. But as she reached for the green tank, he snagged her hand.

"Let me do the rest." Eyes gleaming, he had her out of the tank in four seconds flat and flung her bra aside an instant later.

His heart pumped at the curvy, naked beauty of her. He leaned down to kiss and caress her breasts even as he eased her down on the bed beneath him.

Then he took his time with her. Kissing her throat, nibbling his way once more to her nipples, swathing them with his tongue.

In between kisses and whispers and her hands sliding over him, he remembered that she still wore that tiny peach wisp of a thong. Grinning, he stripped it down along her sleek, tanned thighs and past her pink-painted toes, tossing it across the room, then found himself rewarded by a very long, very hot, sexy kiss.

Bracing himself above her on the bed, every muscle in his body burned with hunger for her. She was slender and luscious, her creamy breasts even more gorgeous than he'd anticipated. As his tongue stroked against her nipples, their rosy peaks pebbled quickly, going hard and tight, as if straining for his mouth, his tongue, his touch. She clutched him, moaning, as he dipped his mouth to them again and again.

"My turn," she said breathlessly, and shifted, pushing

him down with a laugh as he went along and lay flat, grinning at her, one arm resting above his head.

Oh, he was delicious, she thought, kissing and caressing him. The scars on that impossibly hard body only added to the aura of toughness that was simply part of who he was. But his keen, sharp eyes glistened with warmth as she ran her hands over him, her slender fingers and her mouth exploring every muscular inch of his body. He was big, huge, and almost intimidating in size and strength.

But she wasn't afraid of anything about Wes. She knew he'd never hurt her.

Once or twice, she drew in her breath with a little wince of sympathy as she touched the four-inch scar on his chest or kissed one of the many smaller scars and nicks on his arms and thighs and flat, hard belly.

When he surged up over her again, pushing her back down on the bed, he braced his arms on either side of her. He soothed her shock over his old injuries with his warm mouth and deep kisses, then slid his hands and his lips slowly down her skin once more, working his way lower, lower still, to her thighs, then parting them, exploring all of her.

He stroked her inside and out, his fingers gentle, persistent, while he kissed her thighs and then licked all her sweet hidden places until she quivered, until her skin was moist, her heart racing, and her entire body trembling for release.

"You're delicious . . . beautiful . . ." he rasped, lifting his head.

"Look . . . who's talking. I want you, Wes. Now."

"Not yet. Let me savor you a little longer, honey. There's no rush."

"Yes, there is," she murmured. "Trust me!"

"You need to trust me." He grinned and stroked her some more with his tongue, taking his sweet, torturous time.

"Wes!"

"Soon, baby, real soon." He slowed things down, his hands

stroking her some more, then dipping his mouth to her again, wanting to tease her and please her in every way, until she tugged at him, urged him up to face her, and wrapped those long legs around him.

"Wes, don't make me hurt you," she half gasped and half laughed.

His mouth closed over her nipple. "I'm trying to go faster, but I just can't get enough of you."

"I want more of you—right now."

"Likewise, baby." Hell, his body hummed and ached with raw, almost painful need. God, he wanted her more than he'd ever wanted any other woman. Wanted to be inside her, joined with her, one with her. This woman was so damned beautiful in every conceivable way.

So soft and giving. Trusting. He knew she'd been hurt before—physically hurt by her bastard ex-husband, and emotionally hurt by his bullying. The thought nearly killed him.

"You okay, honey?"

"Much . . . better than okay and don't you know it." She let out a breathless laugh that was partly a moan. "Wes . . . in case you haven't noticed, I'm . . . I'm . . . going to pieces here," she managed to pant. As she wrapped her legs more tightly around him, he grinned, and snagged a condom from the pocket of his discarded jeans.

"Damned if you're not the sexiest woman I've ever seen," he said, manning up.

"I'm sure you . . . say that to all the girls."

"Never. Never said it to any girl before." He stared into her eyes and felt something quake inside him, in a place he hadn't even known existed.

Then she arched her back and kissed him with a furious heat that could have set the brown and red quilt on fire.

She smelled like spring and the first day of summer. Her eyes were golden stars in the darkness. Hungry for her in a way he'd never been hungry for any other woman, he pushed deep inside her, cradling her, kissing her sweet lips, hanging on to his sanity as the small room and the bed and the darkness fled, as they rocked together and stroked each other and the mews of pleasure she made drove him deeper inside her, made him hold her tighter, and want her longer.

"Annabelle," he groaned, lost in her, in the softness and beauty of her, in the candle glow of her eyes, and in the feel of her slender fingers gripping him so tightly she stirred emotions and sensations he'd never felt before.

The old cabin drifted away into a far-off blur, and so did the wind outside in the trees. There was only this room, this bed, this incredible, sweet, and fantastic woman clinging to him, welcoming him, bucking and shuddering and coming joyfully in his arms.

Moments or hours ticked by.

Annabelle had no idea exactly how much time. She gasped for breath and for sanity. She'd been almost crazed when he finally slid into her. He was so big. So thick. Her eyes had widened and her knees gripped him. Her arms encircled him with all of her strength. He smelled of leather and soap. He was all rock and sinew and *man* and he'd driven her nearly insane with pleasure.

But he was Wes, and he was gentle—careful not to hurt her. Controlling his needs, seeing to hers. His kiss had been gentle at first but had soon scorched her mouth, and their tongues danced again and again as they came together in a swift, vivid storm that felt like lightning and thunder and heaven rolled into one.

Annabelle didn't remember the last time she'd felt such joy and release and pleasure.

Such a sense of being wanted. Cherished.

"Wes, that was . . . incredible," she managed to murmur afterward, curling into his arms.

"You all right?" His deep voice soothed her into a blissful daze.

"You could . . . say that. I don't think I've ever felt better."

With a grin, he rolled to his side, realizing they'd been making love for a couple of hours. A prelude, he thought, settling himself beside her, holding her close against his still-pounding heart.

She fit against him perfectly, his arm encircling her waist. As if they were made for each other.

Suddenly she lifted her head, smiled sexily at him, in a way that made him crazy with lust—but an odd tenderness also rushed through him. That was something new.

"Wes, let's do it all again. Everything. Before morning."

"You got it, baby." He laughed. "Anything you want. As many times as you want. And as many ways as you want."

She pressed a searching kiss to his mouth that heated his blood all over again and made him grip her tighter.

"I'm going to hold you to that, cowboy."

"Likewise." He touched his lips to hers—a soft promise.

They lay curled together for a while. Entwined. At peace. Sleep slid over her like feathery lace as she rested her head against his chest.

"I really like you, cowboy," she mumbled.

"You don't know how glad I am to hear that," he drawled with a grin; then as she went quiet, he drew back and gazed down. Her eyes were closed, her skin dewy and flushed, her breathing slow and even.

She was smiling, glowing, sated.

And fast asleep.

Chapter Seventeen

"Wes McPhee, you are such a liar."

Annabelle's eyes danced as she refilled both of their coffee cups the next morning in the cabin's kitchen.

He was bare-chested, wearing only jeans and a bod of pure, sculpted muscle. He'd rustled up toasted English muffins and half an orange for breakfast. Near the kitchen door, Treasure was crunching on dog food from a big plastic bowl.

"You got me here under false pretenses. You claimed you had something to show me."

"I did show you things—quite a few things."

Grinning, he braced his hands on a kitchen chair, eyeing her with such a sexy, purely male grin, her entire body instantly came alive with need. The need for him.

"You know what I mean." Her lips twitched as she raised her coffee cup and took a sip.

"Honey, you're about to eat those words. I can prove I wasn't lying."

Striding over to the lone bookshelf in the tiny living room, he seized a couple of slim children's picture books and a DVD she hadn't even noticed the night before, and brought them over, set them down in front of her.

"What's this? *Lassie*?" She stared in surprise at the DVD cover, at the picture books, then shot him a questioning glance.

"Yep. Two seasons' worth of episodes. And the librarian recommended some books. Just look at those photos."

She turned the pages of the slenderest book. Color photos of dogs, big dogs, small dogs, medium dogs. Full-breeds and mutts of every variety. All adorable and friendly looking, all playing with children, or cuddled against children, or licking children's happy faces.

"I did some research on ways people can overcome a fear of dogs, and one way is familiarity. Lots of safe, comfortable familiarity. It takes time, but if you go through these books with Megan, let her study the photos, and keep things light, it might help. Play the *Lassie* episodes on DVD, let her watch. Actually, the kids might all want to watch together. That little Timmy was about Ethan's age."

"Lassie rescued someone almost every week," Annabelle murmured. A smile bloomed across her face. "Did anyone ever tell you you're brilliant?"

"Happens all the time." He chuckled. "Seriously, it's not too hard to figure out. Who doesn't love *Lassie*? There's no guarantees, though," he added, more seriously. "But according to everything I've read, it might help. It *has* helped."

"It's definitely worth a real good try." Annabelle scooped out some blueberry jam and spread it on the second half of her muffin, suddenly feeling happier than she could remember in a very long time. Oh, she'd been plenty happy last night—in Wes McPhee's bed, in his arms—but this morning was a different kind of happy.

It felt so right being here with him. Just the two of them—comfortable together, a warmth flowing between them. There was no pressure, no watching her words, as she'd had to do with Zack. No worrying that she didn't have a lick of makeup on or that she wore only one of his chambray shirts that fell nearly to her knees—and nothing else. He looked at her with warmth and affection and a keen pleasure in his eyes, and she knew he felt the same irresistible pull she did.

And it was simply the two of them on a sunlit June morning. It was simply fresh coffee in big blue mugs, English muffins and jam, and Treasure beneath her chair now, quiet and calm for a change, snoring gently.

Not a bad way to wake up, she thought dreamily. *Close to Wes, his eyes warm on hers.*

For a moment she imagined what it would be like to wake up like this every day. *But that isn't going to happen,* she reminded herself quickly, caution flooding back. The friction of reality setting in had her choking a little on her next sip of coffee.

"Too hot?"

She shook her head at him, still coughing, and set down the mug. "It's perfect," she managed to choke out at last.

But she was lying to herself if she thought everything, not just the coffee, was perfect. She had to keep ahold of things here. To remember that this was . . . a fling. A break from her real life. Not something forever, only something short-lived, totally unexpected, and wonderful.

The fact was, she had three growing kids who needed to be her top priority. She had a job at the community center and dances to choreograph, a parade to help coordinate, and a bridal shower to plan. She had responsibilities and a busy schedule and a small candy business to try to launch so she could keep making ends meet for the kids. . . .

And as for Wes . . .

The truth burned into her heart. Wes was moving on in a matter of weeks.

July Fourth would be here before she knew it, and then, just like the fireworks, he'd be gone.

So don't start telling yourself lies. Making up fairy tales.

Life wasn't a fairy tale. And Wes wasn't some fairy-tale prince. He was a very tough man, a man of action and restlessness, a man who walked toward danger and challenges— and away from connections and commitments.

Get it together, she commanded herself, taking one last bite of the muffin, the way she'd take one last glimpse of him in a matter of weeks as he drove away down Sunflower Lane.

Keep this simple. Nothing's going on here except fun and flirtation—and mind-blowing sex. Start thinking like a real grown-up woman.

Like those women on all the *Sex and the City* reruns she used to watch with her roommate back in Philly. She needed to enjoy one day, one night at a time while it lasted, and not pretend this was anything more than what it was—having a lot of fun and incredible sex with a gorgeous ex-lawman who'd be moving on in a matter of weeks.

Who'd actually helped her get over Zack, and what he'd done to her. Despite Wes's imposing size and presence, despite what he'd done for a living and dealt with on the job all these years in an underworld of danger, not to mention the aura of toughness that defined him, she wasn't afraid of him in any way.

That was a miracle in itself.

After Zack, she'd practically jumped out of her skin at the prospect of a first date with a man, always assessing him, looking for signs of jealousy or control-freak anger . . . or . . . anything that could signal trouble.

With Wes, right from the beginning, she'd felt safe. Safe

enough that she hadn't even brought her Mace along to dinner last night. She almost always had it on her or in her purse at all times, but last night she hadn't even thought to bring it. She'd felt utterly safe the entire evening alone with him, never once even stopping to watch what she said or did.

But don't get in over your head—he's got one foot out the door, a tiny voice inside her warned as she pushed back her chair. Very soon she'd need to deal head-on with the fact of his leaving. But for today . . . for now . . . he was here. . . .

"This may have been the nicest breakfast of my life." She gathered both of their plates and washed them in the kitchen sink. "Still, unlike some of us," she added with a smile—aiming for offhand and casual and normal, as if she had wild, crazy-intense sex with men once or twice a week and not . . . Well, she didn't want to think how long it had been since she'd even invited a man to step inside her house after a date. . . .

"I have some work to get to and it can't wait any longer."

"Would that be chocolate-making kind of work?" Wes watched her sail down the cabin's short hall toward his bedroom door—no doubt to dress in her scattered clothes from the night before. Right now she looked fresh and delicious as a strawberry sundae in one of his clean work shirts and nothing else. He realized he was hungry for her all over again.

"If you need a taste tester—" he offered, but she cut him off with a smile.

"Tempting, but what I need is to *work*. Seriously. Today I need to nail down a new ending to the choreography my tap students are performing after the parade. I'll have to test it out on Megan and Michelle later—if they can handle it, the other tappers should be able to learn it quickly, too."

"What music are they dancing to?" Coffee mug in hand,

he followed her down the hall. For some reason he didn't want her to disappear into the bedroom, to take off that shirt, climb into her own clothes, and leave his cabin. He was stalling, trying to keep her talking, and there—and he wondered whether she knew it.

"'Yankee Doodle Dandy'—of course. What else?" She laughed, and in that instant he was sure it was the most appealing sound he'd ever heard. He almost ached with need just looking at her. She was so pretty. Those long gorgeous legs, totally bare, and those delicately pink-polished toenails.

He fought a strong urge to bundle her up in his arms and drop her back into his bed, to tangle his hands in those wild blond curls and feel her long legs wrapped around him again.

But it was the third week in June—and July Fourth was looming fast. Too fast. He had to keep a handle on this . . . whatever *this* was. Had to fight the almost irresistible urge to convince her to spend the entire day with him . . . to have amazing sex again this afternoon . . . and tonight—and first thing tomorrow morning. To take her on a damned picnic at Sage Creek, of all things, and maybe have sex with her on that thick grass, then take a dip with her in the creek . . . preferably a naked dip . . .

What the hell was wrong with him? He must be loco.

He suddenly remembered he had a session with the kids staying at Jake's retreat today. *Shit,* he thought, glancing at his watch. He needed to be there in less than an hour.

"I'll give you a ride home," he told her when she finished pulling on the dress and tank and low-heeled shoes she'd worn last night. "That track is too rough and uneven for heels."

Treasure rode along with them.

"You should go with her, boy," he told the dog as they both watched her dash up her porch steps and give a little wave before she slipped into the house.

"You're better off with her and those kids. Not with me. You need a home. And love. I need to move on."

Treasure licked his hand.

"Remember the rules, mutt. Don't get attached."

He said it in his sternest tone, but the dog just wagged his tail.

Chapter Eighteen

✦

Wes didn't think anything could distract him from the amazing night he'd spent with Annabelle, but the session at Jake's retreat came pretty damned close.

He'd brought Ethan and his friend Jimmy along. From the moment Ethan heard what Wes was doing today, he'd begged to come, and then Jimmy's mom gave in to her son's pleas and dropped him off at Sunflower Lane so he could sit in on Wes's talk, too.

Those kids! he reflected later. Not just Ethan and Jimmy, but all the boys and girls at Jake's lodge. There was a huge assortment of kids and ages—black, white, Hispanic, Native American, and everything beyond and in between. From eight-year-olds to young teens.

Man, they were quiet and sat real still at first—they seemed very intimidated. But halfway through the session— right around the time he told them about how making a pile of three of anything—rocks, branches, whatever—was the international symbol of distress, they got into it and started bombarding him with questions, wanting to know whether he'd take them camping, and whether they could learn how to pitch a tent and make a fire, and if he'd teach them how to use a compass.

Wes found himself loving every minute of it. Before he even realized it, he'd promised to look into the possibility of taking several groups on a hike before their time at the retreat ended.

The kids crowded around him at the end of the hour, all smiles, and asking a million questions. Only when Jake's beautiful redheaded wife, Carly, popped in and told them it was time for snacks and then riding lessons did they stream out the door.

While Ethan and Jimmy tagged along to get some snacks, Jake came forward with a big grin and immediately started talking to Wes about plans for the prospective hike, perhaps later in the week. Right when he asked whether Wes would be willing to speak to the next group of kids coming in the following week, they were interrupted by the ring of Wes's cell phone. He pulled it from his pocket.

"Hey, I know you're busy." Jake clamped a hand on his shoulder. "We'll talk later, try to figure out a schedule that works for you."

As Jake took off for the barn where another group of kids were saddling horses, Wes read the name illuminated by his caller ID.

Teddy Hodge.

He picked up, noting that Ethan and Jimmy were standing at the corral, admiring the dozen or so horses scattered inside the fence.

"Wes, we got a situation here. Thought you'd like to know." Hodge wasted no time with niceties. His tone was as grim as Wes had ever heard it.

"What's going on?" He wondered whether this had to do

with Clay and his ex-wife and kid. *What now?* he thought with a frown. *What did that asshole do? I should've beat the crap out of him in high school when he talked shit about Annabelle. Instead of letting it go on, looking the other way, barely noticing because I was so hung up on my own damned family problems. Namely Hoot . . .*

But the sheriff's next words made it clear this had nothing to do with Clay Johnson.

"That missing hiker? Turned up early this morning on Storm Mountain," Hodge said heavily. "Couple of hunters spotted him—what was left of him. Not far from Coyote Pass, at the bottom of a ravine."

"Aw, shit."

"Looks like the coyotes or wolves—or maybe a bear—got to him. Pretty ugly scene. The county medical examiner is taking a look, but it appears he must've had a fall, and died from a combination of his injuries and exposure."

"Sorry to hear it." Wes was no longer seeing the kids racing around in high spirits, or hearing the whinnying of horses from the corral.

He was seeing a man in the wilderness, dying alone.

"I don't think he had much experience in these parts, but he did have some other kind of knowledge. I finally learned what he was doing up there. The young man was a graduate student in American history, writing a dissertation on the Old West. Like too many fools before him, he must have got too deep into his research. Seems he was searching for gold—the missing gold bars stolen by the Henry Barnum gang. He had some maps and notes in his backpack. And a list of sources. Everything indicated he was headed for Coyote Pass."

⌒

Word spread quickly that the lost hiker the town had been speculating about for weeks had been found dead.

Rumors that he'd been shot while searching for treasure swirled like dark smoke after a fire. Sheriff Hodge put out the flames, though, releasing a statement that Randy Kirk had died of injuries from a fall and exposure.

A few days later, Kirk's sister returned to claim the body.

"Damn it," the sheriff told Wes the next day in his office. He banged a thick fist in frustration on his desk.

"We scoured those mountains, the valleys, the ravines . . . miles of 'em . . . searched high and low in every nook and cranny we could find, and we never spotted Kirk. Didn't find a fucking thing. If he'd been conscious, able to answer our calls, maybe . . ." He broke off and shook his head.

Wes's mind raced, trying to recall the rugged terrain near Coyote Pass where the hiker had been found. He could picture the ridges and valleys and steep trails of the region in his mind. He hadn't been back up that way in a lot of years, though when he was a kid, he'd been fairly familiar with it. There'd been a swimming hole deemed too remote and dangerous by parents and teachers, but of course he and Clay, Tobe, and his other friends had congregated there. Cougar Rock, the favorite high school make-out spot, was less than three miles from the swimming hole. Wes had wandered the area a whole lot back in the day, alone and with friends and girlfriends, but he hadn't set eyes on it in a long time.

"Teddy, you did your best." There was sympathy in his voice. "He didn't tell anyone where he was headed, and you had a lot of territory to cover. Welcome to my world, times a hundred. Why do you think so many agents in the DEA burn out after ten, fifteen, twenty years? You can only take so much blood and loss, and much of the time, murder and death, before you start to wonder if it's worth it. Any of it. The losses usually add up a lot faster than the wins. But then—coming back to a place like this—"

He paused, glancing briefly out the sheriff's window with its view of Main Street. He could see women in the park, talking, pushing children on swings, and teenagers laughing, streaming into Head to Toe to buy T-shirts and jeans and bathing suits.

"Maybe that's part of why I came back," Wes muttered. "I didn't even realize it at first, but I don't think it was just my grandmother's accident that brought me. I guess I needed to remind myself of a few things. That there's more to life than bullets and greed and bad guys. And that there are still good people and places in this world. Neighbors who care about each other. Families that stick together. Unfortunately," he said in a low tone, thinking of the hiker's brutal death, "sometimes the bad stuff still isn't all that far away."

"I hear you." Nodding, Sheriff Hodge leaned his big frame back in his chair and folded his arms across his middle. "Thank God I have Joanie to go home to every night. And Madison—that's my granddaughter—she lives right here in town. I suspect she and her young man—Brady Farraday—will be tying the knot pretty soon—and then I'm looking forward to some great-grandchildren to bounce on my knee."

His eyes lit up as he mentioned his granddaughter. Wes was sure he'd never seen the sheriff look happier.

"It does keep things in perspective when you have good things going on around you," Hodge continued. "You don't get so caught up in the ugly stuff. Of course, it's the *job*; there's no way around it—but a man needs something to keep the bleakness away."

His words hit home. They rolled around Wes's head, and fell into place. *Yeah.* For a long time, he hadn't let himself think it all the way through—at least not in so many words—but Hodge was damned right. A man needed something . . . someone . . . to keep the bleakness at bay.

Instantly, an image of Annabelle seated at his kitchen table the other morning, fresh and laughing and gorgeous in nothing but one of his shirts, popped into his mind.

He tried to push that pretty picture away as he stood and shook hands with the sheriff.

"Hope the next one's a win, Teddy."

"Me, too. Luckily, we've got a peaceful, decent town here. Good folks. And a nice influx of tourists adding to the economy in the past year," the sheriff added.

Then he gave his head a rueful shake, remembering the tourist who wasn't going to make it back home. "Maybe after the Fourth of July and the parade, we can get an ordinance passed, letting us put up signs on the doors of every restaurant and shop in town. 'Welcome to Lonesome Way but don't wander out in the wilderness if you don't know what the hell you're doing.'"

Chapter Nineteen

~~~

The following Saturday, Annabelle arrived at Charlotte's bridal shower the same time as Tess, who looked glowing and happy and very pregnant. Realizing they were the first guests to arrive, they grinned and chatted excitedly as they walked up the path to the Victorian house of Charlotte's aunt Susie, carrying their covered dishes.

Charlotte's aunt had offered her home for the shower and she greeted them warmly, as did Patricia, Charlotte's mother. She looked bright and flushed with excitement in a pretty floral, cap-sleeved dress. Ushered through the bright, spotless house by the two women, Annabelle and Tess stepped out through a set of sliding glass doors and into a large delightful garden.

"How beautiful," Annabelle breathed. And it was.

Susie Walker's garden was a large, expansive space, gorgeously decorated with streamers and balloons and paper hearts dangling from tree branches. The two long tables where lunch would be served were draped with a lavender lace cloth and bedecked with potted mint plants and slender vases of flowers. Bright pink and cream dishes and glittering crystal glassware sparkled in the June sunshine.

"You did bring your mother's macaroni salad, didn't you?" Patricia asked eagerly, and Annabelle smiled.

"Of course." She handed the casserole dish over. "And chocolates for all the candy dishes and favors. I have the favors in little gilt bags. Also a strawberry pie. I need to run back to the car for all that."

"Your mother brought that macaroni salad to *my* bridal shower," Charlotte's mother told her fondly. "Everyone loved it. It's still my favorite."

Tess handed over her tray of delicate finger sandwiches to Susie. There was tuna salad, chicken salad, and egg salad. Charlotte's aunt divided them into pretty oval silver trays on each table, beside pitchers of iced tea and large cut-glass bowls of fresh fruit salad.

"I'm not sure we have enough food," Tess joked, eyeing the tables, which were beautiful, colorful, and filled with an array of tempting dishes, from cucumber–cream cheese bites to veggie platters, a huge green salad, and deviled eggs.

"Oh, there's plenty more coming." Aunt Susie laughed. "For one thing, my turkey casserole and buttermilk biscuits are still warming in the oven."

Then more guests began streaming in, including Charlotte, lovely and flushed with excitement, greeting everyone and fairly bouncing in anticipation. She looked gorgeous in a bright blue silk dress and small gold heart earrings, and was smiling from ear to ear.

When Sophie and her mother and grandmother arrived, Ava Louise Todd spotted Annabelle immediately, and zoomed right over, her long white braid sweeping elegantly down her back, her wrist still encased in a cast.

"I heard my grandson is babysitting your nieces and

nephew today." Her face beamed. "From what I gather, he's grown quite fond of those children."

"Yes, he has . . . I mean, I think he has. . . ." She found herself stammering. Damn it. Why did the very direct gleam in Mrs. Todd's eyes always disconcert her? Probably because she knew just what Ava Louise Todd was up to, and everyone within hearing distance knew it, too.

Annabelle saw looks and smiles being exchanged between Martha and Dorothy, and several other women, and felt a blush warming her cheeks. "Ivy was planning to baby-sit, but she called this morning and told me she has a cold, so Wes stepped in—" she explained, but Ava interrupted her with a broad smile.

"Of course he did. Wes is a man you can count on in a pinch. And you know those children are in good hands with him. My grandson might look tough as all get-out—some might even consider him intimidating—but he's the kindest, finest man you'll ever meet. Next to Sophie's Rafe, that is," she added sunnily as she noticed the other women listening to the conversation. "And your Jake, of course, Carly. And your dear Travis, Mia," she added, twinkling at the stunning blonde who was Sophie's best friend and married to Travis Tanner. "And then there's your John, Tess. And of course, Charlotte's dear Tim—"

"Gran." Sophie snagged her good arm. "You're right, the men in this town are all paragons. For the most part," she added with a little shake of her head. "I just found your place card. Let me show you where you're sitting—"

"Oh, not just yet, dear. I forgot to mention your mother's dear husband, Doug Hartigan. Such a lovely man, and a big improvement, as we all know, over Hoot—well, I don't mean to speak ill of the dead, but—"

"Mom," Diana interrupted, "let's get you settled. I think the meal is about to start. Would you like some iced tea?"

"I'd love some," Tess jumped in. "Iced tea sounds great. Let me pour you a glass, Mrs. Todd."

Annabelle hunted for her own place card as Charlotte hugged first her mother and then her aunt. Then she embraced Tim's mother, who was slightly overdressed in a lacy sheath and large pearl earrings.

"You all look so beautiful, and everything looks wonderful. Thank you for doing this! You all know I'm superstitious, but today I feel very, *very* lucky, and it's because I have all of you!"

It was a lively lunch, enjoyed by women who'd mostly all known and enjoyed one another's company for years. And after those first embarrassing moments of being startled by Ava's eager endorsement of her grandson's good qualities, Annabelle relaxed and enjoyed herself.

Privately, she thought it was very kind of Wes to volunteer to watch the kids. But it wasn't surprising, now that she'd come to know him. Right before she'd left her house, he'd drawn her into the kitchen for a long, deep kiss that almost made her want to stay right there in his arms. But when she'd finally forced herself to head to the door, he'd helped her load the party food and Charlotte's gift into the car, and the last glimpse she'd had of him, he'd been settling into an armchair in the living room, flipping the tab on a can of Coke, while the kids were already clustered on the sofa, watching an episode of *Lassie* on DVD.

They were all into it, not only Megan. But it had stunned Annabelle that her niece, who was so afraid of dogs, absolutely loved this show about Lassie! She took it all in, fascinated, even shushing Michelle and Ethan as they gasped when something dangerous happened to Timmy, or when they clapped and laughed after Lassie saved the day.

Megan did none of that. She just stared, unmoving, at the flat-screen, and at Lassie, her rapt gaze following the dog everywhere.

"Who made this amazing strawberry pie?" A sweet voice broke into her thoughts. Ava Louise Todd's voice.

She realized that everyone was halfway finished with their coffee and dessert and she'd taken only one bite of Charlotte's mom's famous cream cheese–frosted carrot cake.

"That would be Annabelle." Charlotte grinned. "The only thing better than her strawberry pie is her homemade chocolates." She snagged one of the wedding bell chocolates from the candy dish, popped it into her mouth, then pushed back her chair. "I'm dying to open my gifts. Can I start now? If there's any sexy stuff, I'm just saying, I want to open that first!"

Everyone laughed. Still smiling, Annabelle stood to help clear the tables as the guests began pouring into the house, settling on the sofa and some armchairs and folding chairs to watch Charlotte open her gifts. As she moved toward the sliding glass doors, her arms laden with plates, she saw Diana Hartigan and Sophie had also been stacking dishes to bring indoors. But while Sophie was chatting and laughing with Mia as they gathered up plates and silverware and serving pieces, Diana stood stock-still. Her unreadable but unsmiling gaze was fixed intently on Annabelle.

She looked . . . tense. It was the only way to describe it. *How long has she been staring at me?* Annabelle wondered with a jolt. The very instant Annabelle met her gaze, Diana seemed to freeze. Then, without so much as a nod or a word spoken, she quickly looked away, started toward the house, and slipped inside with her armload of plates and silverware.

She hates me. She definitely hates me. And she hates the idea of my being involved with her son in any way at all.

A weight seemed to anchor deep in her chest as she carried the big fruit bowl toward the house. She tried to ease the pain tightening her throat, telling herself she couldn't really blame Diana. The hurt of her husband's affair with Aunt Lorelei, and the hugely public revelation of it, had spread through Lonesome Way like a dozen wildfires blazing all at once.

That time in Diana's life couldn't have been anything less than agonizing. Aside from the devastating pain of her husband cheating on her, it had been a highly public scandal that had circled through the town, rocking everyone. Not only Diana's closest friends and family knew what Hoot had done, and how much he'd hurt her, but everyone in Lonesome Way knew as well, and even those in outlying areas as far away as Big Timber, Bozeman, and Livingston had probably heard about Hoot McPhee and the wife of Lonesome Way's mayor.

It was front-page news for weeks.

Annabelle understood all that. She was ashamed that her aunt had done something so despicable and caused such pain not only to another woman, but to another family. And she supposed she really couldn't blame Wes's mother for reliving it all every time she saw Annabelle. Even though Diana was now happily remarried, and Hoot was dead, Diana had no doubt been irreparably scarred by her husband's affair.

Even hearing her son's name linked with Lorelei's niece had to shatter the woman with a devastating reminder of that time when her marriage had been torn apart in the most humiliating way possible.

She must despise the thought of Wes being anywhere near me, Annabelle realized.

No small wonder that when Ava had pressed about a possible romance between her and Wes—none too subtly—Diana looked like she wanted to walk out of the room.

Her thoughts were interrupted by oohs and ahhs and laughter. Charlotte was holding up a delicate ivory silk negligee. The older women smiled appreciatively, while the younger ones laughed and applauded. Tess was unwrapping swirls of ribbon and gaily colored paper from the next gift, which turned out to be a set of three cast-iron frying pans, large, medium, and small, along with a cookbook.

Annabelle hurried forward to help repack the opened gifts. There were beautiful candlesticks, lovely crystal bowls, several sets of place mats and matching cloth napkins, a gorgeous silk tasseled table runner, and, from Carly Tanner, a lovely blue, violet, and yellow good-luck-charm quilt.

Annabelle tried hard to focus on Charlotte's delight at each gift, and to forget about the things she couldn't change—including the sensibilities of a woman who'd been hurt beyond repair. Diana McPhee would be relieved soon enough when Wes left for Wyoming and began his new career.

Far away from me. And I'll get back to my own life. . . .

She knew she needed to simply ignore that raw splinter twisting through her heart whenever she thought ahead to the fifth of July—the day Wes would actually leave town.

It would be hard, she knew, but she'd have to get past it.

Thank heavens she was plenty busy with the kids—and a month after Wes left, they'd be getting ready to go back to school. By September there'd be homework and after-school sports and activities. She'd start trying to get her chocolate business launched—in a small way, at first—and maybe she'd find a paying renter for the cabin.

She'd probably be so busy she wouldn't even have time to miss him.

Yeah, like that was going to happen.

Suddenly, she heard a gasp and a scream. Her attention was yanked back to the pretty living room where the gifts were being opened.

But Charlotte wasn't opening anything. She was frozen, holding up a crystal pitcher for all to see, and she was staring. Everyone was staring.

At Tess.

"What just . . . Oh my God," Tess gulped. She grabbed the arm of a chair and sank down. Her face turned pale, and Annabelle rushed to her, as did Charlotte, who stared at the liquid running down Tess's legs.

"Her water just broke," Ava Louise Todd announced crisply. She stood, taking charge as Patricia and Susie rushed forward to Tess's side. "Clear the way. I'm afraid you'll have to leave the rest of the presents for later, Charlotte. Someone needs to get this little mama to the hospital right now!"

"John! I need John," Tess gasped. She looked scared to death.

"We'll get him for you, honey." Annabelle knelt beside Charlotte's mother, and took Tess's hand.

"Are you having contractions?" Dorothy, who'd been the high school principal for decades before she retired, got right to the point of the matter.

"No . . . I'm . . . not sure. . . . I don't think so. . . ."

"Tess, do you think you can walk? Just out to my car?" Annabelle studied her friend's panicked face. "I'll drive you to the hospital right now. I think John should meet us there."

"Take my car," Charlotte's mom piped up quickly. "It's a Chevy and not an SUV. She won't have to step up, just slide inside."

"Towels, we need towels," Charlotte told Aunt Susie.

"Yes! What's wrong with me? One minute." Susie hurried off to the linen closet while Annabelle speed-dialed John.

He wanted to come get Tess himself.

"I'll be there in less than five minutes. Tell her to slow everything down until then." He hung up before Annabelle could say another word.

"I think your husband needs a lesson in female anatomy," Mia's great-aunt, Winny Pruitt, muttered with a snort. "Doesn't he know a woman can't slow things down once that baby makes up its mind to pop out?"

There was sweat on Tess's forehead, tiny beads of it clinging to her hair and skin as everyone pressed around her.

"Let's give her some space, some air." Diana McPhee stepped in, calmly shooing the guests crowding in around the chair where Tess slumped, her eyes wide with fear.

"Don't be scared," Charlotte murmured, kneeling beside her.

"Someone should . . . call the hospital . . . or alert Doc Carson," Tess said faintly.

"I'll do that, sweetie. No worries." Sophie whipped out her phone.

Annabelle felt helpless, and desperate to do something. Then, remembering when Trish had gone into labor with the twins, she suddenly raced into the kitchen, dampened a cotton dish towel with cool water, and returned to dab it around Tess's face. "John will be here any minute," she said soothingly and prayed she'd hear his car pull up right now.

"I know." Tess peered anxiously into her eyes. "It's just . . . so early. I'm only thirty-seven weeks . . . and f-four days. . . . I need to get to thirty-nine weeks! Annabelle, last time . . ." She gulped and couldn't say another word.

"This isn't last time, honey; it's now." Annabelle held the cool cloth to her friend's forehead. "You're close to being full-term. Very close. Your baby just can't wait to meet you face-to-face."

But as she met Tess's frantic eyes, her heart turned over at the panic deepening in their depths.

"Listen to me, Tess—babies come early all the time. My friend Ginger in Philly delivered more than three weeks early and had a super healthy baby boy. They only kept her in the hospital a day and a half. And Trish delivered Ethan twelve days early. No problem."

Still looking scared, Tess managed to nod. "You're right. Everything will be . . . fine. It's just . . . you know. . . ."

"We know, honey." Patricia took her hand and squeezed it gently. "Just try to relax. Take deep breaths."

Suddenly Charlotte grinned. "Hey. Want to watch me open some more gifts while we're waiting for John? That ought to distract you."

"S-sure." Tess tried her best to smile.

"I'm kidding." Charlotte drew in her breath. "But if John doesn't get here in the next two minutes, I might have to bean him with one of those frying pans."

John did arrive less than three minutes later—he must have been going fifty miles per hour, Annabelle guessed— and carried Tess out to his Jeep. He loaded her in, put pillows and towels supplied by Aunt Susie all around her, and, with all of the women either looking out the front window or standing on the lush lawn watching him, took off like a shot toward the hospital.

Annabelle pulled Charlotte aside. "You should open the rest of your gifts," she said when they were gone.

"I know, but all I want to do is go to that hospital and see how she's doing!"

"So do I, Char, but we can't just leave. Your aunt and your mom went to a lot of trouble to make this shower beautiful. You're the guest of honor. Look at all these people and all these gifts," she added softly.

"So what am I supposed to do? Forget that Tess is about to give birth early? She's terrified of losing *this* baby, too!"

"You're right. She is. She needs us, whatever happens."

"So . . ." Charlotte swallowed. "We go?"

"Not yet," Annabelle whispered. "You open your presents and thank everyone—quickly!"

Charlotte began to protest, then looked at the pretty living room packed with guests, and the still-high pile of gifts. She sighed. "You're right. Why are you always right?"

With quick steps, she returned to the gift table and Annabelle moved forward to help unwrap.

"Hurry," she said, so softly only Charlotte could hear, as the guests stopped chattering about Tess and began settling down around the gift table once more. "Open them, Charlotte. Fast. Then we *go*."

Chapter Twenty

Wes had faced fugitives, drug lords, and thugs with an ease born of experience, but he'd never run herd over three active kids for an entire afternoon.

Make that four kids, he thought, as he watched Ethan and his pal Jimmy tossing a ball in the open field that bordered Annabelle's house.

Treasure was out there, too—chasing the ball, retrieving it when they threw it for him, and loping around the field, happy as a puppy.

Megan and Michelle had kept Wes more on his toes than he'd imagined possible, starting from the time Annabelle took off for the bridal shower. They'd been practicing their tap routine for the past forty-five minutes and again wanted an audience. He got the boys to come in and watch for a short time, but soon they rebelled, and he was left to watch the girls tap-dance to "Yankee Doodle Dandy"—minus tap shoes and costume—at least six or seven times.

He was surprised by how entertaining it was. The girls were about as cute as they could be—surprisingly good dancers even at this age, and their smiles just about knocked him out—but it would have been far more entertaining if he were watching Annabelle dancing right along with them.

He decided he might just have to ask her for a private dance performance later. Preferably in a very skimpy costume, if any at all.

She still hadn't come home yet after calling to tell him that Tess was in labor, already at the hospital, and she was headed there, too—unless he wanted her to come home and take over right away. She was worried that he couldn't handle the kids all afternoon, but he'd assured her he'd handled worse and this was a piece of cake.

Watching over kids wasn't exactly his field of expertise, that was for sure, but it was fun, in an unexpected way. Not quite as challenging as a midnight raid, he thought with a grin, as Megan ran over to him and told him breathlessly that they'd practiced real hard and would he watch them one more time?

This time she promised, there'd be no mistakes.

"Sure thing, honey." His heart nearly melted at the way her little freckled face lit up. Michelle had shyly asked him whether he was bored with watching them rehearse. He'd assured her he loved it.

Most of the time, the only way he could tell those two apart was by their demeanor—and their clothes. Plus the fact that Megan was an inch taller, and far more boisterous in general than her sister. She said whatever was on her mind, and had more freckles on her face and scrapes on her knees than her twin.

Michelle seemed to live inside her head most of the time. A thinker, reader, and dreamer, that one. A very sweet one.

"Most boys don't like dancing that much," Michelle commented shyly after he agreed to watch the routine yet

again late in the afternoon. "You don't have to, if you don't
want to."

"I do want to. I like watching you guys do this dance.
Everyone in town is going to love it."

"We're dancing after the parade, though." Megan sighed.
"There's going to be a lot of other stuff going on. Do you
think other people will come to watch, not just all the moms
and stuff?"

"Sure, 'Yankee Doodle Dandy' is the best song of the
Fourth of July. Lots of people are going to want to watch."

"Ethan won't," Michelle piped up. She ran over to the
biggest section of open space in the living room and got into
position for the opening pose of the dance. "He only cares
about basketball, baseball, and the treasure. He wants to go
to the parade just to eat ice cream."

"Who cares?" Megan shot over to join her. Neither wore
tap shoes inside the house. They'd only been practicing the
steps to get the routine down pat. "Watch us just one more
time, okay?"

"You got it. Ready, set, go." He clicked on the music, which
he'd had to download at their request onto his cell phone, and
settled down on the cream and blue sofa, watching and
applauding enthusiastically when they took their bows, admiring Annabelle's clever, fun choreography and the girls' no-
holds-barred energy.

Still he missed Annabelle—and he had a few ideas for
the evening ahead, after the kids were sound asleep. He kept
glancing at the time, wondering when she'd be back.

He may not be used to supervising kids, but they were
easy. Really good kids. Great kids, actually. Still, his admi-
ration for her grew. She was here for them, day in and day
out. Giving it her all. Supporting them and nurturing them.

And she did it all with so much love.

He wished she were back here right now. He had a lot to
tell her about Megan, he realized, as from outside, Treasure

let out several loud, deep barks, and raced madly around the field chasing that ball.

He'd watched three episodes of *Lassie* with the kids this afternoon, and they were halfway through the DVD. He felt encouraged when Megan looked as fascinated as the others and watched the on-screen collie with delight.

But when he asked her if she wanted to walk outside and pet Treasure, she'd quickly shaken her head.

Even when Ethan promised her that Treasure was friendly, and her sister proclaimed she loved Treasure more than anything, Megan set her lips stubbornly and turned away.

"Treasure won't bite you," Wes told her quietly.

"How do you know?"

"Because dogs don't usually bite people unless someone is mean to them or if the dog is hurt or scared. And Treasure isn't any of those things. Most dogs are friendly and love kids. Treasure sure does."

"Lassie loves kids, too."

"You should pet Treasure." Michelle trotted up. She smiled at her sister. "Watch *me*. I'm not scared." Darting outside, she threw her arms around the dog, who immediately sat down and let her bury her face in his neck.

"How about stepping out on the porch with me and we'll sit down awhile, watch Treasure play?" Wes asked, mindful of the reading he'd done, which suggested that gradually getting closer to the animal in small stages was helpful.

"No. He might run over and bite me." Megan's little face was solemn.

"He'd never do that. I promise. And if he starts to run over, I'll tell him to sit and he will. Just give him a chance, honey. Dogs are wonderful and Treasure loves kids. Especially cute little girls."

She shook her head, fear lurking in her eyes. "No. Can I have a cookie now?"

Those anxious eyes were killing him. He let it go. "Sure."

All of the research he'd done had clearly spelled out that overcoming a fear of dogs took time and came in gradual stages. Getting used to being around the dog was key.

So maybe having Treasure out there playing with the boys was part of that, but man, getting the usually fearless Megan within twenty feet of that dog was going to be a challenge. He began to doubt there was any way to rush things along. But he'd really hoped that Treasure would be an integral part of the family by the time he said his good-byes and took off for Wyoming.

It was still a few weeks away yet, he reminded himself as something inside him flinched at the idea of leaving in only a short while. Leaving without Treasure having a home was bothering him. It wasn't anything more than that, he told himself.

He wanted Annabelle and the kids to have a dog to help keep them safe, and he wanted to know that they were all right when he left.

⌒

By seven o'clock Annabelle was home, kicking off her strappy heels, reporting that Tess had gone into early labor, but the child was doing fine and the doctors thought the baby would be here by morning.

The kids all swarmed excitedly around her. Wes met her eyes for a moment as she laughed with relief and then hugged her nieces and nephew, assuring them that in a week or two they could visit the new baby. His chest filled up with some emotion completely unfamiliar to him when she turned to him and smiled. He felt something tight and almost painful, but . . . it made him catch his breath with a kind of joy.

She was just so awesome. For a moment he could only stare at her, and then slowly, coming to his senses, he grinned back.

Ten minutes later he was grilling hot dogs and hamburgers on the grill behind the house, as Annabelle tossed together a salad, chopped carrots and tomatoes, and took out some leftover potato salad. Ethan and the girls were setting the kitchen table, chattering about someday when they'd have ponies or even horses. It wasn't the first time he'd heard them dreaming about that, and even in the short time before he left, it probably wouldn't be the last.

Treasure had finally settled down on the grass after slurping up a huge bowl of water.

But when Wes came around the house with the platter of hot dogs, burgers, and toasted buns, the dog leaped to his feet.

"I'll bring you back a burger in a minute, boy. We'll have to get you home and inside before dark." He started up the steps, then noticed something, a tiny movement at the front window.

Wes's reflexes were quick and he saw the girl at the window just before she ducked away. She was wearing pink shorts and a pink-and-yellow-striped tee. Since Michelle had been wearing blue shorts and a white top a few minutes ago when she ran outside to see how long until the burgers were done, he knew for sure.

The girl at the window was definitely Megan.

A smile touched his lips. He wondered how long she'd been standing there, watching Treasure all on her own.

He felt a beat of hope, the kind he felt when he was very close to breaking a particularly tough case. As happened so often, there was a pattern to how solving cases—and problems—progressed.

The answer was the same for both.

Small steps.

Chapter Twenty-one

❧

"Who's that coming down the drive? I don't recognize that truck."

Diana Hartigan peered out the kitchen window as the sun slowly melted into a luscious pink and gold sky. She'd been too full from all the food at the shower to eat more than a tuna sandwich for supper, but she'd served her mother and Doug a cucumber and tomato salad and the spaghetti and meatballs left over from the previous night.

"Let me take a look." Doug hurried to the front door and opened it, just as the truck in question parked at the head of the drive.

An older man sprang out with the vigor of someone Doug's age—or maybe even younger—and strode up the walk, sweeping off his cowboy hat as he approached the house.

"Evening, sir. I'm looking for Ava Louise."

Doug stepped onto the porch. "And you would be?"

"Ben Adkins. I'm an old friend."

Good Lord. Gazing out the edge of the kitchen window, Ava froze.

His voice was deeper, raspier, but it was the same one she remembered from the days of her youth. Despite his age he'd fairly sauntered up the walkway toward the porch with vigor and a zest for life that rang a bell in her head. His hair was all gray—a deep, steel gray—but it was still thick and he looked broad and energetic and as handsome as ever, in jeans and a flannel shirt and a wide smile on his ruddy face.

What in the world is he doing here? Ava quickly stepped back from the window, her thoughts flying about in confusion. Which was most unusual for her.

She'd been to town a few times since Dorothy and Martha told her Ben was back, but she hadn't seen him even once. Half the town was talking about him, though, speculating about why he'd returned, where he was staying, when he'd show up again. She'd heard he was looking at property-- there were rumors he was going to open a new headquarters for his company.

Why here? Why now?

"Mom, are you all right?" Diana's voice broke into her thoughts. Diana had come to stand beside her. "Do you know that man?"

"We . . . went to school together. We were friends. He's been away for many years."

Ava straightened her shoulders and pulled herself together. He'd startled her, but now she was coming back to herself, and was curious to see why in the world he'd shown up at her door. Years ago, her parents would have thought nothing of seeing Ben or any other young man at her door. She'd had more suitors than she could count on both hands.

But after she'd met Clyde, she'd never taken an interest in any other man.

Doug Hartigan reappeared in the kitchen doorway. "Ben Adkins?" He looked questioningly at Ava. "You know him?

He says you're old friends. I invited him in—hope that's okay."

"Yes, of course." Ava ignored her daughter's surprised expression and tried to look nonchalant. Straightening her back, she swept toward the living room. "Come meet him. I'll introduce you both."

Moments later, she was seated on the chintz sofa in the long, rectangular living room, opposite her onetime best friend, and the boy who'd kissed her at the bottom of a school-yard slide.

Ben stood, his Stetson in hand, as she, Diana, and Doug entered. After the introductions were finished, and after Ben asked with concern about her cast, they all made simple chitchat. For once Ava was impatient with the pleasantries. Ben handled it all with ease, but she noticed his keen brown gaze kept straying to her.

And why not? she told herself. She'd been the belle of this town long ago. Her father had left the Good Luck Ranch to her in his will—it was one of the largest properties in the state. And her beauty, wealth, and horsemanship had been widely known throughout the region.

She liked to think she still possessed a modicum of charm, even for a man as worldly as Ben must be now, if the rumors she'd heard of him held a kernel of truth.

It wasn't long before Diana offered to put up coffee, and excused herself. Doug followed her into the kitchen.

Hmm. Alone with Ben Adkins. Ava's heart wasn't fluttering like a girl's, but it did speed up a beat or two. *Don't be foolish,* she told herself. *He's only a man.*

A good-looking, vigorous man, whose eyes still held a vibrant spark—as she liked to think her own did. A man who wore his simple country clothes easily and well.

Time to get to the crux of the matter.

"So, what brings you back to Lonesome Way after all these years?"

"Ava," he said with a slow smile, "I'm not exactly sure how to answer that."

"Meaning?"

A hearty laugh broke from him, filling the room with warmth. "You always were the most frank and honest girl in town. No game playing, not from you."

She couldn't help but smile. "I like honesty. Respect it. Don't take much to folks who go around in circles, when all they have to do is tell the truth."

Something flickered in his face. "Yes, the truth." Leaning back against the chintz love seat, he almost dwarfed it with his burly size and frame. "I'm not sure where to begin. But let me start with your first question and I'll get to the rest eventually."

"Working up to something?" she asked, a hint of tartness in her tone.

"Maybe I am." He studied her from beneath shaggy eyebrows. "You're still the same, Ava. Still the same girl I remember. Sweet and tart all rolled into one. So let me tell you—and apart from my Realtor, you're the first to know—I'm here hunting for a vacation property for my family. I've got three sons, a daughter, seven grandchildren, and so far, three great-grandchildren. None of 'em have ever been to Montana, much less to Lonesome Way. They grew up on the East Coast. They've heard my stories about home and always wanted to come here and see where I grew up. Well, there's no hotel or resort property in Lonesome Way, so I'm thinking about building a large vacation home where we can all hang out together when the grandkids have vacation from school, or if any of my children or grandchildren and their spouses want a getaway."

Her gaze shifted to his left hand. He wore no ring, but that didn't mean anything.

"And for you and your wife," she said. "How is Margie?"

He didn't flush, look embarrassed, or react in any way

that reflected shame. He shook his head, shifted his cowboy hat from his hands, and set it on the love seat beside him.

"Margie and I divorced after six months of marriage. I remarried sometime later—my second wife's name was Sandra Laughlin. She was a business associate, sharp as a needle, kept me on my toes. Sort of the way you did. She reminded me of you in a way, and we caught each other's eyes. But sad to say, Sandra died seven years ago. Cancer."

"I'm sorry," Ava said at once. "I didn't mean to bring up a difficult time in your life."

"Don't get me wrong. Sandra and I had a good life together, and raised some fantastic kids, but I've grown used to being alone in many ways. Of course, I would have loved her to see this town, but . . . Sandra never wanted to come to Montana. She was a San Francisco girl through and through. Didn't want to venture into the boonies, as she called it."

"Some folks feel that way. Of course, they've never been lucky enough to see what we have here," Ava said softly.

"That's it exactly." Smiling at her, Ben's still-sharp brown eyes crinkled with warmth. He leaned forward on the love seat and held her gaze with his. "I'll tell you, Ava. It's sure good to see you again. You haven't changed."

"Are you blind, Ben?"

He grinned. "You might look a little bit different—we both do; that's for damn certain. But you're the same as I remember. Beautiful, dignified, spirited, And to the point. You always had a special spark about you. A kind of wisdom that went beyond your years. I was crazy in love with you for the longest time."

"Nonsense. You were not."

He stared at her in surprise. "Since grade school." The words sounded sincere, but Ava wasn't buying it.

"Oh, that." She shrugged, her gaze fixed steadily on him. "That day at the slide? We were children."

"Not exactly children. What we felt was not childlike. I never forgot that particular kiss."

Despite her armor, warmth flooded her and she hoped her cheeks hadn't turned pink. She hadn't forgotten that kiss, either.

"We had others," she reminded him, sitting a little straighter in her seat.

"I'm hoping there might be more in the future."

He said the words so calmly, she almost thought she misheard him. Ava smiled sweetly. "You're one of those infernal optimists, I see."

"I didn't get where I am by being a pessimist. I go after the things I want."

Another woman might have blushed, but Ava wouldn't allow herself to do that. "Yes, I've heard you've been quite successful in business. Everyone in town is talking."

"I don't gauge success by business accomplishments alone. I count my family, friends I care about, my values. What about you?"

Ava was surprised by his answer and didn't speak for a minute. Finally she nodded. "The same."

For a moment they just gazed at each other. "Perhaps you haven't changed—in the ways that count," she murmured. "But still . . ."

"Still what?"

Ava could stand it no longer. Despite all her efforts, a blaze of emotion shot through her. She remembered the night he swore he loved her, and how only days later he was gone. She managed to keep her tone cool and even.

"You left town in a big hurry way back then."

Something flashed in those keen brown eyes. Possibly regret, she thought, but it was impossible to be sure.

"One of my biggest mistakes. I acted impetuously when I was eighteen. Out of panic and . . . anger." He cleared his throat. "I'm sure you heard all the rumors about me and Margie. I know I hurt you back then, Ava. For that, believe me, I'm truly sorry."

"If you did hurt me, and I'm not saying it's so, I recovered just fine. You can see that for yourself." She lifted her chin. In her eyes there shone a world of wisdom and life knowledge as well as pride. "But an explanation between old friends after all these years would still be nice."

She knew in that moment he was seeing the same things in his mind as she saw in hers. That sweet kiss at the bottom of the slide in seventh grade.

And that magical starlit night in the barn when they were in high school.

The way they'd touched each other in the hayloft. The way they'd caressed and held each other in the dark. It was only one night in a hayloft, but the words he'd said to her—the way he'd touched her, spoken to her—had stayed in her mind.

Even to this day . . .

Of course, they'd been so young. And witless with passion . . .

Come have an adventure with me, Ava. Let's leave everything behind and explore what's out there in the big wide world. I want you to come with me. I won't leave without you.

But the next day, after the night they'd held each other in the barn, she told him her answer in no uncertain terms—*no.* She wouldn't leave Lonesome Way.

Looking back now, she couldn't deny that she'd been willful. And spoiled. And more headstrong than any of her father's spirited horses, the ones she rode with such confidence.

Now, with the wisdom of years, she could admit that streak of pride and stubbornness in her young self, and her need for wanting everything her own way.

Flickers of regret twisted through her.

"Ava, something wrong?"

"No. Not in the least." But her stomach dropped as she realized how proud and foolish she'd been when she was young. How stubborn.

"Well, honey, I'd like to tell you the truth." Ben took a deep breath. "It's time we cleared the air."

"We never did talk things out the way we should have back then," she acknowledged with a nod.

He leaned forward. "We were both young fools. Our emotions ran us, not our brains. But let me start by reminding you that you never wanted to go steady with me back then. I asked you and you said no. Flat-out no. I talked about a future with you, a future for us—away from Lonesome Way—and you said no."

When she merely looked coolly at him, refusing to either counter or agree with his recollection, Ben shook his head. "Damn, but you were beautiful. And you loved being pursued by every boy in town. It was hard for me to watch that, Ava."

Regret flickered in his eyes. "I was a hothead. I never planned on what happened with me and Margie. I'm aware that's no excuse but . . ." He drew a breath.

"You remember the night Fred Macintyre had that party? His parents had gone to Butte for a family reunion—it was during the time when Frank Kerney and Bob Lewiston were both courting you and you were mad at me for wanting to go to college far away. I was jealous as all get-out of Frank and Bob. You and I had words a week before the party—a very angry fight—you said you'd see as many boys as you wanted to—and I stopped coming around."

Ava nodded. "I didn't go to the party that night. I went to the movies with Frank Kerney."

"I remember." Ben grimaced. "Margie was there, though, and we got to talking—and drinking. Hell," he added, leaning back and running a hand through his hair as the memories flooded back. "Margie sat on my lap all evening at Fred's house. The liquor was flowing, and she and I drank far too much. Matter of fact, I drank myself stupid. Real stupid."

Ava found that her hands were clenched in her lap. Deliberately, she unclenched them. For some reason, her mind was flitting through time. Yes, she remembered it all. She'd been wild about Frank and Bob—they were both bringing her flowers and gifts, flattering her, competing for her. Still, in the back of her mind, well, she'd always thought she'd end up marrying Ben.

There had been a period of a few months where she'd done her best to convince him to attend college in Montana, instead of someplace far away. They'd argued about it. She'd figured if he saw her with other boys, he'd be more likely to come around, and stay right here in Lonesome Way.

She knew she'd been spoiled by her father. He'd adored her, and she became used to getting her way.

"So you're telling me that you and Margie—it was . . . only that one night?"

"That's right," he said heavily. "One night that changed the course of my life. Her life, too, and maybe yours. I'm not saying I didn't know what I was doing—and I'm not using the liquor as an excuse. I accept full responsibility." He shook his head, his brow furrowed, and Ava felt the beginning of sympathy flowing through her as she saw the honesty in those brown eyes she'd once known so well.

"When Margie asked me to meet her at Cougar Rock a month later, I did. That's when she told me she was pregnant."

Ava had heard as much. Rumors had flown around the town like snippets of ribbon whipped by the wind. She didn't say anything, only nodded.

"Damn, she was more frightened that day than any girl I'd ever seen. She was desperate that no one in town ever know. Her parents found out, though, and raised hell. They insisted she leave. Told her she had to go to her mother's family in Spokane. They didn't want anyone here to know, either."

His face grew more somber as the memories rushed back. "I was in shock, but I told her I'd marry her, go with her. Her father probably would have shot me if I hadn't. But that's not why I did it. I knew I was responsible. And she was a mess." He drew a breath, his face tight with regret as he met Ava's gaze.

"I tried to make it right. My life turned upside down, Ava, and so did Margie's. Her mother's family took us to a justice of the peace the day we got to Spokane, and he married us. Then we lived with her family while I looked for work."

Ava couldn't think of a thing to say. She simply sat there, taking in his words.

"There's one more thing you should know. It wasn't a happy time. I mean, Margie and I both tried to make it work, but she miscarried only a month after we were married—"

"Oh, Ben. I'm so terribly sorry." And she was. She closed her eyes for a moment as their sadness touched her. When she opened them again and looked at him, it was with compassion.

"You tried to do the right thing. I respect that. And then . . . something so awful happened." She shook her head. "I know it was a long time ago, but I am sorry—for you both."

"Thank you." He drew a long breath. "Without the child, there was no glue to hold us together. We tried to make things work for a few months and then we just drifted apart. Neither of us were happy. She met someone else first . . . and . . . well, the divorce was mutual. I left Spokane after everything was finalized and switched to a college in New York City as I'd always planned." He cleared his throat. "Only thing is, I'd *planned* on going there with you."

"But that wasn't meant to be," she said softly, trying to fight the dryness burning in her throat.

Ben had made a mistake, but he'd been so young. They'd both been. He hadn't actually cheated on her.

And she hadn't exactly behaved impeccably herself.

"I was so terribly proud back then," she admitted quietly. "And so sure of myself." She'd tried her best to make Ben jealous and crazy so he'd do just as she wished—which was to stay in Lonesome Way.

Because it suited her.

Her father had always indulged her and she'd wanted Ben to do the same.

Had it ever been true love between them?

To this day, she didn't know. They'd been so young, so full of dreams.

But different dreams.

She was older and a little wiser by the time she met Clyde. Still, looking at Ben Adkins now, tall and handsome still, his piercing gaze intent on her, feelings and memories swirled through her in a most confusing mix.

"I was very stubborn and spoiled in those days." She'd never admitted that aloud before, not to anyone. "But you could have said good-bye to me, Ben."

"You're entirely right. I regret that I didn't, Ava. I hope you can forgive me."

Ava recognized the honesty of the boy she remembered in the serious man sitting opposite her.

It all seemed so long ago, and yet, she remembered it so clearly.

"We both made mistakes," she began. "We were foolish . . . young. I know that I was spoiled—"

"Oh, that you were." He chuckled.

Her eyebrows shot up, and she straightened her spine.

"You were also damned irresistible, Ava." He spoke the words softly, ruefully.

For a moment she thought she glimpsed a spark in his eyes. A spark of something that had been there when he'd looked at her long ago. But before she could respond to the compliment, or decide whether to accept it with a smile or a frown, her son-in-law suddenly stepped into the living room.

"Ava, Mr. Adkins, coffee's ready. Diana said to tell you there's apple pie and ice cream."

"I know there's apple pie." As Ava rose from her chair, Ben followed suit. "Seeing as I'm the one who baked it yesterday."

But Ben wasn't taking a step toward the kitchen. "Ava?" He stood, hat in hand, staring at her questioningly.

She realized he wanted to know whether he should stay for pie and coffee, or whether now that he'd said what needed saying between them, she wanted him to leave.

"We'll continue our conversation another time." She smiled at him. "But you should know, Ben, that my apple pie is considered one of the best in the county. I taught Sophie, my granddaughter, how to make it and now she sells it at her bakery in town. A most successful bakery! If you don't come try it and judge for yourself, you'll be making a great mistake." With a gracious smile, she swept ahead of both men into the kitchen.

Doug Hartigan glanced at the older man and merely shook his head. He was used to his very dignified and usually sweet mother-in-law—but she didn't normally put on such airs. Not that he could recall.

"I'll be damned. Thank God that woman hasn't changed." Ben's grin was almost as big as his hat. At that moment he didn't look in the least like a retired CEO of a major corporation. He winked at Doug and, hat in hand, followed Ava Louise like an eager puppy dog into the Good Luck Ranch kitchen.

Chapter Twenty-two

A fever of activity pulsed through Lonesome Way as the Fourth of July drew near. Dawn pearled the sky on a crystal-clear morning with only four days left until the parade. Until the fireworks, the speeches and celebrations, the quilt auction, the dance performances, and the bake sale—all to benefit the community center and raise money for the indoor basketball court.

In her bedroom on Sunflower Lane, Annabelle pressed a kiss to Wes's chest. They lay entangled together on her bed, warm and naked, gazing into each other's eyes. She was quickly coming to the conclusion that morning sex was possibly even more delicious than afternoon or evening sex.

But then, every moment of sex with Wes was wonderful.

The day was perfect, the air still and peaceful. Faint peach light gradually stole the last of the dark. Slowly Annabelle traced her hands and lips across the hard muscles of Wes's chest and down those powerful arms. With a growl, and a sleepy grin, he pulled her atop him.

"Morning, sleeping beauty."

"It really is a good morning." She closed her eyes as his warm hands stroked down her body, as he drew her near and pressed his lips to her throat. Pleasure seeped through her smooth as wine.

"Much better than cereal to start the day," she murmured.

"Understatement of the century."

They kissed, long and deep and slow. Gazing into his eyes, she tangled her hands in his hair and pressed against his rock-hard body. "The kids . . . won't be up for another hour yet," she murmured. "We could go back to sleep . . . or . . ." She brushed a kiss against his shoulder. The sun had barely peeked through the last of the fading stars.

"Let's make the most of it." Wes's eyes gleamed. He rolled over and switched places with her, nibbling and teasing her throat, her shoulders, and her breasts, then sliding his palms down her body. As she practically purred like a cat, his hands parted her thighs.

"Unless you *want* to go back to bed . . ." he suggested teasingly, lowering his mouth to her belly, then lower still, to the sweet spot he knew would make her moan.

"Not what I want . . . at all," she gasped, as his tongue slipped inside her and the world spun. "Sleep is . . . way overrated."

Wes laughed quietly. He loved the way she trembled and tensed and caught her breath as he ran his hands over her. He took his time licking and kissing and tasting her most sensitive places. In the past month, he'd discovered them all. He couldn't get enough of making love to Annabelle. She was not only beautiful; she was so vibrant with her emotions and her pleasures—and the way she touched him was an enticing mixture of bold and tender. She'd discovered just how to make him fight for his own self-control.

He'd been with quite a few women in his day but none of them was anything at all like Annabelle. Not just passionate, but brimming with life, with beauty and determination and a sweet tenderness that brought out something in him he hadn't known existed.

Damn it, he was getting gooey. Sentimental, or something . . .

Get a grip, he told himself. The only thing dampening his pleasure as they made love in her very feminine bed, with the frail pink light of the new day glistening through the room, was the knowledge that he'd be leaving her soon. Leaving those kids, who'd inched their way into his heart. They became embedded a little more each day, which was why he was glad he was leaving soon.

Five days.

In five days, he was going to Wyoming. Leaving this house, and the children Annabelle tended with such love. Leaving Annabelle, with her laughter, her bravery and spirit.

It struck him with a powerful thwack to his gut that he couldn't have ever suspected, that it wouldn't be as easy as he'd first thought. He'd never imagined getting this close to anyone, even her. It had just happened. He'd never felt a pull like this with any woman before . . . ever.

Perhaps because they both knew his days in Lonesome Way were drawing to an end, their morning lovemaking was sweeter than ever. He covered her lips with a last lingering kiss before he pulled on his clothes. Then he eased out the door, moved silently down the hall past the sleeping children's bedrooms, avoided the fourth step from the top, which squeaked, and the third step from the bottom, which creaked, and let himself out of the house with a stealth he'd learned sneaking up on the baddest of the bad guys.

Twenty minutes before the kids even thought about stirring, he was halfway down the path to the cabin. After letting Treasure outside, he put up coffee, poured food for the dog, freshened the mutt's water bowl, and finally lowered his tall frame onto the old porch steps with a mug of black coffee in his hand.

He could get accustomed to all this. The view and the peacefulness. And Annabelle, in his bed. Seeing her in his day and in his night.

Every night.

But he wasn't going to. This life wasn't for him. Though the grasslands were thick and green and the mountains west of Lonesome Way rose majestically in the distance, the road called to him.

It always had.

This was his father's town. The one Wes had left behind. The day he'd taken off on his own, he'd vowed that he'd never live here again.

But as he gazed at the house down Sunflower Lane, all he could think was that the woman who lived there called to him, too.

Not intentionally, but she was in his mind, in his bones, maybe even in his heart, the way no other woman had been before.

He took a gulp of coffee, feeling unsettled. He knew he'd better head out soon before the crazy spell of this town made him loco. When he'd lived here, he'd hated it. But this time around, something had changed.

And he knew what it was.

Annabelle. She and those kids had made him see Lonesome Way through a different lens. Or maybe he was changing, too.

He'd let himself get too close to them. Big mistake. He should probably take off today, not even wait until the fifth. Each day might make it a little harder to break away. Harder for him, and for them.

Gritting his teeth, he realized he needed to finish a few things in the cabin, put another coat of varnish on the floor, sweep out the crawl space in the corner of the bedroom.

Then the place would be in spick-and-span shape for Annabelle to rent out.

He needed to pay a nice long visit to Sophie before he left. And spend some more time with his mother and grandmother. He'd schedule a playdate with Sophie's son, Aiden, make some more memories with the little guy, and spend an afternoon with Ivy. By the time he got around to coming back for a visit, all those kids would have changed so much.

So would Megan and Michelle and Ethan, he realized. They'd remember him, though—he was pretty sure of that. Wyoming was only a hop, skip, and a jump, relatively speaking. Once he and Scott got the business up and running, he could always come back every six months or so, check on everyone. . . .

Six months. A lot could happen in six months.

Then he remembered he still had to convince Annabelle to keep Treasure. . . .

Annabelle . . .

How in hell was he going to leave her? The thought of it made him hurt deep in his gut.

Well, he'd done some hard things before. When it came to it, he'd just go. Quick and clean.

And he'd know better than to take even one look back.

Chapter Twenty-three

~✑~

As Ethan slammed the door of the Jeep and raced toward Jimmy's house that afternoon, Annabelle stepped out to greet Sylvie Collier, Jimmy's mom.

"Sylvie, you're a life saver. Are you sure Corey won't mind keeping an eye on both boys?"

After a fine clear morning, clouds had started to drift in. Though the sky was still bright blue, the weather forecast now reported thunderstorms brewing to the east, and they were likely to hammer their way right into town before dark.

"No problem." The other woman smiled. "I'm leaving in a half hour to get my hair trimmed and tinted at the Cuttin' Loose, but I'll only be gone an hour or two. Martha's completely booked up starting tomorrow, so it's probably now or not at all before the Fourth. Corey does complain a lot when he gets stuck babysitting, but if he wants to keep his car keys, he knows he has to help me out." She laughed.

A special dress rehearsal had been called at the

community center today for all the children involved in dance or gymnastics performances as part of the July Fourth celebration. Annabelle had planned to bring Ethan to the rehearsal with her but he'd insisted he wanted to go to Jimmy's house instead. Apparently a new treasure-hunting book had come into the library mentioning the Henry Barnum gang. There was half a page about them, Ethan told her. Jimmy had checked the book out of the library yesterday.

The boys wanted to pore over it together, and perhaps dig and explore in the little valley that ran beyond Jimmy's backyard. In their imaginations, the treasure could be theirs for the taking anywhere in Lonesome Way. All they had to do was dig.

Corey appeared from inside the house as she was getting ready to drive off. After the easygoing sixteen-year-old promised Annabelle and his mother that he'd keep an eye on Jimmy and Ethan for the next couple of hours, Annabelle drove Megan and Michelle straight over to the community center.

For the next two hours, the excited girls in her class rehearsed, finally taking a cookie break, chattering all the while about their pretty, white fluffy skirts and red tops with blue stars sewn on, and practicing their shuffles and their flap ball changes in their tap shoes, again and again.

Annabelle was calling them back onto the floor for yet another run-through when her cell phone rang.

A moment later, listening to Sylvie on the phone, she froze. Her face turned pale as she heard the frantic tone in the woman's voice, the desperate apologies before Annabelle gulped out, "I'm coming right now."

"Girls!" She spun toward her class, trying to keep her voice steady. "I have to leave. Right now. Go ahead and practice by yourselves one more time and wait right here," she ordered.

Then she raced down the hall to the office where

Charlotte was wrestling with details of the upcoming fall schedule.

"What is it? What's wrong?" Charlotte jumped to her feet in dismay when she saw Annabelle's face. "Is it Tess . . . the baby . . . What?"

"Ethan. It's Ethan and J-Jimmy. Jimmy's brother was watching them today. But Corey's girlfriend stopped over and they decided to drive to Cougar Rock. They took the boys with them! Ethan and Jimmy were supposed to stay close by, but Corey and his girlfriend were doing what every young couple does at Cougar Rock—and they weren't really watching the boys, at least for a few minutes. And Ethan and Jimmy must have wandered off!"

"What?" Charlotte went still, staring at her.

"Corey says he and his girlfriend called and yelled for them. They searched all over and they can't find them, Charlotte. The boys didn't answer back, not even once. Sylvie's on her way to Cougar Rock now. I . . . I need you to watch my class. Please! I have to go find them!"

"Yes! Omigod! Go!" Charlotte hurried to her, her face tight with worry. "I'll take care of everything. Annabelle, maybe you should call Sheriff Hodge—"

"Sylvie's calling him next to see if he and Deputy Mueller can come out and help. After I call Wes, I'm going right over there myself."

"You'll find them. I'm sure they're fine. They were probably looking for that silly treasure and maybe they got a little turned around—"

Annabelle's voice trembled. "They could have fallen, gotten hurt. There's wolves and coyotes and . . . b-bears up there, Charlotte!"

As fear threatened to overwhelm her, she swallowed it back. "Take care of Megan and Michelle, okay?" she choked out. "I don't want them worrying."

"I've got it covered." Charlotte hugged her. "Keep me posted on what's going on!"

No longer trusting her voice, Annabelle nodded. Her heart clutched as she saw that the sky was already darkening with thunderclouds. She dashed out to the parking lot, raced for her car. Before she drove off, she punched in Wes's cell number.

He picked up almost immediately.

"Hi, baby. You know, I had an idea for that hardwood flooring you picked out. It's still back-ordered but I think I can get—"

"Wes, I need you," she blurted, trying to keep her voice steady, but failing. She felt like the world was falling in on her, and she fought for control. "I need you right now!"

"What's wrong?" His tone sharpened.

She felt tears squeezing from her eyes, but she couldn't hold them back any longer. "It's Ethan and Jimmy. They're missing. Wes, I'm so scared! They may be lost on Storm Mountain!"

Chapter Twenty-four

〜

Ominous clouds shadowed the town and the mountains as word spread that Ethan and Jimmy were missing in the wilderness. Friends and neighbors from miles around began streaming toward Storm Mountain to join the search.

Sheriff Hodge was in charge. Several volunteers, including Sylvie, her husband, Dave, Charlotte's fiancé, Tim, as well as Jake and Rafe Tanner, were combing the rocky paths to the north. Wes and Annabelle, along with Travis Tanner, searched to the south. And Deputy Mueller, along with Brady Farraday and half a dozen other volunteers, scoured the trails to the east, always in pairs.

There was no cell phone connection that far up into the mountains, but the sheriff and deputy gave walkie-talkies to Wes and a few others, and they put together a buddy system for all the searchers. They were prepared with flashlights, whistles, and water, and a few had brought first-aid kits.

People didn't get lost all that often in the mountains flanking Lonesome Way, but when they did it was serious business. The tragic search for Randy Kirk was uppermost in everyone's thoughts as they spread out, scrambling across the rough terrain, calling out for the boys who were two of their own.

As thunder began to boom and echo through the mountains, Wes swore at the sky. The damned weather would make it nearly impossible to search once the storm fully unleashed. Everyone combing Storm Mountain would have to take shelter once the rain and the lightning came. The trails would become far too slippery and dangerous, and the search would need to be postponed or dramatically slowed until the downpour passed.

Taking another frantic glance at the dark clouds looming overhead, Annabelle shouted again for the boys. "Ethan! Jimmy! Ethan, answer me!"

Fatigue and tension tightened her face as a scatter of rain splashed down.

"No, not yet. Please, it can't rain yet. We have to find them," she muttered to Wes. They were navigating their way around a massive boulder and onto a side trail that led steeply down toward the remote bluff where Coyote Pass was tucked away. If the boys had headed deliberately anywhere, that was where they'd go. Most of the rumors about that damned gold hinted that it was near Coyote Pass.

That was where Randy Kirk had headed.

She was furious at Ethan in that moment, furious that he'd snuck away from Corey and gone alone with Jimmy to find the gold. She'd told him and *told him* not to ever go off on his own!

Upset and angry and filled with dread, she slipped in her haste on some loose stones and would have fallen if Wes hadn't seized her arm. Steadying her, he tugged her close; then one big hand gently stroked her hair.

"We'll find them, Annabelle. I promise you. I won't stop looking. But I want you to go back home now."

"No. I won't. I can't." She looked shocked, and pulled away, shaking her head. "Not without Ethan, not without both of those boys."

"Look, no one's giving up," he said as spatters of rain began to fall. "Sure as hell not me. The volunteers will need to take cover once this storm breaks wide-open and the lightning hits. They'll have to wait it out, but I'll keep searching, I promise you. In the meantime, you look exhausted. Annabelle, I can't worry about you getting hurt, too. I need to concentrate on those kids."

"I'm not exhausted; I'm just scared. Wes, I'm so scared."

"Honey, I know." He wrapped her in his arms, but she leaned back, gazing at him, her face pale. Tears slipped down her cheeks.

"Trish . . . and Ron . . . They trusted me to keep their kids safe! And . . . I let Ethan go to Jimmy's when I knew Sylvie wouldn't be there to watch them. I never should have done that!"

"He's been there plenty of times before when Jimmy's brother was charged with keeping an eye on them. They never wandered off before. You couldn't have known they were going to do something like this."

"I *should* have known. They're so crazy about this treasure. It's all they talk about. And ever since they heard that Randy Kirk was focused on searching at Coyote Pass, too—oh God, I should have put a stop to it, Wes! I should have put my foot down. . . ."

Her voice cracked. Her eyes were wide with fear and worry and he had to fight the urge to take her in his arms and just hold her, try to comfort her, for as long as it took. But he knew she didn't want that now, and there wasn't time.

"Shhh, baby." He pressed a quick kiss to her forehead.

"It's not your fault. Do you hear me? And it's going to be all right. I promise you. We'll find them!"

A heavier rain began to fall, drumming against the rocks. Annabelle's eyes widened in dismay. Soon the path would be pooling with water, slippery as hell.

"Oh, no! We need to hurry. I'm sure they're headed to Coyote Pass."

"Yeah, but you're not. Annabelle, you're wearing sneakers, not hiking boots. You're not even wearing a decent jacket," he noticed suddenly, scowling at her Windbreaker. "Here, take mine." He shrugged out of it and wrapped it around her. "You don't belong out here in these conditions, and you're going to slow me down. Look, all the volunteers who are sheltering out here, waiting out the storm, will need coffee soon—and food and flashlights in order to keep searching. Go back and try to organize some support for all the searchers. You don't know these mountains the way most of us do—you haven't lived here all your life. Trust me, you'll be more help back there—and I won't be worrying about you."

She wavered. What he said was true—but she wanted so much to race across the rocks and narrow paths, to scream until her voice was hoarse. She started to tell Wes she couldn't go, not when Ethan was still out there, but then she saw his face, those deep green eyes lit with concern for her.

He wore hiking boots and had a pack strapped to his back. He moved quickly and easily through these mountains—he'd had experience tracking and climbing in all kinds of weather and was sure-footed on the trails. He also knew the ins and outs of getting to Cougar Rock—and Coyote Pass—much better than she did. She might have balance and grace from her years of dance training, but she'd never climbed a mountain before, never negotiated a trail this steep or high. She was slowing him down, she realized.

And as a crack of thunder roared across the mountains,

she faintly heard someone calling out for the searchers to take cover. It sounded like Sheriff Hodge's voice.

"All right, I'll go back," she said on a deep breath. "I'll help organize coffee and food and more flashlights and I'll bring everything over to Sylvie and Dave's. They're closest to the trailhead. Be careful, Wes. Find them, please."

"Don't worry. I will. It's a promise." He kissed her quickly, enfolded her in his arms for one more moment, then helped her negotiate back around the jagged rock as rain pummeled down. When they reached the more even path that led to the trailhead, he gave her a quick kiss.

"Take it slow. You'll be fine. Folks are going to need that coffee and some sandwiches."

"Yes. I'm on it."

She met his gaze and for a moment neither of them spoke. Her heart was pounding with fear for the two boys lost, possibly hurt on the mountain. She wondered whether Charlotte had told the twins why she'd left so suddenly and why she hadn't come back for them. Either way, the girls were probably upset.

She tried not to think about that right now, but it was even harder not to think about Randy Kirk, falling to his death in these same mountains while searching for the damned treasure.

Cupping her face, damp with rain, Wes touched his warm mouth to hers. "Annabelle, go get warm. I'll find them, both of them, and bring them home. That's a promise."

He was gone then, moving so swiftly he disappeared almost immediately from her sight as the path wound upward, twisting around boulders and fallen tree limbs and scrub.

"You come home safely, too," Annabelle whispered. But the wind blew her words away into the rush of steadily falling rain.

Chapter Twenty-five

Thunder boomed like rapid gunfire, echoing through the mountains as chill summer rain pummeled the rocks and scrub brush, the weeds and the twisting trails.

Water ran in angry rivulets every which way. The gray glimmer of slashing rain was eerily illuminated by occasional flashes of lightning.

Wes had been searching through the downpour for more than an hour, working his way methodically toward Coyote Pass. Finally, he was getting close. He was headed toward one of the narrowest and most dangerous passes in the range of mountains ringing Lonesome Way, the going now slowed, made even more difficult by the rain and buffeting wind.

At least the lightning had ceased. Although it was his surest lead, he prayed the boys hadn't come this way. It was so steep, so dangerous.

Maybe they'd turned back . . . or gotten lost, then found

shelter in a place easier to access, and safer to travel . . . or . . .

Suddenly he saw something on the ground about twenty feet ahead of him that made him halt. Hope stirred as he scrambled forward, the mountain seeming to shake beneath him during a deafening clap of thunder.

Three rocks were sitting there. Fairly big ones. They were set atop three sodden leaves, holding them in place.

Three of something. Three of anything. A distress signal for those who were lost. That was what he'd taught the kids at Jake's retreat, the day that Ethan and Jimmy had tagged along with him.

He shouted again at the top of his voice. "Ethan!"

No answer, but he moved on, encouraged, looking this way and that, skidding ahead on the slick trail as fast as he could, gripping rocks and branches, finding his footing by pure instinct, experience, and determination.

He hadn't seen any other searchers in a while. Most of them had probably taken shelter. He pushed on. Finally he reached a muddy, jagged path that led downward. Squinting through the rain, trying to make out what was below, Wes thought he could see three more rocks in a tiny pile, but he couldn't be sure.

He called out again, and started down that slick excuse for a path.

His heart leaped as he reached the ledge on the bottom and saw three more rocks placed on leaves. He stared at them as lightning streaked across the pewter sky.

Speeding up as much as he dared, he worked his way past one precarious ledge, then another, driving rain slamming into his face.

He kept going, calling out into the fierce wind, working his way still farther and calling out the boys' names as the sky unleashed its full fury all around him.

Twenty more feet along, and his voice now hoarse as he yelled, he thought he heard a sound from far below.

Was that a voice? It was faint, but still . . .

"Ethan," he roared full-force. "Ethan! Jimmy!"

Thunder cracked, drowning out any chance of hearing a reply. He swore and wiped the dripping rain from his face. Despite the lashing, sideways downpour, he skidded forward as fast as he could.

"Where are you?" he shouted again into the growing darkness, and this time, he heard a faint reply.

"Help! We're down . . . here!" The words came in a thin scream above the incessant rushing sound of the rain.

Head down, Wes charged forward, slipping and sliding, clutching at branches and brush, steadying himself, hanging on to his footing as he hurtled on toward the bottom.

"Don't move! I'm coming down for you. Hang on!" he yelled.

Moments later, he reached them. They were huddled on the ground beside a rock, perched only a few yards back from a ledge with a dizzying drop. Ethan was soaked and shivering, but Jimmy was lying on the sodden ground, his ankle twisted beneath him at a bad angle.

"Jimmy fell. He can't walk . . . or climb. . . . It might be broken!" Ethan threw himself at Wes and wrapped his arms around Wes's waist.

"Everything's going to be all right. I'll carry him back. Jimmy, don't try to move. Ethan, you hurt?"

"N-no." Wes wasn't sure whether Ethan was crying or his face was soaked by rain, but he heard the panicked tremor in the boy's voice.

Quickly he scanned both of them for injuries or signs of shock. They looked drenched and pale and miserable, but aside from Jimmy's ankle, and the pain clenched across his white face, they seemed okay. Shaken, but okay.

Alive, thank God.

"Hold on. I've got some water and granola bars—and a blanket—in my pack. Everyone's searching for you two. Let me give the sheriff our position."

He pulled out the walkie-talkie as Ethan hugged him tighter and Jimmy managed a slight, weak smile.

"Is Aunt Annabelle mad at me?" Ethan asked after Wes checked Jimmy's ankle, gave each boy a bottle of water, and wrapped a blanket around both of them.

"Maybe not mad, but for the next ten years, kiddo, don't plan on being out of her sight."

Chapter Twenty-six

Annabelle remembered about Treasure as she hurtled toward home.

This could be a very long night. Who knew when Wes or any one of them would be back to feed the dog or let him outside?

Shoving her foot down hard on the gas pedal, she sped right past her house to the cabin, then fought her way through the rain and wind to let the dog outside.

She left him in the yard for a moment or two to take care of his business, then called him in, dried him off with a fluffy towel, and put down some dog food and fresh water.

"Wes will be back later," she murmured, and raced back out, locking the door behind her.

Her mind couldn't stop spinning. The moment she was inside her own house, she put up a big pot of coffee, then dug frantically through the shelves for a thermos, and when she found it sank against the counter. Closing her eyes, she drew in a couple of deep breaths.

She had to stop picturing those boys out there on the mountain. Alone, cold, possibly hurt. Pain sliced her in two at the thought.

Please, please, let them be all right.

She knew she had to stay calm. *Focus.* The girls were safe with Charlotte, thank heavens, and she knew she could count on that. She'd call later on her way to Sylvie and Dave's house, and do her best to reassure them.

Focus. Coffee and food. Flashlights. Batteries. Coats? Sweaters?

Blankets!

After pulling out a pound of sliced turkey from the fridge, she grabbed a loaf of bread, fingers flying as she prepared sandwich after sandwich. She'd never worked so fast in her life. When the turkey was gone, she grabbed a jar of peanut butter and another of jelly. When she ran out of bread, she filled a Tupperware container with crackers and slices of cheddar cheese.

All the while, *hurry hurry hurry* pounded through her brain. She grabbed her cell phone when it rang, her throat dry, praying it was Wes, but it wasn't.

It was Diana Hartigan.

She went still at the sound of the other woman's voice.

"Annabelle, we just heard the news about Ethan and Jimmy. It's spreading through town—and everyone is pitching in. Right now we're driving to Sylvie and Dave Collier's place. Sophie and Ava and my husband are with me. We're bringing a chicken enchilada casserole I'd baked for supper and some tuna sandwiches and bottles of water for the volunteers. Martha Davies and Dorothy Winston are on their way to help, too. We're setting up shop to help feed and warm the volunteers until those little boys are safely home."

"Mrs. Hartigan, I can't thank you enough! I'm very grateful." Tears brimmed in her eyes and she had to swallow back a lump in her throat. "I'm bringing sandwiches and coffee, too. I'll be there soon myself."

"I know Wes is out there searching. If anyone can find those boys, my son can. Oh, and my mother would like me to tell you that she's praying for the boys and she is bringing an angel food cake she baked this morning. She thinks the angel food cake is good luck. She says angels are watching over them."

"I pray she's right. Thank you, and please thank Mrs. Todd for me."

"Of course. The roads are slick, so do be careful, now."

She stared at the cell after Wes's mother disconnected.

Her voice hadn't been fuzzy-wuzzy and filled with warmth, but it had been kind and very concerned. And her words had been, too.

Annabelle spared a precious moment to call and update Charlotte just before she began packing up the car.

Charlotte reported that she'd told the girls the truth and they were upset, and very worried about Ethan, but she'd given them a snack and would try to keep them calm until the boys were found.

"I'll call you as soon as we get them back." Annabelle closed her eyes a moment, trying to envision Ethan racing into her arms—and praying it would prove true.

"You'll find them, Annabelle. Have faith. I do. The whole town is searching."

But that hadn't helped Randy Kirk, she thought after she promised Charlotte to keep her posted. Gathering up all the food and coffee, she began ferrying everything out to the car.

She reached the Collier home in record time, despite the rain and wind and thunder. It was gratifying to see so many friends and townspeople streaming in to help. Sylvie told her that even Tess's husband, John, had left her and their infant daughter, Fae, to come out and help search in the storm.

For a half hour she distributed sandwiches, cheese and crackers, coffee, granola bars, and cookies. She was just heading back to the kitchen for more food when three more searchers came in, sopping wet and shivering. Martha Davies hurried over to them with blankets.

"Oh, dear, these are the last of the dry blankets," the older woman muttered.

"That's what I forgot to pack! Blankets!" Annabelle hurried into the kitchen and gazed at Sylvie and Ava in dismay.

"We're running a little short of them," Sylvie admitted. "But I don't think you should go back out in this storm. I can take some quilts off the beds—"

"No, I'm going. I have at least a dozen packed away. Trish never threw out a blanket unless it was threadbare. She always said you never know when disaster will strike—"

Breaking off, she shook her head. She didn't want to think about how she'd let Trish down today. It hurt too much.

"Can you handle things here? I'll be back soon."

She had to keep doing something . . . something to help. She couldn't stand still and wash out the coffeepot and have time to think about Ethan on that mountain. She just couldn't.

Moments later she was racing into the house on Sunflower Lane once more. Darkness had crept in, but the rain was lightening slightly. Her hair and her face were damp and cold, though, as she ran through the night—the air brisk from the storm.

Shivering and chilled, she grabbed her hoodie from the closet and shrugged it on, then bolted up the stairs. Grabbing up a handful of neatly folded blankets from a storage trunk in the closet, she took the stairs carefully and started toward the door to load them into the car.

At that moment, someone pounded on the kitchen door.

Wes! Ethan!

Hope surged through her and she dropped the blankets onto a chair in the hall and flung the kitchen door wide.

"Did you find—"

But a stranger stood there. A tall, strongly built stranger. He wore a black shirt, black pants, and an amused expression on a face that was handsome in a sleazy way she couldn't define. She'd never laid eyes on him before.

"Who . . . are you?"

"Evening, Miz Harper."

His voice creeped her out. It was outwardly pleasant, but had an undertone that made her skin crawl. How did he know her name?

"Who are you?" she asked again. "What do you want?"

Then she spotted the stoop-shouldered man standing just behind him. He was older, his skin swarthy, with a hard, bony face, reminiscent of a skeleton. Thin, stringy gray hair, and the darkest, emptiest black eyes she'd ever seen.

A man without a soul, she thought, chills prickling her spine.

"We're here on business," the old man said, and she caught the heavy Spanish flavor of his accent.

Fear breathed along her skin. She tried to slam the door, throwing all her weight against it, but the tall man grabbed it and pushed it wide, then shoved her backward. As she grasped the kitchen counter to keep from tumbling to the floor, both men slipped quickly into the kitchen.

The older one closed the door behind them.

Then he clicked the lock in place and turned back to stare at her.

That was when Annabelle read the hate glinting in those cold, dark eyes. She took in the cruel set of his mouth. And knew in that instant these men had come to hurt her, maybe kill her. She knew it as if they'd spoken the threat aloud.

As terror shuddered through her, the tall man pulled out a gun.

⁓

"Doc, over here!"

Carefully, Wes set Jimmy down on the Colliers' couch.

The house was still packed with friends and neighbors. They'd all broken into whoops and applause when the sheriff told them the boys had been found and were on their way down the mountain.

Dave Collier, Rafe Tanner, and his brother Travis had been the first ones to meet up with Wes and the boys at the trailhead. Dave took his son in his own arms, and began carrying him slowly down the mountain through the rain as Wes guided Ethan close behind.

"They should go to the hospital," Travis Tanner said as soon as the boys were in the house.

"Jimmy needs to, for sure," Rafe agreed.

"He needs this ankle set," Sylvie whispered, kneeling beside her sobbing son.

"Both boys should be checked for exposure." Ben Adkins spoke up. He'd been enjoying a cinnamon bun and coffee in A Bun in the Oven earlier that afternoon when he'd heard about the missing boys, then had driven out to join the volunteers streaming to the Collier place, asking whether there was anything he could do to help. He'd been handing out water and food ever since.

Now everyone looked at him in surprise, for though he'd grown up in Lonesome Way, these days he was a newcomer. Still, most everyone knew who he was by now, and they all nodded at his words, spoken with the absolute authority of a man accustomed to leadership.

"I agree with Ben." Ava handed Deputy Mueller a cup of coffee—the poor man looked exhausted after having spent more than four straight hours on the mountain. "You can't be too careful with children."

"Right. They both need to be checked out." Wes took a quick inventory of the room. "Where's Annabelle?"

Sylvie glanced up from where she was kneeling, talking quietly to both boys. "She went home a while ago to get more blankets. I'm not sure how long ago, but I'd have thought she'd be back by now."

Frowning, Wes pulled out his cell phone as Dave lifted his son again to carry him out to the car.

"Tell you what, Dave—can you take Ethan, too? Annabelle and I will meet you there," he told Jimmy's father. "I'm going to call her now and tell her we've got the boys."

He knelt beside Ethan first. "You okay with that, buddy? Your aunt and I will meet you at the clinic pronto."

"I want to go with you."

"We'll be right behind you. As soon as I meet up with your aunt. She's worried and I know she's going to want to see you right away."

Ethan nodded, his face weary from his ordeal. "Okay, I guess. But if it hadn't started r-raining . . . and Jimmy didn't f-fall, I bet we could've found the treasure."

Wes gently tousled his hair. "I'll let your aunt tell you what she thinks about that, buddy."

⌒

As soon as he had Ethan comfortably buckled into the Collier truck, wrapped in a quilt with Sylvie riding shotgun on both boys, Wes checked his phone. He'd tried to reach Annabelle several times, but she hadn't picked up—or called him back.

With a flicker of unease, he punched in her number again as he roared away from the Collier home, heading toward Sunflower Lane.

Two minutes later, she still wasn't picking up. What the hell?

Worry chafed at him as he drove. She must be frantic about the boys and she had no idea yet that they were safe. Had she gotten into a crash driving to or from the Collier place? His chest tightened with fear at the thought.

He called again. No answer.

Swearing under his breath, he suddenly remembered that a call had come in two hours ago. The number belonged to Walt Carruthers. Walt had left a voice mail, but Wes hadn't had a chance to check it out yet.

"Now what?" He had a bad feeling as he peeled down the wet back roads toward Sunflower Lane. He clicked on the voice mail message.

"Wes, bad news. You need to watch your back. Call me when you get this."

Wes swore. He knew in his gut that this day was about to get worse as he punched in Carruthers's number, the rain lightening now to a faint gray drizzle.

"What's up?" he asked brusquely as soon as his former boss picked up.

"Hate to tell you this, but they got Sutton. It was ugly."

Sutton? Shit. Wes's stomach dropped. His hand clamped like a vise around the phone.

Rick Sutton had been his second in command on the mission that left Diego's son riddled with bullets in a garbage-strewn alley. Sutton was good. Almost as good as Wes.

He gritted his teeth.

"Where'd they get him? When? And how the hell did they find him, Walt?"

"From all we can tell, Cal Rivers tracked him down night before last in Seattle. Sutton was home with his family. Gated community. Security system, the works. They still got in—and . . ." His former boss cleared his throat.

"They killed Rick's wife, too, Wes. Left the kids alone, sleeping in their beds upstairs, but they shot both Andrea and Rick with a silencer."

Cold shock swept through him. Icy, rigid, mind-numbing shock. Along with fury. For a moment, he couldn't speak.

An ugly silence hung in the air as his mind filled with images of the night a few years back when he'd gone out to dinner with Rick and Andrea in their Seattle suburb. She was a kindergarten teacher, pretty, sweet, and smart. She'd ordered chocolate mousse for dessert, shared it with Rick. They'd held hands under the table.

Iron-hard rage pumped through him.

"When did this happen? You sure it was Rivers?"

"An undercover cop happened to be filling up at a gas station a mile away from the killings—he remembered a man and a vehicle pulling in earlier for gas and cigarettes. The guy fit the description given by a neighbor who apparently saw Rivers leave the Sutton house. They both described him to a T, even the baseball cap that mostly hid his face. Rivers ditched the vehicle within a half hour after the approximate time of the killings. No prints. There's an APB out, but . . . it's Rivers. He's long gone by now."

Wes's eyes narrowed. He'd talked to Rick only a month ago. Had he mentioned to his former partner that he was headed home to Montana for a visit? If he'd told anyone, it would have been Rick. . . .

"If he found Arroyos and Sutton, you're next on his list, Wes. You were the team leader and all. They're working their way up the chain of command, saving the best for last. Wes . . . you still there?"

"Not for long," he rasped. He had to leave Lonesome Way. *Now.* As soon as he made sure Annabelle was okay, he'd make a big enough noise to lead Rivers far away from her and those kids.

He couldn't go to Wyoming yet and team up with Scott Murray, either. Scott had a family, too. He needed to lead Rivers into a trap and turn the tables.

End this once and for all.

His mind was already spinning out plans. Figuring a route that led far away from anyone he knew or cared about.

"I'm hitting the road, Walt. Thanks for the heads-up."

"Keep your eyes open," the other man said grimly.

Wes was already shoving the phone in his pocket. He tried Annabelle again, the knot of worry in his chest tightening by the moment. Could Rivers have tracked him already, have found out he was in Lonesome Way, and where he was staying?

The bastard definitely could've traveled to southwest Montana from Seattle by now—especially if he had Diego's resources.

Suddenly, Annabelle not answering her phone took on a whole new meaning. His muscles clenched with tension. Fear clamped in his gut, cold and hard as a boulder. If that son of a bitch even touched her . . .

Wes floored the truck and whipped down the road. Everything else was forgotten.

Annabelle's face swam in his mind, lovely, gentle, and full of laughter. It was a face he cherished. A face he loved . . .

The tension of the night had cleared for him the moment he found Ethan and Jimmy safe, but now it returned tenfold. He sensed a cloud of death descending.

But his eyes glittered hard as jade in the darkness and he took the turns fast, flooring the truck, gripping the steering wheel in iron fists, and rocking through pinwheel turns on the country roads. He knew that every second counted.

No one he loved was going to die tonight. Not if he could help it.

Chapter Twenty-seven

"Get out of my house. Both of you." Annabelle's gaze was pinned to the tall man's face. She tried very hard not to look at the gun.

"Not going to happen, sweetheart."

The old man pushed forward, swearing, as her cell phone rang again from inside her purse on the kitchen chair.

"Don't touch that," the old man ordered once more. Grabbing the purse, he dug for the phone, dropped it to the floor, and stomped on it with his heel until it cracked.

"Now, pretty lady, where's McPhee? Tell us and you won't be harmed."

"I don't know who you're talking about. You're in the wrong house."

The old man's eyes glistened with contempt. "Don't you lie to us. People who lie to us get hurt very badly."

"I'm not lying." Annabelle heard her voice trembling and she reminded herself she had to stay calm. Fear needed to be channeled into calm—and then action. She needed to keep her mind focused. Clear.

"A man was staying in the little cabin behind my house, but he moved on a few weeks ago. I live alone."

"You'll die alone, sweetheart, if you don't tell us the truth," the tall man growled, his voice rough with impatience. "There's kids here. We saw a ball in the yard."

Stepping forward before she could move, he pressed the butt of the gun against her forehead.

It felt cold. Deadly.

For a moment Annabelle's knees trembled so badly she thought they wouldn't hold her. She could smell his sweat and see in his eyes that he was enjoying this moment, drawing pleasure from her fear.

"Give her ten seconds and no more," the old man rasped. He stood beside the other man now, both of them confronting her.

There was nowhere to run.

"All right. I'll tell you where he is. Just put the gun down." She allowed her voice to quaver pitifully. And took a small step backward.

"Talk. Now," the tall man ordered. But he lowered the gun.

"He headed out to meet someone in Butte. He mentioned the name of the man he's planning to meet with for a few days—I can't remember it—but I . . . I wrote it down on a piece of paper."

As she started to reach into her pocket, the tall man scowled. "Stop right there. I'll get it."

"No. Please don't touch me. It's just a slip of paper. . . ." She froze at the warning in his eyes.

He moved closer. With the gun still trained on her, his free hand stretched down toward the pocket of her hoodie.

He was so close she could see the dark swirl of black and purple vampire tattoos scrawled below his neck. So close she could smell his sweat and see the sheen of his skin. She felt her blood thrumming in her ears as he moved even closer, his fingers grabbing at the pocket of her hoodie.

It was now or never.

Springing into a whirl of action, she shoved his gun hand up and away with her left hand exactly as she'd been taught, then rammed her knee hard into his groin at the same time. Then she slammed her closed right fist into his Adam's apple, using every ounce of her strength.

The big man tumbled backward with a groan of agony that echoed through the kitchen.

"Bitch! You are *dead*!" the old man screamed, leaping forward. He was faster and spryer than he looked, Annabelle realized with a gasp. But terror made her faster. Her fingers had already dipped into the pocket of her hoodie and she yanked out the Mace. One quick blast right between the eyes as she'd been trained to do and his scream nearly burst her eardrums.

She stepped back, her breath hitching in her throat, as the old man covered his eyes with his scarred, dark-veined hands, still shrieking even when he fell to his knees. She was about to dart toward the big man and give *him* a super spray from the canister before he could shake off the pain, but then she saw movement and realized that a third man was running in from the living room.

With a cry, she spun toward this new threat.

It was Wes! Relief made her gasp as he moved like a bullet, mowing down the tall man, who'd just staggered to his feet. Wes punched him in the face, then slammed a fist into his stomach. As the man doubled over, Wes gave him a brutal chop to the back of his neck and his opponent slumped to the floor like a sack of rocks.

A moment later Wes was on him, pinning him down, landing blow after blow. The big man slumped unconscious beneath him.

"Don't . . . kill him, Wes," she gasped, clutching the kitchen table, her voice shaking.

He was back on his feet in an instant, racing to her side, enfolding her in his arms. "Sorry, baby. I'm so sorry I didn't get here sooner," he said thickly, holding her tight.

"You got here just in . . . time. . . ."

"Nah, you had this. Good work, sweetheart. You could teach me some moves."

He squeezed her gently, then let her go, his gaze cold as he trained it on the two men. "Call Hodge, Annabelle. Tell him to get out here right now, okay? Got any duct tape, honey?"

The old man was still coughing, on his knees now, his eyes red and inflamed, his face convulsing with pain. Wes unbuckled his belt and Annabelle ran to the storeroom, grabbing a roll of duct tape from Ron's old toolbox.

"They . . . destroyed my cell phone," she managed as she returned with the tape.

"Sorry about that, sweetheart. I knew something was wrong. I kept trying to call you. Ethan and Jimmy are safe. They're on their way to be checked out at the clinic."

"Thank God!" Her eyes filled with grateful tears as he handed her his phone, and she quickly called the sheriff's office.

Wes first strapped the big man's arms behind his back, then duct-taped the old man to the legs of the kitchen table.

"It's over, Annabelle. It's all over, sweetheart." He came to her again and wrapped his arms around her gently. She was shivering, damn it.

He pressed a soothing kiss to her forehead, his eyes dark with regret. "I'm so sorry, baby. This was my fault. I brought this scum here. I'd give anything if you hadn't got caught up in it. I should have left town sooner—"

"No." She threw her arms around his neck. "Don't say that, Wes. It's *their* fault. Not yours. You saved my life."

"It never should have been endangered." He felt shaken and sick just thinking what would have happened if he hadn't come back when he did. And if Annabelle hadn't fought back, hadn't known how to protect herself.

"Sweetheart, if anything ever happened to you—" His gaze locked on hers as it struck him that he might have lost her for good.

Something turned upside down and inside out within him. He stood frozen, his heart slowing in his chest.

"It didn't," she murmured, touching his face. "Because of you."

As he stroked a hand through her curls, he wondered how in hell he was going to leave this woman. This exquisite, brave, loving woman, who was looking at him with such softness and trust in her eyes. This woman who'd made him feel a kind of peace he'd never known.

But before he could find an answer, sirens sounded far off, quickly drawing closer.

The big man stirred and groaned on the floor.

Reluctantly Wes let her go and pivoted back to keep an eye on his prisoners.

"Soon as Hodge gets this scum out of here, we'll go to the clinic and fetch Ethan. Where are the girls?"

"Charlotte's. Oh, God, I need to call them. They've been so worried."

"We'll pick them up, too. Do you want to get checked out at the clinic? Did they hurt you at all?"

She laughed shakily. "They only scared me half to death."

"They never will again. No one will ever lay a hand on you again. I swear it."

Wes had never felt such a strong surge of emotion—relief, tenderness, love.

Love?

To his surprise, the word didn't scare him. Though he

felt something he'd never thought would touch him, claim him, he recognized it as right and good and impossible to deny. He loved Annabelle Harper.

Leaning down, he caught her lips in his as sirens roared through the night, and came to a screeching halt right on Sunflower Lane.

They held each other, and the danger and the panic and the fear all faded.

Chapter Twenty-eight

⌒

The annual Fourth of July parade turned out better than its organizers could ever have hoped.

The sun shone all day in the huge blue Montana sky, glazing the lavender mountains with sheer light as crowds of people, kids, dogs, and babies lined the sidewalks of Lonesome Way.

Colorful floats and trucks painted red, white, and blue cruised down Main Street. People cheered almost nonstop. Those riding the floats waved American flags, singing "This Land Is Your Land," accompanied by the Lonesome Way High School Marching Band.

The mayor and his wife were dressed as George and Martha Washington on their float sailing down Main Street. Then Madison Hodge, the sheriff's granddaughter and an up-and-coming singer/songwriter, strummed her guitar on another gaily decorated float and sang "America the Beautiful," while everyone in the crowd joined in.

Children walked and skipped in the parade and some rode bicycles decorated with red, white, and blue ribbons. The bake sale table at the very end of the parade route did fantastic business with not only apple and peach pies for sale, but cookies, brownies, peanut butter cups, and Fourth of July sheet cakes—as well as huge blue-and-white-frosted cupcakes with cherries on top.

Dogs walked in the parade, too—even Treasure, who wore a red leash with blue and white ribbons tied to his collar as a grinning Ethan led him along the parade route.

When all the floats had passed by, the entertainment portion of the celebration began. Annabelle's tap class performed at exactly one P.M. The parents and onlookers cheered and applauded after the girls finished their routine, and then a jazz group rushed into the square to perform "It's a Grand Old Flag."

Annabelle rounded up Megan and Michelle, then spotted Ethan and Treasure in the park —Jimmy was there, too, his crutches beside him. She paused a moment to silently say a prayer of thanks. Thanks that the boys were safe, that the men who'd threatened her and Wes were in custody—and that the only place those monsters were headed after their trial was a very long, cold stint in prison.

Life was good. Sweeter than she'd ever imagined it could be. The only thing troubling her was tomorrow.

Of course, she didn't know whether Wes was leaving *exactly* tomorrow—he'd promised his grandmother he'd stay until after the Fourth of July—and Ava had just gotten her cast removed from her wrist yesterday. But if not tomorrow, then most likely he'd be saying his good-byes the next day or the day after that.

She didn't want to think of what would happen after he drove away, out of her life. An emptiness swamped her even when her thoughts wandered forward, trying to imagine that moment. She was trying to enjoy today. The parade, the celebration, everyone in her family safe and healthy, and the cabin ready to be occupied by a paying tenant.

She had much to be thankful for. But . . . *crap*. She blinked away the threat of tears burning behind her eyelids as she walked over to the park.

Today, focus on today, she ordered herself fiercely.

"Penny for your thoughts." Wes appeared suddenly beside her and handed her an ice cream cone. He looked hotter than the July sun with his long legs encased in faded jeans, and a white T-shirt that had a small American flag emblazoned in the center of his muscular chest.

"Whoa, what's wrong?" The grin faded abruptly and his expression turned to one of concern.

"Nothing. I'm just thankful. For the way everything turned out."

"Yeah, me, too." He kissed her, a kiss that lingered on her lips and made her melt into him, but he drew back as Megan and Michelle suddenly raced up to join them.

Annabelle took a lick of her ice cream.

"Can we stay in town and watch the fireworks tonight?" Megan asked eagerly.

"Please," Michelle pleaded. They were both smiling from ear to ear, still wearing their sparkly patriotic costumes, and Annabelle knew how they felt.

Beautiful, special.

That was how she'd felt when she'd danced and performed.

"Sounds like a great idea to me," Wes answered, then glanced at Annabelle for confirmation. "How about I take you all to dinner at the Double Cross; then we'll come back and sit on the grass in the park, watch the fireworks. What do you say?" he asked Annabelle over the girls' screeches of delight.

Despite the heaviness in her heart, she couldn't help but

smile. "I say yes." She wanted this to be a special day for all of them. The girls and Ethan would miss Wes, too.

Treasure barked suddenly, and broke away from Ethan, who was loosely holding his leash.

"Treasure, come back," the boy shouted, but the dog dashed over to Michelle, who threw her arms around him. When she plopped down on the grass, he sat beside her and licked her face again and again.

Megan was staring at her sister and the dog. An intent stare. There was fear in her face, but something else, too. Excitement, eagerness, along with wariness.

"Megan . . . honey, are you okay?" Annabelle knelt beside her niece as all around them, music swelled. The marching band was playing "Party in the USA."

"I want to pet him," Megan said so quietly that Annabelle thought she must have heard incorrectly.

"You . . . what?"

"I . . . want to try to pet Treasure." The little girl looked up at her, with her lips set in determination.

"Well, then, why don't you call him over to you, honey?" Annabelle stayed beside her, hope rising in her heart. "He'll come to you. I bet he'll even lick you."

Megan drew in a breath. "T-Treasure, come!"

The dog leaped toward her, his tail wagging at a speed that would make a state trooper switch on his siren.

But Megan suddenly screamed as the dog bounded within touching distance.

Fortunately, Treasure froze immediately, scared by her cry. He stood just within arm's reach, looking uncertain as she gasped and grabbed onto Annabelle's arm.

"It's okay. Why don't you try going over to him, Megan? Nice and slow."

Her niece seemed to steel herself for something very difficult and dangerous.

But then, before she could move, Treasure leaped again, landing in front of her. His tongue shot out, licking her cheek. Megan yelped at the sudden appearance of the dog right in her face, but the cry quickly turned into a laugh as he rolled over onto his back, his front paws waving in the air.

As her laughter faded, the little girl in the sparkly costume knelt down and tentatively began to rub his belly.

The dog writhed, rolling back and forth in ecstasy.

"Wow. Miracles do happen," Annabelle breathed, as a small, pleased laugh escaped her niece.

Wes wrapped his arms around her waist. "Don't I know it. I'm standing beside one right now."

She felt warm and flushed all over as he lifted her long hair and kissed her neck. Heat tingled through her. If only there weren't three hundred people roaming around, including Ethan and the twins, she'd pull him down onto the grass and jump his bones right now.

Here they stood in the center of town, looking like a couple, a happy couple, and all the while she knew it was a false impression. Why was he bothering? Wes cared about her—yes. She knew that.

He liked making love to her, yes, he did . . . almost as much as she loved making love to him.

But it didn't mean anything to him beyond the moment. Tomorrow or the next day he was moving on. She wondered whether he'd take Treasure with him, or if now that Megan seemed to be conquering her fear, he'd leave the dog with them.

She swallowed hard and steeled herself to accept the inevitable.

One way or another, he was going away. Any day now. *And that will be that.*

Chapter Twenty-nine

By the time Annabelle tucked the kids into bed that night, the last of the fireworks had long disappeared from the sky.

The night was very dark and very silent, no stars visible and only a sliver of moon. It cast a pale, silvery gleam over her gardens and Wes's black truck parked in the driveway.

She paused a moment outside the twins' room and gazed at Treasure, curled up at the foot of Megan's bed. The girls had argued for ten minutes over who got to sleep with him this first night that he stayed in their house, and in the end, Annabelle had flipped a coin.

Megan won.

Wes poured her a cup of coffee as she sailed into the kitchen.

"You're a genius, do you know that? Treasure's sleeping in Megan's *bed*!"

"Nothing genius about it." He grinned. "Did a little reading, that's all."

"Don't be modest, cowboy; it doesn't suit you." With a smile, she walked right into his arms and kissed him on the mouth.

Unfortunately, their long, deep kiss was interrupted by the chirp of her cell phone. It was Charlotte, stressed out about wedding plans. Her wedding was at the end of the month and the bridesmaids' dresses still hadn't come in for fittings.

And, Charlotte told Annabelle, Tess thought white roses were more elegant and romantic than pink, but Charlotte had read that white flowers were unlucky in a wedding bouquet. What did Annabelle think?

It was difficult to think at all because Wes had led her into the living room, set her coffee cup on an end table, and pulled her down atop him on the sofa. His hands roved over her, his mouth was tasting the sensitive skin at her throat, and what he was doing to her blocked out all thoughts of flowers, colors, and bridesmaids' dresses.

"Annabelle, are you listening to me?" Charlotte demanded suspiciously, when she heard a soft moan on the line.

"Not really, Char. S-sorry. Can I call you back tomorrow?"

"Oh, no. Yes, I mean, *yes*, call me tomorrow. Sorry; far be it from me to interrupt young love. Go for it, girl." Charlotte laughed, apparently forgetting to be stressed for a moment. "Make some fireworks," she ordered, and then clicked off.

"We should go upstairs and lock the door," Annabelle managed to whisper a few moments later. "One of the kids might wake up and come downstairs for a glass of water."

"Shit. You're right." Grinning, Wes stopped unzipping her jeans and sat up.

"What time is it? Oh . . . too early for bed, I guess. Let's grab our coffees, sit outside on the porch for a while first. The night's young."

She glanced at him in surprise.

"There might be more fireworks," he explained with a grin.

"Not in Lonesome Way. Once the fireworks are done, they're done. Usually by nine o'clock they shut it all down."

"Yeah, well, let's sit outside anyway. There's something I want to talk to you about."

Her stomach rolled. Here it came. She suddenly didn't want coffee.

She didn't want anything but the strength to hold back tears when he told her he was leaving first thing in the morning.

Uneasily she sat down on the porch step and took a gulp of coffee, tightly gripping her mug. When Wes settled close beside her, she tried to swallow past the lump in her throat.

"Nice night," he said.

"Yes, a little dark, but—"

"A good night for fireworks."

"Except I told you, the fireworks are over." Managing a smile, she set her cup down on the step beside her and took a deep breath. "Don't make small talk, Wes. I know what you're going to say. It's okay. I won't go to pieces on you."

"Go to pieces? What do you mean?" A frown crossed his face. He set down his cup, too, and glanced at his watch.

Was he already counting the minutes until he could leave?

"I know you're heading out tomorrow morning. Or the next day . . . or . . . are you going *tonight*?" she asked suddenly, her throat going dry.

"Annabelle, you've got this all—"

"I won't cry—you can tell me," she interrupted him. Two tears squeezed out of her eyes and rolled down her cheeks. Mortified, she brushed them away with the back of her hand. "I'll . . . m-miss you, but I'm a big girl and I knew how this would end—"

"Annabelle, baby." Standing suddenly, he grabbed her

hand and pulled her up, too, then took her in his arms and held her close.

"Stop, honey. I love you. I'm not going anywhere."

"You . . . *what*?"

He bent and kissed her lips, a quick, hot kiss that made fireworks go off in her heart. "I love you more than anything in this world. And I love those kids. And maybe even your dog—"

"He's your dog," she said quickly, stupidly, confused by the words she thought she'd heard.

"*Our* dog," he said firmly. "If you say yes."

She couldn't believe what he seemed to be saying. She stared at him. "Yes to . . . what?" she asked cautiously.

"To the question I'm going to ask you. I've done a helluva lot of things in my life, but I've never done this before. I love you, Annabelle. More than anything or anyone. I didn't even believe in love, not for me. And then *you* came into my life."

"You came into mine." Her heart began to beat faster and a smile spread across her face, lighting her eyes with hope.

"Now you're getting the idea." Smiling, he stroked a strong finger gently along her cheek. "You've changed everything. I never thought this would happen to me, not love . . . or you . . . or anything I feel when I'm with you."

He caught her hands in his, holding them gently. "I'm calling my buddy Scott in Wyoming tomorrow and telling him I'm opening the business right here in Lonesome Way. If he wants to invest or to move here and be partners, or to work something else out, that's fine, but you're here and those kids are here and that dog is here and—you get the idea. You guys come first. *We c*ome first. I'm staying. And not in that cabin, either. Right here with you. If you want me, that is. Uh, damn. Hold on."

He broke off, looking toward the sky. "What the hell?" he muttered in the darkness. Dropping her hand, he glanced at his watch again.

"Wes?"

"Sorry, I . . ." He looked up impatiently at the sky once more, frowning. "Where the hell—ah. Finally. It's about time."

Confused, she saw him break into a wide grin the same time the night suddenly exploded with *boom boom boom*. Annabelle nearly jumped out of her skin.

Fireworks?

The night lit with dazzling light and colors—glittering red, pink, and golden sparks—hundreds of them—shooting through the sky. Then they suddenly shifted and drifted and formed words.

Words that blazed against the blackness.

MARRY ME, ANNABELLE.

The pink, red, and gold sparks melted into the night and disappeared.

Fireworks! She gasped in shock, even as Wes pulled her closer against his side. Her stunned gaze was still pinned to the sky, where the words she'd thought she'd seen had vanished.

There was another *boom boom boom* and the words *I love you*, shimmering in silver against the darkness.

Before she could speak, a dozen more booms filled the night and formed a giant red heart that glowed with fiery sparks before it melted away.

She turned to him, dazed.

"F-fireworks," she gasped.

Wes dropped to one knee. His grin faded, and he looked very serious. Suddenly there was a ring in his hand. She stared down in shock at the enormous princess-cut diamond that shimmered like a huge sparkler on a silver band. Blinking in disbelief, she stared down at him, kneeling before her.

"Really?" she gulped.

"Annabelle, I love you so much."

Her heart caught in her throat and she couldn't breathe.

"Baby, I want to spend my life with you. Please, will you marry me?"

"I'd be crazy not to!" Kneeling down beside him, tears of happiness streamed down her cheeks as he cupped her face in his hands.

The night had gone quiet now, but for the two of them.

"I don't know how you managed to arrange those fireworks, but I loved them, Wes. And I love you so much."

"Exactly what I hoped you'd say." Grinning, he surged to his feet and took her hand in his, lifting her up to stand beside him. Gently he slid that amazing ring onto her finger. Annabelle's eyes glowed more brightly than any of the sparks that had lit the sky.

"Yes, I'll marry you," she whispered, and kissed him until they both had to come up for air. "Yes, yes, and yes," she breathed.

"Gonna hold you to that, honey." He caught her against him and stroked a hand gently through her hair. For once his glance was dark and serious. "I don't know what I'd do if you'd said no."

"I say yes. I'll always say yes."

And then they held each other tight and sealed the deal with a kiss that left them both without breath to speak for a very long time. When Wes carried her inside, up the stairs to her bedroom, he set her down on the bed, then turned the lock on the door.

By the time he turned back she was naked from the waist up and tearing at his shirt.

"I think I'm gonna like being married," Wes drawled.

"I *know* I will." Annabelle laughed, tracing her hands along the muscles of his powerful chest and soaking in the sight of him.

Those were the last words either of them spoke for a very long time.

Chapter Thirty

"Am I calling too early?"

Wes's mother stood at Annabelle's door two days later as Annabelle was rinsing the breakfast dishes. Diana looked casual and pretty in beige pants, white sandals, and a pretty, pale green top.

Annabelle was barefoot, wearing cutoff shorts and a gray T-shirt.

"Too early? Um . . . no. I mean, not at all. Please come in, Mrs. Hartigan."

To say that Annabelle was stunned to see her was an understatement. Wes had taken Ethan and the twins down to the cabin only ten minutes earlier. He wanted to show them how he was going to turn it into an office for his new company, and where he was going to build a new barn.

She still couldn't quite believe it. Right after they'd broken the news to the kids that they were getting married and going to be a family, Wes had sprung another surprise on all of them, including Annabelle. He intended to buy a couple of horses for the kids.

As a wedding gift.

"I'm thinking we might get a few more down the road," he told Annabelle after the kids ran outside with Treasure, elated by the news—probably almost as elated about the horses as the fact that Wes and Annabelle were getting married.

"If we have some more kids, we might need more horses," he pointed out casually.

"You want more kids?" She stood stock-still. "There's three already. I never thought . . ." Her voice trailed off.

"Do you want more?" he asked, suddenly serious.

"Yes, but—"

"Then it's settled." His grin reached all the way to his eyes. "I vote we start trying tonight."

"There's something so irresistible about a man who knows what he wants and goes for it." Smiling widely, she stepped into his arms.

Now, alone in the kitchen with his mother, she wished he and the kids were back here. It was awkward being alone with Diana.

She knew that Wes had called his family first thing this morning to tell them they were invited to a wedding. Diana had invited him, Annabelle, and the kids over for supper at the Good Luck Ranch tonight.

But she hadn't expected Diana to come to Sunflower Lane.

This can't be good, Annabelle thought, her stomach clenching. It would've been so much easier to face Wes's mother with a houseful of other people instead of just the two of them.

"Please sit down. Can I get you some coffee, Mrs. Hartigan?" She felt flustered and was trying hard not to let it show.

"You've already done enough, Annabelle. I don't need anything more."

Annabelle froze. What did that mean?

"I'm sorry. I don't understand."

Diana's face broke into a huge smile as she stepped closer and clasped Annabelle's hands in hers. "I can't begin to tell you how I prayed for this. I saw the way my son looked at you when he first came to town, and I prayed so hard."

"Wh-what?"

"Wes has been gone so many years, Annabelle. These past weeks mark the longest time he's been home since he turned eighteen, and I'm so thankful he's back. I prayed something might blossom between the two of you the moment I heard he was living here at your cabin. I finally had a small ray of hope that he might somehow end up staying here in Lonesome Way."

"You . . . did?"

"Do you remember that day at A Bun in the Oven—when my mother hinted that the two of you should get together? And everyone in the bakery was listening? I was so on edge that day!" Diana laughed. "I was terrified she'd offend you and make you want to steer clear of Wes. I was afraid to even hope that she could be right and that you might be the one. . . ."

She broke off, her eyes suddenly moist with emotion. "There's always been something special about you, Annabelle. What you did, coming back here to take care of Trish and Ron's children. That's so admirable. I've seen how dedicated you are to them, and I think you're a wonderful young woman, and I can certainly see why my son fell in love with you."

"B-but . . . I don't understand. Mrs. Hartigan, I noticed you looking at me sometimes, but then you turned away whenever I glanced at you. I thought you were unhappy that Wes was staying at the cabin and that we were spending time together."

"Not at all!" Diana smiled, and touched Annabelle's arm.

"Well, I admit that when you first moved back here, just seeing you in town did bring your aunt to mind. I felt the same way about your sister for quite some time. But I got over that. I dealt with it," she said with a shrug.

"Of course, you and Trish were no more responsible for Lorelei's actions than I was for Hoot's. It may have taken me some time to get accustomed to that idea, but I promise you, once the thought struck me that you and Wes might grow to care for each other, I was afraid to do *anything* that might influence the outcome. I didn't want to jinx it, or push it or upset the applecart in any way." Her mouth twisted in dismay. "I'm sorry if you thought I was unkind."

"No. Never unkind. But . . ." Annabelle drew in a breath, trying to reconcile her impressions with Diana's words.

"I'm thrilled that you don't object," she began, but Diana smiled widely and interrupted her.

"How could I object? I'm proud of my son for his good taste in choosing a woman with such character. And as for Ethan and the twins? You'll all be welcomed warmly into our family. The more, the merrier. Doug and I couldn't be happier about this and I know I'm speaking for Sophie and Rafe as well."

"That means so much to me." Annabelle swallowed hard and impulsively hugged Diana Hartigan. "Your son is the finest man I've ever met."

"Thank you." Diana kissed her cheek. "I'm proud of him," she said softly. "And proud that he chose you."

For the rest of the day, Annabelle walked around in a radiant kind of daze. She and Charlotte met at Tess's house and she got to hold Tess's adorable little daughter, Fae. After that she showed her friends her ring, and asked them to be bridesmaids at her wedding.

"Wait, when are you getting married? What month?" Charlotte demanded, ready to jump in with a lucky date.

Since Charlotte's wedding was at the end of July, Annabelle and Wes had decided on mid-September.

"Hold on, let me look that up." Charlotte punched the buttons on her phone with lightning speed. "Don't mean to be a downer, but it's very important that you choose a lucky . . . Wow, listen to this. 'Married in September's golden glow, smooth and serene your life will go.'"

"Works for me." Annabelle winked at Tess. Then she laughed as the baby made an adorable cooing sound. "Fae agrees. Oh, God, I want one of these of my very own. Boy or girl, I don't care. She's precious, Tess."

"First things first." Tess handed her daughter back into Annabelle's arms, grinning as the little girl cooed again, and blinked up adorably at the person holding her. "September will be here before you can blink. We'd better start planning this wedding. Where do you want to get married?"

"That much is settled." Annabelle felt a rush of warmth and joy.

"Believe it or not, Diana Hartigan invited us to have the wedding at the Good Luck Ranch. Her mother was married there, and she and Doug were, too. Just like Sophie and Rafe. It's such a beautiful place. I never imagined that Wes would agree, but he did! He wants us to carry on the tradition. The ranch and this town used to remind him of his father, but not anymore. He said Hoot's ghost can't touch him or us. And he's over letting his father's memory affect the way he lives his life. Wes stayed away for so long because coming home reminded him of his father. But now . . ." She beamed. "Now he says this town feels like home. And the Good Luck Ranch will be filled with everyone we love. No ghosts allowed."

"Then what are you waiting for?" Charlotte grinned. "You need to go to town and order some invitations! September is right around the corner."

"It's only the sixth of July." Annabelle laughed at her.

"Time flies when you're in love," Charlotte countered. "I'm going for my fitting today. Come with me to Big Timber and we'll look at dresses! Tess, you can bring Fae. I can tell she's all girl. She's going to love shopping as much as we do."

Tess's eyes lit. "You're on. I haven't been out of the house in weeks."

Annabelle felt like she was going to burst with happiness. There was so much to do, but all of it was wonderful.

Wedding dresses. Invitations. Flowers and candles, a wedding supper and champagne. This was real. As real as the love she and Wes shared.

"Let's go right now." She jumped up. Joy floated through her.

She couldn't wait to walk down the aisle and into Wes's arms.

Chapter Thirty-one

～

The day of Annabelle and Wes's wedding dawned clear as a glass of fresh springwater. A September breeze whipped down from the Crazy Mountains to ruffle the cottonwoods, but by four o'clock when the guests arrived and cars filled the driveway leading to the house, the wind had settled and the air held only a slight nip.

Autumn in Montana was as lovely in its own way as summer.

Upstairs in Sophie's old bedroom, Annabelle stared after her two junior bridesmaids as they kissed her on the cheek for luck and then romped out into the hall. She felt a lump in her throat when they started down the stairs, hand in hand.

In frothy pink dresses of lace and tulle, Megan and Michelle looked like tiny angels.

"You okay?" Charlotte asked, touching her arm.

She blinked back happy tears. "I just wish that Trish and Ron could be here, could see them. And see Ethan in his tux, carrying the ring."

"What makes you think they can't?" Tess asked gently.

Annabelle dabbed at her tears and smiled through them. "You're right. They know. They're here. They have to be."

Diana entered the room, beaming and elegant, her fair hair gently streaked with gray, and a flush of excitement brightening her face. "Reverend Kail is ready. Everyone is here. Are you ready?" she asked Annabelle with a smile.

"Ready? I can't wait another minute."

Her mother-in-law-to-be hugged her warmly. Then everyone chuckled as Annabelle sailed toward the door.

"Wait, Little Miss Bride, we go down first, remember?" Charlotte laughed. She smoothed the pale gray skirt of her dress. "I know you can't wait to marry the guy, but hang in there another minute, okay?"

Laughing, Diana slipped out the door first. Tess and Charlotte walked with Annabelle out to the landing; then they continued down the stairs, all smiles.

Standing at the top of the staircase as her best friends finished their descent, Annabelle felt her heart zoom. Wes stood waiting for her at the bottom.

He wore a black tux, a burgundy shirt, black tie, and a cowboy hat. So tall, so dark, so handsome.

So mine, she thought, her heart flying in her chest.

So many people she loved filled the lovely old ranch house. The twins were waiting below for her; so was Ava in a soft blue lace gown, and her friend Mr. Adkins beside her. He looked very distinguished in a tux. Ava had asked whether she could invite a guest, an old friend, but judging by the way the man's gaze rested on Ava—with a slight mistiness—Annabelle had to wonder if sometime soon another wedding might take place in this beautiful old house.

She smiled at the thought and at that moment, Wes looked up and saw her.

His hard, handsome features softened as he took in her cocktail-length, sophisticated ecru lace gown, her long legs, and knock-'em-dead stilettos. She didn't know whether he noticed the diamond drops at her ears, or her hair tumbling to her shoulders in a mass of curls.

But the way he grinned, his eyes lighting as they locked on her, touched her very soul.

She started down the steps and floated toward her future.

"I love you," Wes whispered right before the ceremony began. His words proved true for all to see when moments later he enthusiastically obeyed the reverend's order to kiss the bride.

"I don't have the words to tell you how much I love you. I don't know if I ever will," he told her huskily as the guests erupted into wild applause.

"I love you more," she whispered back, throwing her arms around his neck. While thunderous clapping and words of congratulations engulfed them, Doug Hartigan began passing out flutes of champagne.

Annabelle brushed her hand against Wes's cheek, knowing this was real, but feeling like it was a dream.

Later—much later—after a gorgeous buffet dinner, and an entire table laden with desserts—they danced their first dance while the guests watched, smiling, and Megan and Michelle, giggling, danced with each other in a corner of the dining room.

"I'm so lucky I found you," Wes said softly, kissing along the shell of her ear.

"I'm lucky you did, too." Lifting her face to his kiss, she knew it was true.

This man, this town, and their new family together was everything. Everything she could ever want.

Ethan had gone searching for treasure, but there was no need. The treasure was right here.

Happiness and home and everyone she loved was here, right here in the Good Luck Ranch house—in this town called Lonesome Way.

Turn the page for a preview of
another Lonesome Way novel from
New York Times bestselling author
Jill Gregory

Blackbird Lake

Available now from Berkley Sensation!

LONESOME WAY, MONTANA

Carly McKinnon's day had been cruising along just fine—a perfectly calm, typical, somewhat slow Wednesday in her Spring Street quilt shop.

Until late afternoon when she heard the news that Jake Tanner was back in town.

Suddenly, everything seemed to freeze for a full thirty seconds.

Of course she could still see Gloria Cartright, finished with her afternoon shift at the Lickety Split Ice Cream Parlor, thoughtfully fingering some new calico fabric on the shelves at the far side of the shop. She could still hear the sound of light traffic outside on Spring Street, and she could feel her own breath catch hard in her throat at the mention of Jake's name.

But she couldn't move, couldn't speak, couldn't *think*— not until the first ice-cold shock of the news had settled into her brain.

"Jake Tanner . . . are you *sure*, Laureen?" she finally asked her assistant, struggling to keep her voice calm and her face composed, as if she were talking about the chance of rain tonight or today's ninety-nine-cent caramel brownie special at A Bun in the Oven bakery.

"Jake Tanner?" Gloria shook her head skeptically. "That man hasn't been back more than a handful of times in the past dozen years. Not since he first fell in love with rodeo."

Shoving the bolt of calico back on the shelf, she eyeballed Laureen as if trying to ascertain if the other woman knew what the hell she was talking about.

"Well, I didn't say *I* saw him." Laureen Rowan glanced back and forth between Carly and Gloria, the small paper bag from Benson's Drugstore containing her new red lipstick and a pack of sugarless gum still clutched in her hand. "But Deanna Mueller is positive she did. The second I stepped into Benson's just now she rushed over in a big hurry to give me the scoop. Deanna was at the gas station filling up her minivan when Jake cruised by in his truck. She said there was a big dog leaning over his lap, its head hanging out the window. I never knew Jake to have a dog before, but Deanna insisted they were headed for Sage Ranch. Turned onto Squirrel Road right quick, she said. Deanna swears it was him. She told me, who else could it be, no one is as handsome as that Jake Tanner."

Tell me about it, Carly thought. A flush of heat raced through her body.

"Well, duh. That's for sure." Gloria nodded knowingly. "That man is smokin'. And he's all over the TV these days, between the rodeo coverage and those beer commercials of his." Her bright little black pepper eyes brimmed with interest. "I know if I was a dozen or so years younger, *I* wouldn't think twice about climbing between the sheets with him."

"Carly?" Laureen moved toward her boss in concern. "Hey. Are you all right?"

It was only then that Carly realized she was biting her lip, her hands were clenched, and her neck felt as tight as a washrag twisted in the clothes dryer.

"Sure. Fine," she said airily, forcing her lips into a smile, casually pushing a thick strawberry blond curl back from her usually dreamy green eyes.

"Well, you don't look fine. You look like you're going to fall down in a dead faint or something." Laureen studied her carefully, her own round, pretty face worried. Forty-four and divorced, she was the proud mother of two mutts and three cats, all adopted from Lonesome Way's overwhelmed shelter.

Laureen didn't know how to say no to a sad pair of feline or canine eyes. She had a heart as big as Montana and Wyoming combined. With chin-length white blond hair and hazel eyes she was still as pretty as she'd been in high school when she was named prom queen, but she'd gained twenty pounds since her divorce—and had convinced herself she was too fat to ever attract the attention of a man again. But still . . . Tonight she had a date with a rancher from the nearby town of Big Timber.

A blind date that had been set up by her sister-in-law in Butte.

Laureen had been insisting to Carly all week long that this was going to be her very last shot.

No more dates, blind or otherwise. They never panned out, not a single one of 'em. If this guy didn't call her back, Laureen was done.

"Maybe you should sit down. I'll get you a glass of water. There's a bad flu going around Billings. Could be the bug made its way here and you caught it."

"No, I'm . . . okay. It's just . . . I didn't get much sleep last night. Emma kept waking up," Carly lied.

It was only a half lie, though. Her eighteen-month-old daughter had woken up several times after Carly put her to bed, but it had all happened long before Carly went to sleep for the night.

A semi-lie is okay, she assured herself shakily. *Especially in extreme circumstances.* And Jake Tanner coming home to Lonesome Way—definitely an extreme circumstance.

She felt her heart lurch. Memories burned through her, along with a sprinkling of guilt and a pinch of unease. That thick, longish, jet-black hair. All those rock-hard abs. The slow, sexy kisses trailing down her throat . . .

The man had returned to his hometown only once since she had moved there from Boston nearly two years before—and even then he'd hit town for only a day. Which was one of the reasons she'd felt comfortable settling in Lonesome Way in the first place. Because Jake hardly ever came home. He'd told her as much that one night they'd spent together in Houston.

And that's what everybody always said.

Jake Tanner was a roamer through and through.

But his family was all here. His brothers, Rafe and Travis, along with their wives, Sophie and Mia, and their children.

All of whom were Carly's friends. Some of the nicest and best people she'd ever met. The last time Jake *had* come home—when Mia and Travis's daughter, Zoey, was born a year ago—Carly had heard in advance that he was coming in for a day to meet his new niece and had made sure she and Emma lay low.

Of course when she'd decided to move to Lonesome Way she'd always known Jake might drop into town on rare occasions for a visit, but most of the time she relegated that possibility into the far recesses of her mind as she savored her own sense of peace and delight with small-town life.

"I bet he's here for his niece's birthday party." Gloria's dark head bobbed up and down. "Zoey Tanner turns one this weekend. I have it on good authority that Travis was none too happy when Jake said he wasn't going to be able to make it to her party."

"You're probably right," Laureen said distractedly. She was digging out her new, very red lipstick from the drugstore bag and ripping at the packaging with her nails. "Everyone knows family means everything to the Tanners. Jake must've got wind Travis was pissed and changed his mind."

Panic whipped through Carly. She felt breathless and a little sick to her stomach. She and Emma were invited to Zoey's party.

If Jake was there, they wouldn't be able to go.

But that was the least of her problems. . . .

She needed to get home. To hold her daughter. To think.

But it was only four thirty and she didn't normally close Carly's Quilts until five. Gloria looked like she wasn't going anywhere, not while this juicy topic of conversation was on the table. And Laureen—Laureen seemed to have forgotten all the urgency of her big date tonight as she drew a mirror out of her purse and began applying her new lipstick with the careful precision of a surgeon performing a lobotomy.

Time to remind her about that date, Carly decided desperately.

"I know you want to get ready for tonight, maybe get a manicure, wind down, or whatever, so maybe we'll just close up early," she began with what she hoped was a breezy smile. Moving briskly across the shop, she began folding bolts of gingham and calico left on the long table beside the shelves and gathering up pattern books the few customers of the day had been browsing through. "I want to go home and check on Emma, too—what with her getting up so much last night. Just to make sure *she's* not coming down with something."

True enough. Emma *had* been restless last night. She probably sensed her daddy was headed to town, Carly thought wildly, knowing the thought was totally irrational.

Nervousness flowed through her like a chill autumn wind sweeping down from the Crazy Mountains.

Stop it. Pull yourself together. She gulped a couple of breaths and dug deep, searching for the hard-won serenity and sense of peace she'd worked so hard to achieve over the years.

Her own childhood hadn't exactly been a picnic—more like an odyssey of lonely confusion, uncertainty, and fear. But now, at thirty, all of that was behind her. She'd built a life here for herself and her daughter—a life that was solid and steady and filled with the warmth of this tight-knit community. Nothing was going to change that.

She reminded herself that Jake didn't know about Emma. He had no clue that he even *had* a daughter. Much less that she and Carly were living in Lonesome Way.

He probably doesn't even remember *me*, she thought, drawing a breath.

Jake Tanner had women falling all over him in every town from here to Alaska. But he was the last man to ever want any ties, any family of his own, any kind of commitment—except to the rodeo life.

He'd made all that very clear the one and only night they'd made love.

What am I talking about? We didn't make love. We had sex. Intense, incredible, rock-the-world and light-up-the-night-with-fireworks sex.

It was the lone one-night stand of Carly's entire life. She'd acted completely out of character. But then, she'd already downed two glasses of wine at the bar of that hotel in Houston and was sipping a third, trying to expunge her lying, psycho ex-boyfriend from her head, when she spotted him.

Jake Tanner. In all his hot cowboy ruggedness. He'd seemed like the ideal candidate to eject Kevin Boyd from her brain for good.

So when Jake glanced over from across the lobby, cocked

an eyebrow, and grinned that sexy cowboy grin, she'd made the first impulsive move of her life.

She'd downed the third glass of wine and gone for it.

The next ten hours had been momentous in every way. But then, of course, there had been nothing. Zip. No phone call from him a day or two later, no *maybe I'll see you again sometime.* Just nothing. Slam, bam, and . . .

Of course, she'd known that was exactly how it would be. She'd counted on it, even. He'd made it clear over dinner in the hotel restaurant that he wasn't the kind of man who was into long-term relationships or commitments or anything remotely hinting at permanence.

And we both wanted it that way, she reminded herself, trying to thrust Jake Tanner and his sexy smile, lean, powerful body, and impossibly hunky muscles from her mind.

That one night they'd spent together in his cushy Houston hotel suite had been, for her, all about rebound sex, pure and simple. They'd made crazed, incredible love all night long. And every bit of it had helped her to forget just a little more about her scumbag ex.

She'd discovered only four months earlier that Kevin Boyd had lied to her. Not just once or twice, but the entire time they were together. It turned out Mr. Fancy Schmancy genius architect wasn't divorced after all. And he wasn't a good, upstanding guy, searching for a serious, stable relationship as he'd claimed.

Just the opposite. He was married. With children! Three children, to be exact, one of them a two-month-old *infant.*

Carly had gone numb with shock when she discovered the truth. Kevin was a player. A liar. An elegantly good-looking blond jerk with a high IQ and a talent for hiding his wedding ring.

It had taken her long enough, but she'd finally started to grow suspicious and followed him one day when he left her apartment.

She actually caught him with his family, after he'd told her he was headed to the airport and an out-of-town consultation with a new client.

Watching in horror, her knees had sagged as Kevin hugged twin little boys who looked to be about eight or nine, scooped a pink-clad baby girl into his arms, and embraced a woman in a stunning Chanel suit. She'd grabbed onto a brick storefront for support as she watched them all bundle into an elevator in an exclusive doorman building that was *not* the place she'd thought was his home.

It was definitely not the apartment where she'd spent countless nights in his king-sized bed, where dozens of designer suits, pairs of slacks, shirts, and polos hung in the walk-in closet. An apartment always stocked with gourmet food and wine and an extensive collection of antique clocks and timepieces, where expensive works of art hung on all the walls.

And in that last huge fight with Kevin at *her* apartment in Boston she'd glimpsed a side of him she'd never seen before.

The angry, snarling, bordering-on-violent side.

Mr. Genius Architect didn't even think what he'd done was wrong! Even when she'd forced him to admit to his lies, to admit he'd told his wife he was traveling on business all those days or nights he spent with Carly, he'd shouted at her, and then snatched up the crystal ballerina sculpture her college friend Sydney had given her for her birthday. Even as Carly screamed, "Don't!" he hurled it at the brick wall behind the fireplace, shattering the exquisite dancer into a thousand shards.

He'd screamed that everything he'd done had been for *them*—so *they* could be together without the financial messiness of a divorce.

In shock, Carly had stared at the man she'd thought she knew. Listened to him try to gloss over his lies—all the things he'd said and done to make her believe that he was working tons of overtime at the office or conducting out-of-town meetings with clients.

When all along he'd been home with his wife and kids.

It was devastating to discover what an idiot she'd been. A naïve, gullible fool who'd swallowed hook, line, and sinker all his crap about the stresses of being an overworked, in-demand architect. She'd believed him when he claimed he couldn't have dinner with her regularly or attend her friends' parties—or even leave town for a romantic weekend getaway—because of a killer schedule and his boss being a demanding pain in the ass. She'd nearly thrown up when she learned there was a *Mrs.* Boyd—and a young family to boot.

At first Carly had been sickened, but that had quickly turned to fury. Fury not just with Kevin but with herself. She'd concluded that either she was as dumb as a brick or she'd inherited her mother's knack for picking losers. That making stupid romantic choices must run in her family, like allergies or cancer or freckles in other families.

Bad romantic karma was *in her genes*.

And she'd figured out one other thing—she wouldn't have a chance of finding peace again until she found a way to exorcise that entire fiasco with Kevin from her head.

So when she'd flown to Houston on business several months later and run smack-dab into Jake—tough, drop-dead sexy, rodeo champion Jake—whom she'd met briefly years before when they were both kids—she'd suddenly lost every single one of her brain cells and had done something stupid, something crazy, something she'd never done before in her life.

One-night stands were *so* not her thing.

Caution. Good sense. *Those* were her things.

But that night . . . that one amazing night . . .

There *should* have been no consequences, she'd thought faintly several weeks later when she stared at the results of her home pregnancy test.

True, she'd gone off her birth control pills after the fiasco with Kevin, swearing she'd never get seriously involved with another man again—but she and Jake had used condoms that night.

And yet . . .

A baby had been growing inside her. Emma.

Now a vivacious little blue-eyed charmer, eighteen months old—Emma was bright, active, and more precious to Carly than all the stars in the sky.

From the instant she first saw her daughter, Carly had never, ever thought of Emma as anything but the most treasured gift in the world.

So pull it together, she ordered herself again as she caught Gloria staring at her, while Laureen scooped up coffee cups from around the homey quilt shop with its walls of buttery warm yellow and its floors of burnished wood. *If you don't, the moment you get home, Madison might see something is wrong. And Emma could sense it.*

Emma's daytime babysitter, Madison Hodge, was a smart, down-to-earth twenty-year-old who adored Emma just as much as Emma loved her. Carly didn't know how she'd ever get by without Madison. A former pageant princess, this girl worked harder than anyone Carly knew. When she wasn't babysitting Emma four days a week, she was working toward her online degree in childhood education and playing keyboard in a local country band at night.

"Closing up early works great for me," Laureen was drawling. "I can use the extra time. Maybe I can fit in a really intense workout and lose twenty-five pounds before eight o'clock. Ya think?"

She headed toward the sink in the back of the shop, the cups hooked on her fingers. "This isn't going to turn into anything, you know," she called over her shoulder. "After tonight, I'm never going to hear from this guy again. He's probably expecting a skinny girl. A size two. Or four. You watch, when he sees me, he'll run fleeing into the night."

"Stop." Carly managed to drag her thoughts from her own worries. "Don't talk that way. You're beautiful, Laureen. You're stunning. And smart. And amazing."

"You're my friend. You have to say that."

"Well, *I* think you could stand to lose a few pounds," Gloria chimed in, sauntering toward the shop door. A grandmother of three teenagers, she was small and as skinny as a scrap of tree bark, and her bright orange sweater, the color of a ripe pumpkin, hung loosely on her wiry frame. "But some men think more pounds is just more to love. So you need to think positive. And hope this date of yours likes red lipstick, because that one you bought is awfully red. I'm just sayin'."

In typical Gloria fashion, she yanked open the door and was gone.

For a moment there was dead silence. Laureen and Carly stared at each other.

"Can you believe her?" Laureen finally gasped.

"Don't you dare pay any attention to a word she says," Carly ordered.

"Tell me the truth. Do *you* think the lipstick's too red?" Laureen's hazel eyes locked on Carly. The lipstick she'd carefully applied was full-on, red-carpet red, a lush, richly voluptuous color that looked bright and prettily vivid with her fair hair and creamy complexion.

"No way. It's perfect. Gloria's just being Gloria. Go home. Primp. I mean it, Laureen. Drink a glass of wine, and have fun tonight. I'll expect a full report tomorrow."

"No way. *You* go home." Setting the cups down with a clatter on the countertop at the rear of the shop, Laureen hustled up to the front where Carly was putting away the toys scattered around the small children's play area.

"I'll close up." Her red mouth was firmly set. "*You* check on Emma—that's a whole lot more important. My date isn't until eight, so go. Go see your daughter."

Straightening, Carly took another deep breath. "You sure? You don't mind?"

Laureen grabbed the stuffed Big Bird from her. "Get outta here, boss."

Carly didn't have to think twice. Grabbing her purse from beneath the front counter, she managed a quick, grateful grin. "That does it. You're officially employee of the month."

"Last I heard, I was the only employee, this month or any other."

"That makes you the best. Every month." It was all she could do not to sprint to the door. "This guy better treat you right tonight or he'll answer to me," she called over her shoulder.

"Yeah, what are you going to do? Stitch him to death?" Laureen gave a small huff of laughter before the door of Carly's Quilts clicked shut behind its owner.

Then Carly was bolting across Spring Street toward her Jeep, her tan wedges tapping the pavement. A cool September wind nipped down from the mountains, tousling her thick, curly mane of strawberry blond hair, making her shiver in her sea green cotton sweater and jeans.

I'm not *going to have a panic attack, I'm* not, she told herself, taking deep breaths, repeating the mantra over and over, trying to turn her mind from every disastrous thought.

It was hard to get in enough air, though, and she felt a little light-headed. But she hadn't had an attack in years, hadn't even had one when she found out about Kevin being married, or when she discovered she was pregnant. She certainly wasn't going to have one now. . . . She couldn't *let* herself have one now, not after all this time. . . .

She had nearly reached her Jeep when she heard Martha Davies's voice call out from behind her.

"Yoo-hoo. Carly! Where's the fire?"

Can't get away with a thing in this town. Carly's stomach clenched. Turning, she managed a smile for her foster mother

Annie's cousin, the eighty-something owner of the Cuttin' Loose beauty salon, waiting as Martha bore down upon her, beaming. A long purple knit skirt swished around the older woman's legs and a turquoise crocheted sweater covered her tall, spare frame. Not a smidgen of gray showed in her chin-length hair. It was freshly dyed a light blondish auburn and gleamed with reddish highlights in the autumn sunshine.

Martha was famous in Lonesome Way for changing her hair color the same way some women changed shoes. But her heart was as steady as a rock. She was Emma's god-mother and, now that Annie was gone, the closest person to family Carly had left in the world.

If not for all the times she'd accompanied Annie on visits to see Martha in Lonesome Way over the years, Carly might never have discovered the town that had become her home.

"I was just on my way to find you," Martha went on briskly before Carly could respond. "Closing up a little early, honey, aren't you?"

"I wanted to squeeze in some extra time with Emma." Leaning forward, Carly gave the older woman a quick kiss on the cheek. She hoped Martha couldn't sense the tension flowing through her. Martha might be in her eighties, but she still ran her business with a firm hand and was as sharp as a toothpick. "It was a slow day; you know how it goes."

"Oh, honey, you bet I do." Martha's dangling jet earrings swung as she shook her head in annoyance. "Wouldn't you know, Georgia Timmons canceled her tint at the last minute and now I have twenty minutes to kill before my next client comes in for a manicure and cut. What am I supposed to do, twiddle my thumbs?"

She stopped grimacing suddenly and stared at Carly with sharply narrowing eyes. "You know, you look sort of tense, honey. Everything all right? Emma isn't sick, is she?"

"Emma's great. She blew me about fifty kisses when I left this morning. I'm just tired." Carly hated lying but she could hardly tell Martha that Emma's daddy had breezed into town. Even Martha didn't know that Jake Tanner was Emma's father. No one knew. And Carly intended to keep it that way.

"Can I give you a call later?" She edged toward the Jeep. "Madison needs to study for an exam, plus she has a gig tonight. I want to let her leave as early as possible—"

"That's exactly what I want to talk to you about—Madison! Can I switch days with her and watch Emma tomorrow instead of Friday? I'll be shorthanded Friday and have a full day of appointments booked, including two perms and three manicures. But I don't want to miss out on any time with my little miss."

Ever since Emma turned one, Martha had insisted on having Emma spend the day with her at least once a week and then sleep over that night at her apartment. She'd even bought a crib that fit into a corner of her small living room and had sewn a gorgeous quilt for her goddaughter. Emma always squealed in excitement at the sight of "MaWa"—and not just because each time she slept over at MaWa's apartment there was a new toy or doll waiting for her.

"No problem—or we could skip this week if it would be easier for you—"

"Not a chance." Martha waved her hand, an amethyst and jet bracelet jangling cheerfully on her wrist. "I look forward every week to having my time with her. And—I bought her a little something new. I can't wait to give it to her."

"You don't have to buy her things all the time, Martha." A mixture of emotions rose in Carly, an overwhelming combination of guilt, love, and tenderness for this woman who had taken her and her daughter so deeply into her heart and woven their lives into hers. "Emma loves you for you, not because you give her—"

"Shoot, don't you think I know that, honey? I *like* buying things for her. Gives me a kick to see her face light up. Never had a little granddaughter of my own. And it's my business if I want to spoil her, isn't it? I think Annie would want me to do just that. Remember, it's *your* unpleasant job to say no to her now and then—not mine." Chuckling, she turned back toward the Cuttin' Loose. "You go ahead now. But don't forget to tell Madison," she instructed over her shoulder.

"I won't."

For a moment Carly watched the older woman saunter back toward her shop. There was a lump in her throat as she studied the tall, retreating figure. Martha had always been so kind to her, so kind to Emma.

Just as this town had been. . . .

Drawing yet another long breath that was supposed to be calming, she climbed into her Jeep, snapped her seat belt, and roared out of her parking space a lot faster than she'd intended.

She couldn't believe any of this. That Jake Tanner was here, that this was really happening. But the sick feeling in the pit of her stomach brought reality vividly home.

From *New York Times* bestselling author
JILL GREGORY

Blackbird Lake

A LONESOME WAY NOVEL

When rodeo champ Jake Tanner returns to Lonesome Way, Carly McKinnon is not happy about it. The last thing she wants is Jake finding out about their daughter. Since their one-night fling years ago, Carly has been a great parent on her own, and doesn't need Jake shaking things up. When Jake learns the truth, he wants to be a part of Emma's life even if he's not going to be a part of Carly's. But the attraction between them won't be so easily denied...

PRAISE FOR JILL GREGORY

"For tales of romance and adventure that keep you reading into the night, look no further than Jill Gregory."
—Nora Roberts, #1 *New York Times* bestselling author

"An amazing talent."
—Catherine Anderson, *New York Times* bestselling author

jillgregory.net
facebook.com/LoveAlwaysBooks
penguin.com

M1499T0514

*A woman comes face-to-face with a love from her
past and finds the chance to heal…*

From *New York Times* Bestselling Author

JILL GREGORY

Larkspur Road

A LONESOME WAY NOVEL

Fifth-grade teacher Mia Quinn expected a tranquil summer in her hometown of Lonesome Way, Montana, sewing
for her quilting group's exhibition fund-raiser and caring
for her rescued dog, Samson. But all her plans for a relaxing break are thrown out the window when Travis Tanner—the boy who broke her heart in high school—returns
to town with his ten-year-old adopted stepson.

Now an FBI agent, the boy Mia once knew is now well
over six feet of male muscle—and he still has the power
to make Mia lose her train of thought with just a glance.
When Travis asks her to tutor his troubled son, Mia
quickly discovers that the sparks between them are hotter
than ever. As danger comes to Lonesome Way and family
secrets come to light, will Travis and Mia realize that love
can be even better the second time around?

jillgregory.net
facebook.com/LoveAlwaysBooks
penguin.com

M1261T0213